BLUE BLOOD FOR LIFE

BOOK 2 IN THE MY BLOOD RUNS BLUE SERIES

STACY EATON

NITEWOLF NOVELS

Blue Blood for Life

Book 2 in the
My Blood Runs Blue Series

Written by
Stacy Eaton

****

Nitewolf Novels

This book is dedicated to
My Gemini Justice Sisters: Kristin & Amy

ACKNOWLEDGMENTS

This book came easily after writing *My Blood Runs Blue*. The story line almost wrote itself as I typed the words onto the pages; but through it all, I had many people who helped support and encourage me along the way.

My husband is at the top of my list. You were always willing to take over the household chores as I lost myself in the world of Fawn Hollow Township and the drama of Kristin and the gang. I thank you for your patience and willingness to do so much while I appeared to be doing so little, staring at my computer while only my fingers seemed to be moving autonomously. I know you totally understand that my brain was going a mile a minute while I sat there.

To my sweet daughter who only got more excited as my book was being completed. Her words have always been encouraging and the look on her face as she spoke about my book to others made me feel humbled, to say the least. She even managed to sell a few to teachers at her school. Someday, she might be my agent; until then, she will have to wait to even be able to read them. I love you, Little Button!

My two Gemini Justice Sisters, welcome to Fawn Hollow Township. I truly hope you enjoy how I portrayed your friendship and assistance in Kristin's life. You have all given me so much support and being able to put two great friends into my book, so that Kristin knows the friendship that I do, was incredibly important to me. I hope you all enjoy it, and thank you for being there for me to rant, rave, and basically lose my mind as I wrote this book. You ladies will never know how much you mean to me.

Since the publishing of *My Blood Runs Blue* in April of 2011, I have met so many wonderful authors who have helped encourage and assist me in my writing.

To the rest of my family, thank you for your words of support. Thank you for all of the excitement that you have shown for the first book, *My Blood Runs Blue*, and for the shared excitement of knowing that a sequel is coming out. I am proud to call all of you my family, and I hope that I continue to make you proud of me.

To my followers and readers...Thank you. Thank you for taking the time to get to know my writing and for coming back to read the next story in the saga of Officer Kristin Greene. Please be sure to visit me on my website to find out what's new and when the next book will be released.

www.stacyeaton.com

CHAPTER ONE

KRISTIN

"What are you doing there, man?" I spoke out loud to myself as I looked out the window of my patrol car. Someone was slipping between the houses across the street from where I was parked. It was a quiet night in the township, and I was looking for a car or two to pull over, but this looked as if it was going to be more fun. The guy was about five hundred feet away and hidden in the deep shadows of the moonless night, but I could still see him. Not every perfect detail, but I could make out enough of him to know that he was probably doing something that he shouldn't be doing. My keen eyes could take in things that a mere mortal person could not. Most mortals probably wouldn't have even noticed the guy from this far away.

I pushed the button to lower my window, reaching out with my sense of hearing to listen and see if there were any other telltale signs of the man being up to no good. A muffled cracking of glass told me, why yes, he was indeed doing something that he shouldn't be. I grinned and quietly opened my car door, glancing around to make sure no one was in the vicinity. I slipped into the darkness of a nearby tree, still listening and keeping an eye across the street. The windows

1

of the house were dark, and there were no cars parked in the driveway.

The quiet tinkling of glass falling to the ground reached my ears and I scanned the area again before darting across the roadway. I could not only hear and see better than mortals, I could move faster and quieter, too. I made it across the street within a second and slid up against the side of the house, stopping again to listen. The sound of someone grunting and huffing made me pause. I heard the sound of things scraping and realized he was probably trying to hoist himself up through a window.

I was about to peer around the corner to see if I could stop him before he got inside, but an emotional barrage slammed into me. It invaded all of my senses and almost made me gasp out loud. *Damn it, Alex! Not now!* I thought. I sent back an irritated feeling to let him know I was not happy with the interruption at this exact moment.

Alexander was my mate. Well, he was supposed to be. While we had completed the first part of our mating, we had not completed the second—the step that would make me a full-fledged vampire. It was also the part I was avoiding. I wasn't ready for it yet. As quickly as I had sent off an irritated response, Alex returned an even more irritated one right back, almost demanding that I respond to him. It was a mental ping-pong match that frustrated me to no end sometimes. I shook my head and yanked up the walls around my mind, shutting him out completely. The ability to put up those walls was something that I learned to do very quickly. If I hadn't, my mind would have been an open book to any vampire who wanted to listen in. It would also have been wide open to Alex's demands.

And I don't do demands.

I turned my attention back to the stranger. By this time, he had managed to climb into the house, and I could hear him moving around the room just beyond the window. I started to round the corner and got a whiff of the coppery sweetness of fresh blood. My instincts kicked in, and my front canine teeth started to tingle with anticipation. I spun back around the corner, taking a second to get my feelings under control and keep them in place. As long as I focused carefully, I could keep myself in check. I rounded the corner and moved to the window. On the edge of the windowsill was a small amount of fresh blood. The guy must have cut himself when he climbed through. I tried to keep the tempting metallic scent out of my nose, but it was hard. I needed to rein in the natural feeling that came with smelling warm blood, an intense feeling of hunger that comes as the sweet, coppery scent passes through our sensitive noses.

Once back firmly in control, I took a peek inside. The man had turned on a small flashlight and was digging in a drawer. The small beam of light was not strong enough to be seen outside the window by any human. He pulled open a jewelry box that sat on the dresser and I heard his quiet, "Bingo!"

He snatched a pillow off the bed, ripping the pillow out and throwing it to the floor. He started dumping the contents of the jewelry box into the pillowcase.

I quietly pulled my cellphone off my duty belt and moved back around the corner to text my partner, Mick. *325 Newtown—front door —wait.*

It took a few seconds before he responded back, *ENRT,* which meant that he was en route to my location.

I kept an eye on the guy inside the room while I waited for Mick to show up. My eyes kept flitting over to the blood droplet. I needed to make sure I fed when I got off duty. It had been too long. While I waited for Mick, I sent him another text message. *Burg in prog—one subject inside res—advise.* This told him he needed to call it out on the radio and tell our dispatcher where we were and what was going on. I couldn't take the chance of turning on my portable radio and letting the guy get spooked quite yet. I wanted to wait for my partner to get here.

The guy inside the house was now digging through the closet looking for valuables. I knew in a minute or two he would probably head on to the next room to see what else he could find.

While I waited for Mick, I briefly thought about Alex and how pissed off he was going to be that I shut him out, again. There would be hell to pay later, but I was getting used to that. This was not the first time I'd shut him out because he was demanding that I do something. I wasn't sure how long it was going to take before he realized I wouldn't bend to his demands.

I heard a car's engine racing down the street; by the deep sound of it, it was a patrol vehicle. I waited until it stopped and I heard the car door open. I could hear the mobile radio in the distance and our dispatcher acknowledging that we were on scene. It was too low for the burglar to hear it inside the house though.

I waited until I knew that Mick was about into place before I put my plan into action. I pulled my flashlight slowly off the back of my duty belt, stepped up to the window, and shined the light inside. I didn't shine the light for my benefit. I did it for his. Like a deer in the headlights of a car, the guy spun around with sheer panic in his eyes and froze. His wits took their time coming back to him and I felt his adrenaline spike. He stood up from the crouch he was in, and I felt the wheels begin to turn in his head. He looked over his shoulder at the door behind him, then back to me.

"Drop the stuff and come out the window," I said to him in a very calm, professional police voice.

He looked around again, and did exactly what I figured he would do. He turned to run out the bedroom door. I pretended as if I was going to climb in through the window, and that got him moving faster. He spun around and took off down the hall. I knew he would either try to run out the front door that would be the furthest from me or hide somewhere in the house. I'd give him a minute to see what he did.

As I started back around the side of the home, I heard rattling around in the front part of the house, and then the sound of a door opening. I smiled. Bad guys were so predictable. A second later, I heard Mick say very calmly but forcefully, "Police, put your hands up and get down on the ground."

"Fuck!" The guy's voice reached me as I turned to the front side of the house. I watched his wide eyes staring down the barrel of Mick's Glock. Very slowly, he got down to his knees and put his hands behind his head.

I stood in front of the guy and leaned down so that I was just inches from his face. "Bingo," I said quietly to him, and he rolled his eyes.

I laughed as I walked around him and smacked his wrist with one of my steel handcuffs. The ratcheting sound that the cuffs made as they slid into place was an awesome sound. I pulled his arm behind his back and grabbed the other wrist to pull it down and lock it into place.

"Up," I told the guy, who sat on his knees staring at the ground. He was probably trying to figure out what he could say to get himself out of this. He stood, and I led him over to Mick's car. I pushed him up against the side and started to pat him down. I pulled a screwdriver from the front pocket of his black hoodie, and a pocketknife from the front pocket of his jeans. Once I was sure there were no other weapons on his person, I opened up the rear door and told him to watch his head as he climbed inside. He looked up at me for a second. When we made eye contact, I saw not fear or anger, but resignation in his eyes. He lowered them and climbed into the back of the car. I closed the door and turned to find Mick watching me.

"How do you do that?" he asked me quietly, his head tilted to one side.

"What?" I pretended not to know what he was talking about. This was not the first time he asked this question. I shifted away and tried to walk past him, but he grabbed my arm and stopped me.

"You know what, Kristin." He held my arm, and I tried not to sigh as I faced him. He was the same height as me, but twice as wide. There was not an ounce of fat on his solid muscular frame. His dark brown eyes were slightly narrowed as he studied me. I could see the questions he wanted to ask, but I could not answer them. How could I tell my mortal partner what I really was?

"Really..." I laughed, although it was shallow. "Why do you always think it's more than just me being lucky?" I shrugged as if it was no big deal.

"You know you can tell me what's going on. You can trust me,

Kristin." He said it quietly, and I laughed again, this time much deeper. Man, he had no idea what he was asking for.

"Mick," I started, and then took a deep breath and shook my head. "There is nothing to tell, my man, nothing to tell." I pulled out of his grasp easily and went back to my truck to grab my camera and start processing the scene. I might have caught the guy at the scene, but I still had to prove that a crime was being committed and that he was involved in it for the justice system to work.

"Someday you are going to trust me, Kris," he called out as I walked away. He paused and waited for me to answer. When I didn't, he said, "I'm gonna take this guy to lockup. Want me to pick up coffee on the way back?"

"Yeah, I'll process the scene real quick, and then meet you back at the station," I called out over my shoulder, avoiding eye contact. I needed to start being more careful. Mick was such a quiet guy, and sometimes it was the quiet ones you had to worry about.

Over the last couple of months, my ability to locate crime in the making had been pretty consistent, especially with drug busts on traffic stops. I'm starting to think I might need to be a bit more careful to avoid suspicion. If Mick was starting to question how I found all of this stuff, it wouldn't be long before other people wondered, too.

I grabbed my camera bag out of the car and turned on my radio to make sure I didn't miss any calls while I was processing the scene. I went back inside the house through the front door, since the guy had been nice enough to leave it open for me on his way out. Carefully, I took pictures of the bedroom he had been in, made a list of the items he had thrown into the pillowcase, swabbed up the blood that he had left on the windowsill, and made some notes. Before I left, I put a business card in the front door with a note on the back telling the residents to contact us as soon as they arrived home. They were going to be surprised when they found their bedroom window busted out. Luckily, it wasn't supposed to rain tonight.

The radio was quiet right now, which meant I could probably take my time on my paperwork without being called out to anything else. I might be able to move fast and hear things that others couldn't, but paperwork was paperwork, and it didn't matter who you were. It took the same amount of time to do it.

On my way back to the station, I slid open my cell phone and found three missed calls and several text messages from Alex. I groaned. I knew he was going to be really pissed off that I not only shut him out, but ignored his calls, too. Not that I had done that part on purpose. My phone had been on silent so as not to alert the burglar. I figured since Alex was already pissed off, I would wait till later to call him back. I really didn't want to get into it with him tonight.

I got back to the station shortly after Mick arrived and tried to get situated in our designated area so that I could get the paperwork done. Our station was a small old ranch house that had been donated to the township by a developer. It wasn't much, just a couple of rooms with nowhere near enough storage, but it was quiet, and it was our home away from home.

I could tell that Mick was watching me. I had my back to him, but I knew the feeling of having someone stare hard enough at me that I could almost physically feel them touching me. My mind was still closed up from Alex, but if I let down the walls, I'm sure I would have been able to hear Mick's thoughts. They were practically verbal already. I tried to lose myself in the paperwork, but I kept feeling his eyes on my back. Finally, I took a deep breath, spun around in my office chair, and looked him in the eye.

He turned away as if he was embarrassed to have been caught, but then he met my gaze again. We sat there for a little while waiting for the other to talk. Finally, he tilted his head again and simply said, "How?"

So many questions were burning through his mind. I could sense them and make most of them out now that I was concentrating on him. Vampires were pretty good at reading the minds of others, especially humans. If I were a full vampire, I wouldn't have had any trouble figuring out what he was thinking, but as it was, I was still a half-breed, although I was more vampire than human now.

"Mick, I don't know what you want me to tell you. I'm in the right

7

place at the right time, that's all." I held my hands out in front of me as if I was begging him to believe me. I was actually able to say this with a straight face, because it was basically true. I had to be near the crime in order to know it was happening. It wasn't as if I could be on the other side of the township and know something was going on down here. I had to see or hear something first to be alerted to it.

"Kristin, for the last couple of months, I've noticed a difference. It's not just the crime you find or the drug busts you've made. It's you. *You're* different." He looked me up and down, as if he was trying to figure out how I might have changed.

I laughed and shook my head. "Mick, I am no different today than I was a couple of months ago. I'm just me, enjoying my job, and that's it." The lie tasted bitter on my tongue, but I couldn't tell him the truth. None of my friends knew the truth.

He shook his head vehemently. "No, there is something else. I'm not the only person to notice it either. The chief was talking about it the other day."

"Henderson was talking about me? I never even see him. Why would he think there was something different about me?" I haven't seen my chief in several months because I was only working night shifts. He very seldom had a reason to come out at night. I was experienced enough to deal with the serious incidents we might get at night and always advised him by phone of anything he might need to know about right away.

"He hears things, Kristin. Come on, you can't expect him to sit in his office, read all of your arrest reports, and not wonder what's going on. Almost every shift you work, you're busting someone for some major crime. How much dope have you gotten off the street in the last two months? Three, four hundred thousand dollars worth?"

It was actually over half a million dollars, but I wasn't going to correct him. It would only validate his point.

"You are catching people doing things that we never caught before. Well, not until we actually investigated it. Now we don't need to investigate. You catch them while they are in the act, and the county hasn't seen this many drug busts in years." He was examining his brown paper coffee cup, spinning it in his hand as he spoke. Finally, he looked back up at me and asked me once again, "How?"

I watched the logo on the cup spin around one more time before I answered. "Mick..." I stopped and sighed. How could I tell him? How could I say that I was immortal? That I had powers beyond that of a human? Vampires were the stories of the night, scary tales of blood-drinking creatures that killed humans for food. How could I explain to him that I was one of those creatures, and while we didn't kill humans, we did drink their blood.

Before I could come up with a response, the radio mic keyed up and called Mick for an ambulance call. *Saved by the static-filled male voice, at least for now,* I thought.

He guzzled the rest of his coffee and stood up to leave. As he turned away, he called over his shoulder, "We're not done with this. You are going to explain to me what's going on. We've worked together too long, and I deserve to know." He stopped and gave me a pointed look before heading for the door.

Jesus. Another demanding man! I watched him hit the green button on the wall that released the magnetic lock in the door. The door closed behind him with a small thud and a click, indicating the magnets were locked again. Crap, how was I going to handle this?

Two hours later, my paperwork was finished, my photos were uploaded, my reports were printed, and my criminal complaint was completed and ready for the court. I sat back and stretched my arms over my head. Swinging myself slightly left and right in the chair, I thought about the fact that I needed to call Alex. He had called me three more times while I was busy with paperwork, but I had refused to answer.

We'd been together now for three months. The first month had been bliss. We spent much of it getting to know each other, learning about each other. Then month two came along and Alex started pushing a bit, wanting to move our relationship along and complete our mating. I was able to push it off during month two, but now that we were almost at the end of month three, Alex was making it well known that he was not happy about waiting much longer.

I once told Alex that I was a cop and my blood ran blue. I thought he had understood that. I thought that he would understand my passion for the job and that I wasn't ready to stop working to complete the last step of our mating.

I took a long, deep cleansing breathe before I opened myself up to him. I could feel his frustration coming across our bond loud and clear, actually clearer than my portable radio normally was. I could picture him sitting in his office, looking at the bank of computer screens behind his desk. He would be staring at them, not seeing them. Waiting…just waiting for me to call, and then we'd start the conversation all over again.

While I could feel his emotions, I could not mentally speak to him at this distance. He was up in Poughkeepsie, New York, and I was in southeastern Pennsylvania. That was too far for us to communicate telepathically, but we could feel each other's feelings, especially if they were strong; and right now, his were really, *really* strong.

I took a deep breath and hit his name on my cell phone. It was two rings before he answered. "You need to come home," he said in his deep, mellow voice.

"Alex, I am home," I answered as I looked around the patrol room of my station.

CHAPTER TWO

ALEX

"Damn it, Kristin! Answer your phone!" This was the third time I called her in the last two hours. I spun around in my office chair and stared at the bank of eight computer screens behind my desk. Screens that showed me what was going on in the building and what was happening at several locations around the country. With the push of a button, I could change any of the monitors to show a different location.

I sat there staring at them, but not seeing them, wishing the whole time that Kristin would answer the damn phone or call me back. Her shift would be over soon and, knowing her, she was probably knee-deep in paperwork from another arrest that she'd made tonight. I didn't really know what she did at work, but she had commented once or twice about how many arrests she'd been making recently.

I knew Kristin hated it when I tried to tell her what to do. She was a strong, independent woman, sometimes too strong, and she didn't like to be told what to do or when to do it. Sending that emotional outburst to her earlier was a bad way to deal with this, and I knew it instantly, especially the moment her walls snapped up. I was so frustrated with things that were happening, and I needed her to understand how important this really was.

It wasn't just that I wanted her here with me. Of course, I did. It wasn't that I didn't want her to finish the mating process with me. I wanted that more than anything. But there was something happening around us, and I felt that she was in danger. We were both in danger.

Three months ago, when Kristin chose me over Julian, I had been happily surprised. I'd loved her for over forty years, although technically, I had only known her as Kristin for three months. Forty years ago, I had fallen in love with Calista, but had put our relationship to the side thinking I had time, and she had found Julian while she waiting for me to come around.

I stared unseeingly at the computer screens in front of me. Julian, or Jules as his friends called him, used to be my best friend. Well, actually, he still was, but we had gone through a tough time all those years ago when Calista had chosen him over me. I know now that it had never been planned and only happened because I hadn't made Calista my mate when I should have.

When Calista and Julian got together, my world felt as if it had fallen apart. So I'd thrown myself into my work with a vengeance and became the head of the VMF, the Vampire Military Force, the group that regulates vampire activity around the country. It also stood for Virtual Military Force, and that was the security portion of the company that worked with human and vampire customers alike.

Julian and Calista had been happy, or so I'd thought. They'd had a daughter named Anastasia, and to all eyes, appeared the perfect family. That was, until Damon had come knocking. Damon was Julian's son, and he killed Calista and Anastasia right in front of Julian, who had been helpless to stop it from happening. He blamed himself for thirty-five years.

There was only one good thing that had come of her death. Damon hadn't had the necessary time to stake their hearts after he ripped out their throats. Since he had not staked them, their souls had been reborn within other half-breeds. This was something we only believed could happen. No one had been able to confirm it with absolute certainty. Not until Kristin.

So it was thirty-five years after they died that everything changed.

Call it fate, call it destiny, or call it weird. I don't care what the hell you call it, but Julian stumbled upon Kristin while working a case looking for Damon. Ironically, Kristin was also working the same case, but as a half-breed police officer who was investigating Damon's latest kill. She had no idea what she had gotten herself into when she responded to the scene that night.

I clenched my jaw as I remembered how Kristin had immediately been drawn to Julian again, even without knowing who or what he was. That first night that I'd seen her again with my own eyes, I'd been shocked. Not only had her soul been reborn, but it was as if her entire being had come back almost exactly the same. Even her scent was duplicated—sweet sugar mixed with creamy butter. Although she looked and smelled the same, she was a lot more headstrong than she had been as Calista.

When I had interrupted Julian and Kristin kissing in the parking lot, things got even more interesting. It wasn't long before I had to explain to Kristin what we were and what she really was. It was only a day later that she came face to face with Damon. He had figured out that she was a half-breed and wanted to take her out, as he was trying to do with all the other half-breeds and female vampires that he could find.

The thing about Damon was that he blamed Julian for creating him, and for forcing him to live life as a vampire. He thought that if he killed all the half-breeds and women vampires, then we could no longer reproduce naturally. When he came for Kristin, she almost didn't make it. It had been a close battle, but Julian and I had been keeping an eye on her. We all worked together, along with Kristin's dog Garda, to keep her alive and end Damon's existence for good.

I thought that when that was over, Kristin would go to Julian. I figured she would fall in love with him again. During the fight with Damon, she hit her head pretty hard and all the memories of Calista had come back. She went to Julian after she woke up and told him that it had been her fault that she, Calista, had been killed. She had tried to help Julian find Damon, thinking he was only trying to make peace with his son. She hadn't known that Julian was trying to find

Damon to kill him. By admitting that, she had released the guilt from his shoulders. They also discussed the fact that they both knew it had been wrong for them to mate all those years ago. The way it was done had been wrong and put a great strain on their relationship. They said good-bye to each other, and she returned to find me packing my things. That was three months ago.

Since then, we had started the process; she carried my blood, and I carried hers. It bonded us, made us able to communicate with each other even when we were apart. I was very good at feeling the emotions of the people around me, especially with those I shared blood with. With Kristin, it was even stronger than with some of the children I had sired. I had sired quite a few children over the two hundred and seventy-five or so years I had been a vampire, but I never truly mated with anyone.

There was one step that kept us from finally being a completely mated couple. It was to have a child together. I know now that she was not overly excited about the whole prospect of bearing a child. She made it perfectly clear, over and over, that she was not ready. I knew she thought that was what I wanted to speak to her about tonight, but there were more important things to worry about right now. Her life...my life...our existence, period.

I picked up my cell phone and dialed her number. Again, it went to voice mail. I didn't bother to leave her a message. She would see that I had called. Once more, I reached out for her emotionally, trying to be calm, but knowing that my frustration and anger were getting the best of me. She was still closed off, holding up the mental wall to avoid my feelings.

I tossed my cell phone onto the desk and took out some paper to write two letters. When I finished, I pulled out two envelopes and put the papers inside them. I sealed them and put Kristin's name on the front of one and Julian's name on the front of the other. Then I tucked them into the appointment book on my desk. If something happened to me, someone was bound to find them.

As I sat back in my chair and spun it around to look at the computer screens, I felt her reach out to me. She was pretty calm, calmer than I expected after all the phone calls and text messages I sent her. I looked down at the phone and answered it on the second ring.

"You need to come home," I said simply, not meaning for it to be a demand.

I heard her sigh on the other end before she answered, "I am home."

I knew what she meant about her work being her home. She devoted herself to her job. To her, it was who she was and, as she had told me before, her blood ran blue in her veins even if it looked red.

"Kristin, I need you here. There are things going on that you need to be aware of, and it would be better if you were here." I wasn't going to make the mistake of saying "home" again, even though we did have a house here together. We also had a house in Fawn Hollow Township where she worked.

"Alex, I can't come there right now. I'm working." She said it as if I didn't already know that.

"I'm not talking about right this second. This is your weekend off. I need you to come up here tomorrow night as soon as you can. How are you doing with daylight? Can you still venture out?" I knew that as a half-breed sunlight would not hurt her, but we had shared a lot of blood, and I knew that it would have an effect on her pretty soon.

"Yes, I can still handle sunlight in the late afternoon, but Alex, I took a shift tomorrow night, and then I have a party to go to. I told you about that. It's Mick's thirty-fifth birthday party on Saturday night, and I can't miss my partner's party."

"When did you pick up the shift? When I talked to you yesterday, you weren't scheduled for it." I was getting angry. I didn't want to have to explain all of this to her on the phone. I wanted her to be here where I knew she was safe.

"Alex, really! I sent you a freaking text earlier today about it. Do you ever read what I write, or do you have selective eyesight like most men have selective hearing?" She was pissed, too. I thought back quickly and remembered about the text, but I had been busy with other things and dismissed it quickly.

"Yes, I got it." I tried to calm my voice. "Look, Kris, this is important, and we need to talk face to face. I need you to come home. I need you to be here with me." She was probably going to get even angrier now that I just said "home" again. For some reason, she hated to think of our house here in Poughkeepsie as home.

"I can't. We're short staffed right now, and we have a lot going on. I'm not going to do that to the guys just because you want to hash out this whole mating thing again. We've talked about it over and over. I'm not ready for that. My job is too important to me to stop right now. I thought you understood that."

Now I was the one getting angry again. "Kristin, this is not about that. God, woman, you can be so damn hardheaded sometimes. This is something else entirely. Something that you really need to know about and I don't want to talk about it on the phone."

"I'm sorry, Alex, but I'm not going to make it up this weekend. I'll come up midweek when I have a couple days off. Maybe I can get one of the guys to grab one of my shifts then and stay an extra day. I'm sure whatever it is can wait a few more days."

"Damn it, Kristin! This can't wait. Look, if you won't come here, then fine, I'll come down there. Expect me tomorrow night." I shook my head at how obstinate she could be. "I'll call you when I get to the house."

"Whatever, Alex. I'll see you then. Look, they're calling me. I gotta go." I could hear in the background that they had indeed just called her. As she went to hang up the phone I heard her voice drift away from the line as she answered on her lapel mic, "Thirty-One-Paul-One," then the phone went dead as she ended the call.

I closed my eyes and put my head back on the leather chair I sat in. If only she knew how important this was. I had to get to her before they did. I had to keep her safe. I hoped like hell that tomorrow night would be soon enough.

CHAPTER THREE

KRISTIN

I woke up around four in the afternoon. I wasn't sure if I wanted to even look at my cell phone. How many times would Alex have tried to get a hold of me while I slept? I sighed and rolled over, lifting the phone from the charger dock. I only missed one call and had two text messages, none of which were from Alex.

My two girlfriends, Isabell and Olivia, had both sent me messages to make sure I was going to the party tomorrow night. I shot off responses to them that I wouldn't miss it for the world!

I lay back in bed and looked around my room. I sold the little ranch house that I used to live in before I met Alex and was now living in the local VMF house. It was more appropriate for me to live here, seeing as the bedrooms on the top floor had no windows to affect my sleeping or cause me ill effects from the sun.

The room was decorated in rich, dark oak wood and deep purples, something I had insisted on updating when I moved in. It was about the only big change I'd made to the house. Well, other than altering the rear door so that Garda, my Shiloh Shepherd, could come and go as he pleased. He loved our new home. There were three stories for him to investigate and get lost in. Plus acres of land for him to run and chase the small critters that came out from the woods that surrounded the house on all sides.

It was a beautiful house, mostly done in stone, with wood accents. A magnificent staircase ran down into a stone foyer with a large crystal chandelier hanging over the entrance. The thing I liked best was I didn't have to clean it. There was staff who came in a couple of times a week to clean the rooms and stock the kitchen.

Damn, kitchen, I forgot to eat last night. Crap! My back cracked as I rolled out of the bed and stretched my arms over my head. On my way downstairs I realized that it had been almost three days since I last fed. With the reaction that I'd had last night to the blood droplet, I berated myself for waiting so long. Inside the stainless steel fridge there is a panel that if you slide it up, you will find a compartment that holds bags of fresh blood, courtesy of a special blood bank. A quick snip, pour it into my favorite mug, and punch some buttons on the microwave, and I was on my way to a gourmet meal, liquid style. My fangs were heavy in my mouth as the scent of blood filled the air. I really needed to stop waiting so long between feedings. When the ding toned on the microwave, Garda ran through the doggie door from outside. He must have heard it, too. He jumped up to greet me, and it wouldn't be so bad if he wasn't about a hundred and thirty pounds and taller than my five foot five frame when he stood on his hind legs. As it was, I got pushed back against the counter and almost spilled my breakfast.

"Gee, you didn't miss me, boy, did you? Get down." He immediately listened and walked over to lie near a stool, assuming I would sit down. I followed his lead and climbed up onto the seat, watching as he lay there panting, his caramel eyes shining brightly up at me. Garda had been instrumental in my life.

He was my companion after Trevor was killed. Trevor had been my human husband and a police officer. He'd been killed accidentally in the line of duty by one of his own partners. It still hurt to think about, how couldn't it? Trevor was my love and my life for several years.

Garda had also been a big part of keeping me alive three months ago when Damon tried to kill me again. He was actually the real reason I survived. If Garda hadn't jumped to knock me out of Damon's reach, I would have been killed.

When Garda knocked me over, I struck my head and was knocked unconscious. When I woke up, I realized that the blow not only gave me a nice lump and a headache, but it also gave me memories of a past life. Everything that had happened to my soul as Calista filled my mind. So many memories had crushed down on me, but none more important than knowing the truth about how Calista and Anastasia had died. It hadn't been Julian's fault, it had been mine, or Calista's really.

Julian...I closed my eyes. His friends all called him Jules, because it shortened his name. I had a different reason for calling him that. To me, his eyes were the color of sparking jewels, dark sapphires and rich aquamarines. I had always gotten lost in his eyes, not only as Calista, but as myself.

I had not seen Julian in three months, not since I confessed the truth about the night Calista died. I missed him, and despite the fact that I was mated to Alex, I loved Julian, too. There was an incredible chemistry between us that we couldn't explain. When we were close by, we gravitated toward one another. That was what had brought us together over forty years ago, that wild chemistry, and we both knew that it was wrong. I sipped from my mug, letting the tangy sweet blood flow over my tongue and down my throat to sate my thirst. My reaction to Julian is probably the reason Alex kept Julian busy in other parts of the country, and away from me. I had no doubt that Alex did not trust us together, especially until the mating was complete. Part of me had to agree with him.

I absently pet Garda for a few minutes thinking about how I had not heard from Alex yet. That was rare. He was probably even more upset than I anticipated if he was willing to come down here. I tried to reach out to him mentally to see what he was feeling, but there was just a brief sense of tension about him; he was keeping himself pretty closed. Whatever. I'd deal with him later when he arrived.

I walked into work later that afternoon to find Thomas waiting for me. He was just coming off the day shift, and we spent a few minutes talking about his shift.

Tom was one of our newer officers. He was young, in his early twenties, eager to work, and always excited to get involved. I could imagine Tom going places in his career, as long as he didn't burn himself out.

With shop talk over, Tom went on to tell me about this new girl he was seeing. He mentioned that he was bringing her to the party the next night, and I honestly was looking forward to meeting her. I liked Thomas, and knowing he was happy was a good thing.

It was a bit later that night as I was driving up to a residence for a domestic, that I got an intense emotional outburst from Alex. It washed over me so quickly that it took me by surprise. Normally, they start to invade my mind slowly; this was like a bucket of cold water thrown on me.

It came out of nowhere, and it was intense enough that I had to stop in my tracks halfway to the front door. Was there something else going on around me, or was this really coming from the blood bond? I scanned the area, but saw nothing out of the ordinary.

Anger replaced the surprise, and I knew it was the blood bond, it was Alex. Why the hell was he so pissed off now? I huffed; I didn't have time to deal with it right now. I slammed the walls up around me. I didn't have time for Alex's temper tantrums, not when I had a man and woman physically fighting twenty feet away. The call ended up not being as bad as it had originally been dispatched. The husband and wife were arguing over a report card their child brought home, and the wife slammed a glass onto the table. The husband, in turn, grabbed the glass and threw it across the kitchen where it shattered. Both parties lost their tempers, and it was just a matter of someone stepping in and calming the situation down.

When I left, the husband had the broom in one hand and an arm wrapped around his wife as he apologized and kissed her temple. How I wished all calls could be so easy. My cell phone rang the moment I opened my car door. I figured it was Alex ready to give me a tongue lashing for blocking him out, but much to my delight it was one of my best friends, Olivia.

"Yo...what's doing?" I said by way of greeting.

"Hey, girl! Not much; you working?" she asked me.

"Yeah, but I'm only working a half shift. I get off at midnight. Why?" I pulled out of the driveway and decided to do some basic patrol while we chatted.

"You wanna meet Izzy, Kat, and me later for a drink?" She sounded down, and I wondered why they were going out tonight, when we would all be out tomorrow night for Mick's party.

"Not sure that I can. Alex is supposed to come down. He's pissed off that I wouldn't come up this weekend. I'm not sure when he's getting in, and I think we need to sit down and talk." I blew out my breath heavily.

"Is he still on the kid kick?" she said, and laughed.

I returned the laugh while I answered. "Yeah, something like that."

"Fine. If for some reason you want to come find us, we'll be down at Joe's Bar. I really gotta let off some steam." She sounded upset.

"What's going on?" I knew her too well, and I had a feeling I knew what this was about.

She sighed into the phone loudly. "Nothing...Well, it's just him again. He's back to his same crap. Doesn't want me working the job, wants me to stay home barefoot and babysitting his kids."

Yep, exactly what I thought. The guy she was dating had been awesome for a while, but all of a sudden, he decided that police work was a man's job and since she was a woman, she would be better off at home raising kids. I hated guys like that.

"I kind of figured that was it. Look, if Alex doesn't get in till late, I'll head down. I'll shoot you a message when I get off." We said our good-byes and hung up.

Olivia, or Livy as I called her, worked for a police department next to mine. We'd been best friends for a couple of years, and I was feeling guilty about the fact that I had never told her what was really going on in my life. She had no clue, and neither did Izzy or Kat, our other two really good friends. The only friends who knew were Gina Marie and her husband Brendon.

The only reason they even knew was because they were both vampires. Gina Marie and Calista had been best friends way back when. Gina Marie is also the one who helped me over the last several months when my life turned into a whirlwind. It was her daughter's homicide that I'd been investigating when I met Julian and Alex and learned who, and what, I really was.

Thinking of Alex, I knew I'd better check on him and see if he had calmed down yet. It only took a quick thought to let down the emotional wall. I reached out for him, but could feel nothing. He must have been really pissed to put his wall up and close me out completely. I tried to call him to find out when he would be down here, but his phone rang four times before it went to voice mail.

"Hey, Alex, just calling to find out when you are going to be down here. Give me a call when you get the message." I hung up, not mentioning anything about the earlier emotional barrage he had almost drowned me in.

Midnight came and I still hadn't heard from Alex, so I decided to meet up with the girls. I shot Alex a text to let me know when he got in and I would meet him at the house. I tried to reach out to him one more time, but again found his walls up as tight as Fort Knox.

*Whatever...*I went home, changed clothes, and took off to meet my friends.

When I walked into Joe's Bar, it was dark and smoky. It was one of the rare places where people could smoke indoors, and tonight, there were a lot of people smoking. Lucky for me, smoke wasn't going to harm me, but as I looked around, I saw a lot of humans who could easily be in the running for lung cancer.

As I scanned the room, I picked up on a presence unlike that of a mortal. There was a vampire in here, sitting on the far side of the bar. She was watching me, and when our eyes met, I knew she had pegged me for what I was. She tipped her lips in the semblance of a smile and turned away. I had no clue who she was, but since I was still new to this whole dark world, there were a lot of people I didn't know.

I studied her while I had the chance. She had strawberry blond hair similar to my color, but hers was much longer. I couldn't see much detail about her face with her turned in the other direction. As I approached, a strange feeling came over me. It was almost as if she was calling out to me, but not. I rolled back my shoulders and tried to deny the internal pull that came from being close to her. I wasn't in the mood to figure it out. I had enough on my mind, and my first priority was to find my friends.

I saw Izzy, Livy, and Kat at a small table in the corner and made a beeline over to them. What a crew we made, all so different. Livy was now sporting long dark hair; she had a habit of changing her hair color and style quite often. She was the shortest of us all, and although she was petite in height, she made up for it in strength and a wild personality. She had a very exotic look about her, dark and sexual, and she was forever getting the eyes of every man in the room. If she kept her mouth closed, and her shirt on, she could have almost any man in the world. It was the rare male who could handle the extreme language that fell from her lips or the twelve colorful tattoos that adorned her body under her clothing.

Izzy was a dirty-blond and around my height of five and a half feet. She was the sane one of our group, for the most part. She had a sweet, innocent face and relaxed features that just screamed, *"I wanna have fun."* She wasn't a police officer, but worked closely with us as a juvenile probation officer. She loved working with kids, but didn't have any of her own yet. She had always been afraid to take that particular plunge, but we'd had conversations recently that suggested she might be coming around. She was the one who was always lighthearted and quick with a joke, where Livy was the dark one.

Kat was the glue that held us all together, the anchor to our reality. She had shoulder-length blond hair and was the one in our group who liked to watch. She was quiet, reserved, and showed intelligence and strength in her blue eyes. She watched, listened, and kept us from doing stupid things—most of the time. She was also the administrative assistant at my police department and was constantly on me to make sure my paperwork was completed on time so that she could do what she needed to do with it. She kept me in line, on and off the job.

I smiled at my friends, glad that I had decided to come out, and climbed up on the empty stool at the table. Before I could even get all the hellos out, a cold bottle of my favorite lager clunked down on the table before me. The bartenders knew us well and made sure we were always taken care of.

We spent some time catching up on the usual gossip of our lives. Livy talked about her boyfriend and the general consensus at the table was to ditch him now before he became more of an idiot. Kat enlightened us on the plans for her next cruise with her husband, and Izzy confirmed that, yes, she and the hubby were going to start working on a family, finally. When the talk of Izzy starting a family came up, I automatically thought of Alex. I reached out for a second and found that he was still closed off.

I was a bit perplexed about this. Alex normally didn't shut me out for long, and this had been close to six hours. I checked my cell phone to make sure I hadn't missed his call or a text message. There was nothing.

"I thought Alex was coming down tonight," Olivia stated as she looked over the table at me. "He's supposed to, but I haven't heard from him. Can't seem to reach him either." I looked at my cell phone, making it seem as if that was the way I tried to communicate with him. Now was not the time to let them know we spoke without words.

Izzy shrugged. "Maybe he got busy. You've told me before his company keeps him busy." She was trying to be positive, I could tell. She must have picked up on my concern for him.

I was about to reply that was probably exactly what happened when I got hit with a wave of emotional pain so intense I almost fell off my stool. It felt as if someone stabbed me in the chest, but it wasn't me; it was coming from my bond. I gasped and grabbed the edge of the table to keep from collapsing off the stool. Dizziness washed over me as I gripped the edge, trying not to damage it with the strength of my hands.

I must have looked horrified because all three of my friends reached for me with surprised looks on their faces. They were almost as shocked as I was, as they said nothing. I tried to take in a breath, but the pain was so intense that I couldn't seem to get the smoky air into my lungs.

Deep, dark, intense pain radiated through my mind, centered in my chest, and then moved out along the limbs of my extremities. I closed my eyes and tried to absorb the pain without it affecting me more. Alex. What the hell was going on with Alex? Was he hurt? This amount of pain had to be physically inflicted, and with this level of intensity for a vampire, it had to be severe.

The emotional burst lasted only about thirty seconds, and then it was gone. It didn't fade away; it was just there, and then it wasn't. I opened my eyes and found all three of my friends staring at me with startled looks on their faces.

"Alex," I said as the air finally whooshed into my lungs.

What just happened? I picked up my cell phone with shaking hands and punched up Alex's contact information. As I was about to bring the phone to my ear, I felt the internal pull again along with a shiver up my spinal column. I spun around in my chair and made eye contact with the female vampire that had been at the bar. She was heading toward the door, a cell phone to her ear, her serious eyes locked on me.

Just as she reached the door, she paused and shot me a crazed look, as if she was ecstatic over something. I couldn't hear the words she spoke on the phone because my ears were ringing, but I could read her lips. I would have bet a million dollars that she said, "Yeah, she just got the message." Then she turned and disappeared out the door.

If I had not been in shock, I would have gotten up and gone after her, but as it was, it was all I could do to hold the phone to my ear and will the ringing in my ear to be answered.

Izzy reached out for me as I hit the END button. "Kristin, what's going on? Are you okay?"

I scanned the table; they all looked concerned, but not as

25

concerned as I felt. I set my phone down with trembling fingers. "No. Something is wrong with Alex."

CHAPTER FOUR

ALEX

Julian called right after I spoke with Kristin. I told him to get on the first plane back to Poughkeepsie. Julian and Gabe were working down in Florida on the case, but I needed him here. I needed him to help protect Kristin and be my right hand on this. If there was anyone I could trust with protecting her and helping me, it was Julian.

I knew he still loved her, just as she still loved him. It was one of the reasons why I'd kept him busy in other parts of the country and not in our area. I figured with more time, they would eventually move apart. I wouldn't have to worry as much once we were fully mated, but I was unsure of when that would actually happen.

Julian was surprised to be getting called back so soon, but understood something was up when I wouldn't give details over the phone. I told him that I planned on heading to Fawn Hollow after he arrived and was briefed. He said he'd meet me at the office as soon as his plane landed.

I went back to my house and tried to sleep, but there were too many things going on right now, and this case was about to crack wide open. Some information had trickled back to me that the vampires we were investigating knew we were on to them. Word filtered down that if we didn't stop investigating them, they would come after me. Normally, I would not be concerned about that, but they didn't stop at threatening me—they threatened Kristin, too.

That was unacceptable!

I dozed on and off, and when I got up I started tying up loose ends so that I could take off to Fawn Hollow as soon as I spoke with Julian. I'd packed ahead of time and was in the office when I realized I had forgotten something back at the house. Julian's plane wasn't landing for another hour, so it made sense to run back now, rather than wait till after Julian arrived. I might be cutting my time short for nighttime travel if I did that.

I was lost in thought as I climbed in the elevator, wondering how I was going to convince Kristin to take me seriously and come back with me. As I stepped out of the elevator and into the basement garage, I knew I wasn't alone. I could feel the presence of four other vampires. They were hidden in the shadows, and I went into fight mode immediately, my body tensing, my senses alert.

Two of them approached me. Both of them dressed in dark fatigues and masks. I noticed that the other two held rifles. Bullets wouldn't kill me; slow me down, yes, but not kill me. Unless they were titanium and platinum bullets, then they could do some very serious damage. These people were vampires, not humans, so it was very likely that the ammunition they were using was not the run of the mill sports store selection.

I stood still, watching and waiting for them to approach me. As they got closer, I saw one man reach behind him and pull out a hand-gun. I tried not to be concerned as he pointed it at me. His emotions were calm, but an edge of excitement laced through him.

"We warned you, Alexander, and now we are going to show you how serious we really are." The man who was pointing the gun fired a shot right into my chest.

It was not until the projectile hit me that I realized that it was not a firearm with bullets, but a tranquilizer gun. I thought as I fell to the ground that I would have had more time. As I hit the hard cement floor, anger bloomed within me.

I was furious for not being more careful. I didn't even look at the security monitors in my office before I got in the elevator. I was pissed because Julian didn't know what was going on, or that he needed to protect Kristin, and scared to death knowing that they would now go after her.

I lost consciousness as my head hit the ground, seeing her beautiful face in my mind as everything went black.

When I woke up, I had no idea where I was. I lay still, trying to listen to what was around me. I could not make out any sounds, and I slowly opened my eyes. It was dark, and it appeared to be some kind of enclosed cell. I wasn't worried about the dark, I could actually see better in it than in bright light.

As my eyes adjusted, I reached out and realized my arms felt extremely heavy. My wrists hurt, and I felt the metal bracelets wrapped around them. I was betting that they were a combination of platinum and titanium alloy. That combination of metal would drain a vampire of strength and mental powers.

I wasn't able to lift my arm all the way up, but I could slide it to the side and made contact with a metal wall. *Damn.* I was probably inside a lead and steel cell. There was no way to communicate with anyone on the outside.

My mind was still foggy from the tranquilizer they had given me, and I was having a very hard time keeping my eyes open and my thoughts in a direct pattern. A few seconds later, my eyes fell shut again, and I drifted back into a drug-induced sleep.

When I woke again later, I was able to keep my eyes open longer, and the fog in my head felt clearer. I didn't want to waste what strength I had by moving around with the heavy metal bracelets on, so I remained still and tried to pick up on any sounds or movement coming from outside the cell.

I'm not sure how long I lay there before the sound of an opening lock made me turn my head and the door opened. Bright light burst through and I clamped my eyes shut against the assault on my senses. As I tried to open them to adjust, another sense caught on something coming through the door, and an intense pain started in my throat.

The smell of fresh, warm human blood was coming from just outside of the door. My body was instantly reacting to the need of being in pain and wanting to feed. The smell of the blood was intoxicating and washed over me like a refreshing rain shower. My throat ached, and my canine teeth extended and throbbed. I tried to focus on the light and block out the smell.

At the same time, I fought to keep my emotional wall up. I didn't know how much I had sent to Kristin earlier, and I didn't want to alarm her now. I needed to protect her the best way that I could, and keeping my pain and hunger away from her was important right now.

Two tall, solidly built men came into the room and grabbed me by the arms. They dragged me out of the cell and into a brightly lit cement room of some kind. Maybe it was a basement. I got pushed down into a hard wooden chair where bright hot lights were focused to blind me after being in the dark. I tried to keep my eyes up and open, but the best I could do was to keep looking down at the ground away from the lights.

A man started to speak from behind me, and I tried to look over my shoulder. The sight that caught my attention stopped me in my tracks. Against the cement wall was a human man, slumped over. His neck was punctured, and blood was leaking down onto his shirt. He was still alive. I could hear his heart beating and see the pulse of the blood as it exited the vein in his neck. I closed my eyes at the urge to fall to my knees and take his vein into my mouth.

When the man behind me spoke again, I tried to pull my thoughts away from the human so that I could hear what he was saying.

"Good, she's there. Let me know if she gets the message." He flipped his phone closed and walked over to me.

I knew who this man was, but I had never personally met him. He was the lowest form of scum in the vampire world. He was ruthless, utterly uncaring about the loss of human life. He only used them to further his own means, no matter the cost.

His eyes were a steel gray, dark and evil looking. He had dark hair that was short and wavy. He was wearing a black suit and looked as if he was dressed for dinner at a nice restaurant, not for being down in this basement with a human bleeding to death five feet from him.

"I told you to stay away from me, Alex. I told you, *'I don't bother you, you don't bother me,'* but you didn't listen, now did you?" He towered over me as I slumped in the seat, my arms hanging heavy at my sides from the weight of the metal bracelets.

"Fuck you, Burke," I said through a sneer. I might have been slumped in the chair, but my mind was reeling with thoughts of what I wanted to do to this vampire.

"No, you are not my type, but..." He put on an evil smile, the color of his eyes lightening slightly.

"Stay away from her. You just stay the hell away from her! She has nothing to do with this!" Adrenaline surged through me, but I made sure not to let my wall fall.

"Oh, doesn't she? Do you not know what your little woman is up to these days? Funny! But you see, Alexander, you are in no position to tell me what to do right now. In fact, what you are going to do is actually help me send a message to her. You can communicate with her emotionally, right?" He turned around and picked something up from a table behind him. I couldn't see it because it was behind the bright lights.

"I'm not doing anything for you. She has nothing to do with any of this. If you weren't bringing attention to yourself, I wouldn't have had to come after you. Kristin has nothing to do with this." I was trying to figure out what he had picked up, and nothing I pictured was any good.

He turned back around and laughed. It made me furious, and I wanted to jump up out of the seat and tear his head off.

"You really have no idea what she is doing, do you? Alex, the man of such control, can't control the woman in his life. How ironic is that?" He laughed again. "I'm done talking to you right now. Let's just send her a little message, shall we?"

He walked up to me, and before I could even think of moving, he stabbed me in the left side of the chest with a metal stake. Not close enough to my heart to kill me, but close enough to inflict tremendous pain.

The stake went into my chest, and the searing pain of it caused me to drop my mental wall immediately. In the back of my mind, I knew that Kristin was getting slammed with the pain almost as surely as I was. I could not control it or even attempt to block it. I couldn't do anything at all besides be conscious of the fact that the stake had done its job: a message was sent.

About thirty seconds after the stake went in, he pulled it out. I fell forward, willing myself to stay conscious. I tried to breathe through the pain, but the stake had gone into my left lung, which made it hard to inhale. I would heal, but with the type of tool that they used, and my weakened state, it would be hard for even me.

The two men came back to pick me up, and Burke's cell phone rang. He answered it on the first ring and put it on speaker.

"Yes, Angelina, did the message go through?" he asked into the speaker.

"Yeah, she got the message," said the female's voice on the other end.

"Good. Keep an eye on her." Burke smiled at me. I could hear it in his voice. My head was hanging down, and all I could think about was how much it must have just affected Kristin.

I was dragged back into the cell and dropped onto the bed unceremoniously.

"We'll see you again soon, Alex. Rest up, we have quite a few more messages to send to her." He laughed as he shut the door with a loud bang.

As I lay on the cot, tears ran out of the corners of my eyes. Not from the pain I felt, but for the pain that Kristin would be feeling and for the confused state she must be in right now.

Julian...please get to her soon, I prayed as I passed out for the third time that night.

CHAPTER FIVE

KRISTIN

To say that I was shaken from what happened tonight would be a fair assumption, but in reality, I was emotionally turned upside down. It had been over an hour since I felt Alex's pain and there had been no other emotions to come my way over our bond. I tried Alex's phone over and over again...but it just kept going to voice mail. I didn't have Julian's phone number, and I didn't even know who else to contact. There was so much I didn't know about the man...Why hadn't I taken the time to find these things out?

Livy, Izzy, and Kat had followed me home. After they saw me go through the emotional downfall, they refused to leave me alone. They had no clue what really happened, but they knew it wasn't good.

I told them I was fine, but they knew I really wasn't. For once, I didn't want to fight with them about it. I didn't want to be the strong one and pretend as if I could handle everything. I was wiped out, and having my friends close by was what I wanted, what I needed.

We all came back to my house, and, for the first time in a long time, I felt cold, inside and out. I turned on the gas fireplace in the living room and watched Livy yawn out of the corner of my eye as she sank down onto the couch.

"How come you never seem tired at night, Kris?" Livy asked as she tried to stop a second yawn.

I shrugged a shoulder. "I work night shifts; my body got used to being up at night. You know you are more than welcome to go crash in one of the guest rooms." I peered at her quickly.

"Nope, I'll stay right here where you are." She hesitated before she went on. "I'm not sure what happened tonight, but it was like you were in serious physical pain there for a little bit, and then it just vanished." She was holding her head up with her hand, and looked so tired.

"Yeah, what's up with that?" Izzy asked as she pulled her feet up under her on the other end of the couch. Izzy and Kat didn't look much more awake than Livy did. Both of them had light purple circles under their eyes.

My look encompassed them all, going back and forth between them a couple of times before I sighed heavily and turned back toward the fireplace. I stood in front of it, watching the flames flick up into the air.

For a few seconds, I lost myself in the dancing flames. They were always moving, rolling, jumping, and sparking up into the air. What would it feel like to step into the beauty of them, I wondered.

"Alex is in trouble." I didn't turn around. I kept my eyes trained on the bright flames dancing in front of me. I knew that behind me they must be looking at one another, waiting. I heard someone yawn, Izzy maybe.

"How do you know that?" Kat asked.

I didn't say anything at first and tried to figure out how to even start. "Wow..." I looked down at the floor, shaking my head. I focused on the fireplace again before I continued. "I wasn't sure when or how I was ever going to get into this with you all, but I guess tonight is as good as it gets." I turned around and looked at them, their eyes all wide as they glanced at me and each other. I sat down in one of the leather wingback chairs.

"It's about damn time!" Livy said.

Izzy laughed. "Yeah, we kind of thought there was a story going on here, but we knew you would tell us when you were ready."

I laughed halfheartedly. It would figure that they knew something was going on. My lifestyle was hard to hide, especially from my best friends. I knew that if my partner Mick was picking up the changes, then my close friends had to know something was going on. To be honest, I was actually surprised they hadn't cornered me before tonight to make me give up the dirt.

With another look around, I made my decision. It was time. And if I was going to unleash this bad boy, these guys needed a drink. I went to the liquor cabinet, collected four glasses, and poured some Firefly vodka into them.

"I'm good. I don't need anything to drink," Izzy said from the couch.

I chuckled and put the cap back on the bottle. "You might want to rethink that in a few minutes." I came back to the sitting area and handed one to Livy, who immediately took a drink, and then set Izzy and Kat's on the coffee table in front of them.

I took a long gulp of mine and leaned back down in the leather wingback chair; the material crinkled under my weight as I contemplated while staring into the fire again. As the vodka burned my throat, I wondered where I should start my tale of truth.

"Damn, this must be one hell of a story!" Izzy laughed abruptly.

I studied her for a few seconds. "Okay, look..." I blew out another heavy breath through my lips. "This isn't something that you all will ever be able to talk about, especially to anyone outside of this house. I'm deadly serious when I say that." I took a second to pointedly look each one of them in the eye. "Do you guys all understand that and promise you will keep it quiet, no matter what?"

They all nodded, but said nothing. They were probably afraid that if they did speak, I might stop talking.

"So here's the deal..." I took a sip of my Firefly and inhaled again to gather my courage. "You guys remember three months ago when I was investigating that girl's death, right?" Another nod around the room and they still remained silent.

"Well, you also know that is when I met Alex and Julian. They were also investigating the incident, but for a different reason. The person who killed that girl had killed a lot of other people. In fact, he had been killing people for almost forty years."

"Wow…a serial killer and you got to work on the case?" Livy was impressed. "Why didn't you say anything about that before?"

"Doesn't Alex own a security company? Why would he be involved in a homicide investigation?" Izzy asked.

"Well, to answer both of your questions, it's because of what the killer was. He wasn't your regular run-of-the-mill guy just out on a killing spree. The guy was killing other people who were like him."

"What, was he killing other criminals?" Kat laughed. "If that was the case, you should have let him continue."

"No, not criminals." I chuckled softly. "Man, I don't even know how to say this." I shook my head and downed the rest of my drink. I got up and refilled it. Before I sat back down I glanced at Livy's glass and saw she still had a fair amount and Izzy and Kat hadn't touched theirs yet. They would be downing theirs very soon.

No one said anything until I was seated again. "Just say it. It can't be that hard," Livy taunted. She was always the one to be point-blank. No skirting the issue with her.

A burst of laughter tore from my throat. "Man, you have no idea what you are saying." I chuckled nervously. "So, how much do you guys believe in the paranormal?"

"What, like ghosts and demons, that kind of paranormal?" Izzy asked.

"Yeah, kind of like that, only deeper; much deeper." I looked her straight in the eye. "What about vampires?" I said quietly.

The room got silent, then Izzy looked at Livy. They both turned to stare at Kat. I waited for someone to say something. Thirty seconds ticked by and I was about to open my mouth to speak, when they all broke out in hysterical laughter.

"You're kidding me! Right?" Livy said between breathes.

My face was sober, my eyes a light gray; a color meant to say that I was very intent, and deadly serious. I remained still, only allowing my eyes to move. When I didn't answer Livy, the laughter began to die down and I felt the emotions kick up in the room. Confusion and a little bit of fear began to fill the space we occupied. "Are you telling me there are actually vampires out there?" Izzy questioned softly. I honestly don't think she wanted to know the answer.

I nodded twice.

"Like blood-drinking monsters of the night?" Livy queried.

"Undead people who can't go around garlic and don't go out in the sun; that kind of vampire?" Kat queried.

"Yeah, except for the garlic and the undead. Well, they exist too, but they aren't part of this story." I flicked my hand to shove that question away.

They all shared another look, and then turned back to me as one. Their eyes were huge, and I watched Izzy actually glance at the glass on the table. It wouldn't be long before she reached for it. Kat picked hers up and sipped. I almost laughed at the face she made as she tried to swallow it.

"Okay, so assuming you are telling us the truth, what does that investigation have to do with vampires?" Livy asked.

The emotions in the room had grown tense, fearful, and excited all at once. I wasn't surprised that the excitement was coming from Livy. I studied her for a moment and shook my head. I couldn't help but snort at her.

"Yes, I'm telling you the truth. Dawn was killed by a vampire." I didn't want to mention that Dawn was a half-breed and that her parents were both vampires. That wasn't my information to give, and I wouldn't give out more than I had to.

"Okay...wow!" Izzy's blue eyes were wide.

"Um, okay," Kat said scanning the room for who knew what. "You neglected to put that part in your report."

"Katherine, could you imagine what the chief would have said if he read that in my report? He'd be putting me out on psych leave in a matter of minutes." I hung my head and stared at the hard wood floor.

I was really trying hard not to dip into their minds, but their thoughts were so loud that I could hear bits and pieces of questions pouring out of them without trying. The biggest one they were all trying to figure out was if I really believed what I was saying, or if I had lost my ever loving mind.

"Look, guys, I am telling you the truth. I know you don't believe me, but it is true. Julian and Alex were here looking for Damon, the vampire that was doing the killing."

"So, Alex and Julian know about vampires, too?" Izzy asked skeptically. She reached for her glass, but didn't drink from it, yet.

"Yeah, they know about them." I was watching Izzy, but could see Livy and Kat off to the side swallowing their drinks.

"Are they the ones who told you about them? Is that how you know? Have you ever seen a vampire, or is this just the story they are telling you?" Livy was getting into her police interrogation mode, firing off questions rapidly. She had put her feet down onto the floor and was leaning forward, excitement wafting off of her.

Enough with dancing around the issue; I needed to just get this out in the open. "Alex and Julian know all about vampires, because that is what they are." I held my breath after I said that to gauge their reactions. Livy's mouth dropped open and Izzy took a hefty slug from her drink. Kat was already taking a sip as I spoke and tried not to blow it out of her mouth while she choked on it.

"You're dating a vampire?" Kat asked me once she could talk again.

"You are not!" said Izzy right after Kat had asked the question.

"Yes, I'm dating a vampire. Well, it's more like I am mated to one." I looked at the fireplace again. The flames leaped higher, snapping softly as they did. I would be officially mated if I would just go ahead and get pregnant already. A small wisp of panic went through me then, thinking about Alex. Where was he?

"Mated to one? What the hell does that mean?" Livy asked. "You're married to him or something? Does he drink your blood? Wait! You let him drink your blood, don't you?" Her eyes were huge as she asked that.

"You do NOT!" said Izzy and Kat at the same time. Before I could answer anyone, Olivia spoke up again.

"Okay, tell me, is it as hot as they say in books? You know, when you let someone drink your blood?" Livy looked as if she was going to jump up and ask to be a victim if I said yes. I stared at her with my mouth hanging open.

"Olivia, I am *not* going to answer that." I peered at Izzy and Kat.

"Look, it's hard to explain what the mating is, but in a way, yeah, we are married, in a vampire way, that is, or we will be when we finish the mating process." *If we finish it,* I thought to myself. No, I wasn't going to think like that. Alex was going to be fine.

"I am so confused. Are you confused?" Izzy looked at Livy, then over at Kat. Kat nodded, but Livy had a thoughtful look on her face.

"Look, can you guys just sit and listen for a little while longer? Let me just explain a bit more and it should all start making sense." They nodded and sipped their drinks; I noticed that Livy's glass was almost empty now and I got up and poured her some more.

"When I was investigating the case, I met Julian. For some reason, Julian and I were instantly attracted to each other. The chemistry was like…like…damn amazing, just amazing." I stopped for a second as the memory of Julian's tongue sliding over my lips, entering my mouth, dancing with my tongue, filling my senses. I could almost smell his sweet cinnamon scent around me. I closed my eyes for a second to block it out.

"You were attracted to Julian? Then why are you with Alex?" Izzy asked.

I stared at her. "Do you want to hear the story or what?"

"Fine, go ahead. I'll save the questions for later." She upended her drink.

"Thanks. Anyway, when Julian and I met, it was like I had known him before. His eyes and his smell were so familiar. Of course, I thought it was all strange and didn't understand it, but he figured it out."

"Smell?" Live wrinkled her nose. "What does he smell like?"

I took a deep breath in through my nose. I could still smell it in my mind, the tingling scent of leather and cinnamon. "Cinnamon. He smelled like cinnamon and leather." I opened my eyes. God, I needed to stop thinking about him like that.

"So what did he figure out?" Kat encouraged me to continue.

"While I was trying to figure out who murdered Dawn, I started to pick up on some strange things, and none of it made sense to me. Julian and I went out to dinner one night to discuss the case, but things just got even stranger. It was like this magnet was pulling us together." I stopped for a second, remembering that night. "I couldn't seem to focus on work, and neither could he. We ended up leaving the restaurant before we even ate dinner, and then we stood out in the parking lot and kissed."

I briefly allowed the picture back into my mind. I could almost feel it, and could still remember his scent rising up to meet me while his arms were wrapped tightly around me.

They were all staring at me with wide eyes. "Yeah, I kissed him, and it was freaking awesome. Anyway..." I cleared my throat and continued. "After we kissed, he called me Calista. I was kind of taken aback with that, and it was at that very moment when Alex showed up and got into a heated argument with Julian. Alex was upset that he was kissing me, and he called me Calista, too."

"Who's Calista?" Izzy look as confused as I had been.

I glared at her for two seconds and then continued with my story. "I got really pissed, and then left them both in the parking lot. Alex came to my house later that night and explained things to me. He told me Calista was Julian's mate from forty years ago. She was supposed to have been with Alex, but Calista and Julian got together behind his back. Calista and her daughter were killed five years later by Damon. Damon is the same guy who killed Dawn. Keeping up with me?" I was talking faster now, spilling all that had been inside of me for months.

They all nodded, so I went on. "See, the thing is, to kill a vampire, you have to bleed them out quickly, like cut open their neck. You need to do it so they can't heal quickly enough. Or you can stake their heart. If you stake the heart, the soul is lost forever. If you just kill one and don't stake the heart, their soul will be reborn in another person."

I gave them a second to consider it, and I was not surprised when Livy asked me, "Was Calista's heart staked?"

"No," was all I said as I looked her straight in the eye.

I saw Izzy flipping her head back and forth between us. I knew that Livy was figuring it all out. I could feel her brain putting the pieces together. I kept waiting for her to say it.

"You're Calista, aren't you?" she said quietly.

I nodded slowly not taking my eyes from hers.

"What? Wait a minute, what am I missing?" Izzy asked and looked at Kat. "Do you understand this?" Kat shook her head.

Livy turned to Izzy. "She was Calista, and that Damon dude killed her, but didn't stake her heart. Calista's soul was reborn into Kristin." She made it sound like the easiest thing in the world to understand.

Izzy stared at her, and then she eyeballed me. "What are you saying?"

Livy ignored the question from Izzy, excitement oozing from her pores. "Are you...?"

I moved forward in my seat, resting my elbows on my knees and holding my glass between both hands tightly. I clenched my eyes closed to gather my strength then lifted my chin up and down slowly.

At first she didn't move. She didn't say anything. She just stared at me. Izzy was still looking back and forth at us. She hadn't figured it out at all, and her confusion was filling the air. When Livy finally spoke, I was not surprised, but Izzy and Kat sure were.

"You're a fucking vampire!"

CHAPTER SIX

JULIAN

I was quite surprised when I received a phone call from Alex last night telling me to come back to headquarters immediately. While things had gotten better with Alex recently, we still hadn't seen each other face to face since the night that I ended Damon's existence. All of our conversations had been over the phone or by e-mail.

After I got off the phone with Alex, I explained what was going on to Gabe. I told him that he should stay and keep an eye out for any more people coming or going from the import/export business we were watching. These people were bringing in more than just artifacts and merchandise.

Gabe was content to stay there, and I told him depending on what was happening, I would either return or send someone else down to assist him in a day or two. Gabe was a like a happy-go-lucky kid who took everything in stride and sang country songs even when there was no music to sing along with. He was glad to do what I asked.

My plane landed late in Poughkeepsie, and I turned my cell phone on once we were at the gate. No calls or e-mails from Alex.

After grabbing my garment bag from the luggage area, I headed out to find my truck. When I stepped out of the terminal, a cold breeze blew up against me and I shivered. I swore as I walked to the parking lot that I would give up living in the north and move down where the warm breezes and soft sands were right in your backyard. It didn't matter that I couldn't enjoy the sun. The nights were just as nice being near the warm ocean.

I tried calling Alex when I got into my truck, but there was no answer on his direct office line or his cell phone. Maybe he had stepped away from his office for a minute.

I pulled up to the building and parked on the street in front instead of going to the employee parking garage underneath. Being as late as it was, there was plenty of on-street parking. I climbed out and walked up the stone steps to the three-story office building that housed the VMF.

The bottom two floors were the central security business. They did everything from personal home security to bodyguards. The third floor was reserved for the vampire affairs, and the people on the first two floors just assumed the third floor was upper management.

There were quite a few people in the building at this time of night, most of them monitoring computer screens or talking on the phones to people about what they were seeing on those particular screens. I nodded to a few people as I entered and made my way to the elevator that would take me up to the third story.

A code was needed to access the third floor, and when I entered the elevator, I punched it in and watched as the metal doors slid closed silently.

As soon as the doors opened, I noticed it was quiet for this time of night; but then again, this was a Friday night, and most of the vampires that worked up here were probably out enjoying the start of the weekend.

I made my way down the hall and stepped into my office for a minute. I flipped through the stack of mail that sat on my desk; nothing that needed my attention. I took a deep breath and willed myself to relax before I set off to see Alex.

In the months since I'd last seen him, I tried to put distance between what happened with Damon and my feelings for what happened with Alex and Kristin. Kristin…I closed my eyes to the pain and longing that I still felt for her. Would it ever go away?

It felt as if I had lost her again that night on the pier. When she told me that she was the one to search out Damon and had brought him to the house to see me, I'd been stunned. I couldn't believe she would do something like that, and it had all been because there were problems between us. She was trying to make things better, but as much as we loved each other, and as much as our souls seemed mated, we both felt guilty about how we had gotten together. How we deceived Alex.

I pulled my shoulders up straighter, stepped out of my office, and headed to Alex's at the end of the hall. I stepped inside and knocked on the doorjamb, but his office was empty.

"Alexander? Are you in here?" I called out, but I already knew he wasn't. I couldn't feel his presence. I walked into his office and looked around. His suit jacket was thrown over a chair, and his cell phone sat on the desk, its blinking light showing he had messages. A bad feeling spread through my gut.

I picked up his phone and touched the screen. I slid my finger over it to show me the missed calls, and the bad feeling intensified when I saw how many there were. Thirty-one, and over half of them were from Kristin. I set the phone back down and walked behind the desk.

I didn't see anything out of place. I flipped over a page on his calendar. Then I saw two envelopes, and I slowly picked the first one up. It had Kristin's name written on it. As I held it in my hand, I looked down and saw the second envelope had my name scrawled on the front.

My hands shook as I put the first envelope down and retrieved the one addressed to me. I closed my eyes. Something was wrong, I could feel it. I sank down in the chair behind the desk and ripped open the envelope, pulling out the paper.

Jules ~

If you are reading this, then something has happened to me. This case has blown open, and I know that Burke is behind the whole thing. He is not only threatening me, but he is now threatening Kristin. Go to her...protect her. You and Trent are the only ones I can truly trust. Do not let Burke get to her. Do what you have to do to protect her, Jules. If she is in a lot of pain because of me, either you or Trent break the bond. Do not allow her to suffer because I am. Do whatever it takes to protect her...I trust you to do the right thing.

~ Alex

I HELD the letter in my shaking hands. He wanted us to break the bond? Damn! This was worse than I thought. I shut my eyes and tried to calm myself, that last sentence running through my mind over and over, until I pushed it aside to focus on the other parts.

Burke had threatened Alex? How had Burke figured out that we were watching him? And why would Burke threaten Kristin? I looked at my watch. Thanks to my plane being late, it was getting too close to dawn for me to head down to Fawn Hollow. I would have to go first thing after sunset tonight.

I put the letter down on the desk and picked up the one to Kristin. My hands were still shaking as I thought about what all this meant. Alex knew something was about to happen to him. He had known enough to write this letter and tell me to break the bond. Fuck! This was not good. Not good at all...

I set her letter down on the desk and turned around to face the computer monitors. I used the mouse to rewind the digital surveillance system. Quickly, I pulled up the video feed from around the building during sunset. I wanted to see when the last time Alex had been on camera and where.

I scanned through the video feed until I found where Alex entered the garage not too long after the sun had set. He had been dressed in his normal attire of a suit without a tie. I could see him walking from where he parked his car in the underground garage. I glanced over to the other side of the desk where the suit jacket was thrown over a chair. It was the same suit.

Alex entered the elevator. A different monitor showed him

standing in the elevator looking tense. A separate camera showed him walking off the elevator and down the brown and beige carpet in the hall to his office. There were no cameras in his office.

I sped up the feed to skim through the time when he was inside his office. Several hours later, he stepped out of his office and went back to the elevator. His sleeves were rolled up, I'd never seen him leave his office that way. His stride was quick, and I slowed down the feed to watch as he got back in the elevator and pushed the down button. He had his keys in his hand.

The elevator door slid open at the basement level, and Alex stepped off. He took a couple of steps forward, and then stopped. The angle from this camera only showed the bottom of his legs, from the backs of his knees down. I checked a couple of other camera angles but found they were all blacked out. My heart began to thud.

I watched the feed from inside the elevator. Alex stood there for just a few seconds before he staggered back as if he'd been hit with something. I watched him fall to the ground, and my heart skipped a beat. The elevator doors closed just as a pair of black boots stepped into the camera's view, blocking any further visual of what had happened and who had taken Alex.

I jumped up from the desk and ran down the hall to the elevator. Punching the button, I paced in front of the elevator until the doors opened. I jumped inside and pushed the basement button over and over, as if it would make it move faster.

When the elevator doors slid open on the ground floor to the garage, I pulled the gun out of my waistband from behind my back and looked around. I knew whoever kidnapped Alex was long since gone, but I wanted to be sure. I looked out the door and took a few steps out, scanning the area. I felt no other presence there. Alex's silver BMW was still parked in his normal spot, and only a few cars were left in the lot. Those cars probably belonged to the overnight crew working on the first two floors.

I searched the ground for any clues that might have been left. Carefully, I took a few steps forward and saw a drop of blood on the ground. I touched the now dried blood and lifted my finger to my nose. Chemical...He was hit with a chemical of some kind.

"Damn it!" I growled as I looked around for any more pieces of evidence that might have been left, but there were none.

I turned around and climbed back into the elevator. I closed my eyes and prayed. *"Dear God, please let Kristin be safe."*

CHAPTER SEVEN

KRISTIN

"You're a fucking vampire!" Livy's eyes went wide, but I don't think it was from fear.

"What?" Izzy said quietly.

I peeked at Kat and saw her staring at me with wide blue eyes and white knuckles around her glass. I hoped she didn't break the glass and cut herself. Now would not be a good time for blood to be in the room. I was hungry.

"Yes, I'm a vampire. Well, I'm still actually in the transition process, but I'm more vampire than human now." I said it matter-of-factly. I leaned back in my chair, trying to appear relaxed.

"You drink blood? You kill people?" Izzy said quietly. Fear radiated off of her. I wasn't surprised.

"No! I don't kill people! Yes, I do drink blood. The blood I drink is purchased though. I don't go sinking my teeth into people's necks, well, except Alex's."

Izzy looked at my mouth. I wanted to laugh, but held it back. "Do you like, have fangs?" she asked at the same time Livy said, "That's kind of hot, if you think about it."

I laughed at Livy as Izzy looked at her mortified. "That is soooooo not hot!"

Kat had yet to comment. She was watching us all with wide eyes. Finally, she looked down, and then right into my eyes. "So that's why you have been catching all the bad guys lately, huh?"

I chuckled at Kat and said, "Yeah, that's kind of why. My senses are much stronger than that of mortals."

"Mortals, huh? So we are just mortals now. What are you, like, immortal?" Izzy's emotional state was starting to calm down, but she was still uneasy.

"Yeah, I'm kind of immortal, although I can die. It's just harder to kill me." I continued to watch Izzy's face. She took a bigger drink from her glass and tried not to gag on the alcohol.

"So if you don't kill people, where do you get the blood?" Livy asked.

"I buy it. Since Alex and I are mated, for the most part, we do share blood, and it makes me stronger; especially right now. His blood is important to keep me moving through the transition, but human blood keeps me alive. Isabell, relax." Izzy was looking totally freaked out, and I saw Kat sit up a little straighter in her chair.

"I get blood from a special blood bank. It gives me what I need, although I still eat regular everyday food right now. Once I finish the transition, I won't need normal food, although I will still be able to eat it." Kat's face was scrunched up as if the conversation was grossing her out.

I had to give Izzy credit as she took it all in. She was doing a damn good job holding it together. I knew that this would be the hardest for her.

Livy was quieter than I had expected, but it wasn't long till she broke her silence with a barrage of questions. I could only laugh.

"So, what else can you do? Are you like super strong? Can you run crazy fast? Can you go out in the sun? Wait, that's why you only work nightshifts now. You can't go out in the sun!" She looked instantly appalled.

"Right now, I can go out in the sun. Once I finish the transition, it will be uncomfortable. You have to be a vampire for a very long time for the slightest rays of sun to make you go up in flames." I eyed her carefully.

Kat and Izzy remained quiet, but I noticed that the fear had dropped in the room. I waited a few more seconds before I went on. "I am strong, really strong, and, yeah, I'm fast. I can hear, see, and smell better than I used to. I can also hear thoughts, or I'm getting better at reading thoughts anyway. It takes a while."

"You can hear our thoughts?" Izzy almost looked as freaked out at this as she was about the whole vampire thing. "Wait, let me clear my mind. What am I thinking about?" She closed her eyes and concentrated.

"Izzy, you're too much. Peanut. You're thinking about your dog and wondering if I drink animal blood." We all laughed as the tension lessened more. Izzy ginned at me, a bit embarrassed. "No, I don't, to answer your question. Look, so that you all relax a bit more, I try to stay out of your heads. I don't want to invade your privacy. Understand that, okay?"

"So what else can you do?" Livy asked me, cocking her head to the side. Her brown eyes were all bright and excited.

"I can feel emotions," I said quietly.

"What do you mean you can feel emotions?" Kat said.

I looked at her. "Right now, you are not exactly scared, but you are uneasy, although you have calmed down a lot over the last few minutes. Izzy is still kind of freaking, and Olivia thinks this is all pretty funny." Livy grinned from ear to ear.

I took a moment to reach out again to Alex, but once again there was nothing. It was more than just his wall being up; it was almost as if he was gone. Fear twisted through my veins. *Alex...Where are you?*

Izzy was watching me. "So you can feel emotions. Can you feel Alex? Is that what happened earlier when you said something happened to him?"

"Yes, it was something like that. Alex has a great gift of feeling emotions from just about everyone, and he is able to send them to me. Because of our bond, I can send them back to him. Tonight, I got hit with Alex's emotions, only these were not like anything I have ever felt before." I spun the glass around in my hands. I was fighting hard not to start shaking.

"What was different about it?" Livy asked.

I took a deep breath. "It was like someone was torturing him, and I think it was meant to be a message to me."

"You? Why you?" Kat asked. I noticed that she finished her drink and put the glass down on the table in front of her.

"I don't know. Alex was supposed to be on his way here. He said he had something important to talk to me about. I figured it was because I was putting off having a child. Somehow, with what has happened, I am beginning to think there was something else he wanted to tell me, but I didn't want to listen."

I closed my eyes. Damn...my headstrong self had once again screwed up. I should have listened to him. Should have gone up to see him, and maybe he wouldn't be where he was, wherever that might be.

"I just wish I could reach him, but it's like he doesn't exist anymore," I said quietly.

Livy, always the tactless one, said, "What, like he's dead?"

Izzy and Kat both yelled at her to shut up.

"Kristin, he's not dead. Look, something is up, and, hey, I don't know, maybe he's just not communicating with you because he's upset with you," said Kat.

I had to get in touch with someone. Julian. I wish I knew how to get in touch with Julian. He would know what was going on.

Out loud I said, "Yeah, you guys are right. I'm sure he will be here soon." I knew that was not the case, but I didn't want to add any more stress to my friends. I couldn't pull them into this any further. What they knew now was dangerous enough.

"Look, why don't you all get some sleep. I'll wake you guys up if I find out something." I stood. Everyone needed a break; all three of them looked exhausted.

Izzy was the first to stand, and she walked over to me. "Kristin, I'm glad you told us. I'm not going to lie and say I'm not totally freaked out about this, but I'm glad you finally told us what is going on." She hugged me. I was careful to turn my head away from her. I was stressed, and I needed to feed. I knew it would not go over well if I dug my teeth into her neck.

As if knowing what I was thinking, she pulled away fast. "You won't bite us, will you?" She laughed nervously.

I chuckled. "No, Isabell, I'm not going to bite you. I have never drunk from a human vein, and I don't intend to start tonight."

"Okay, good." She stepped back and stretched. "Man, I'm exhausted."

Kat and Livy gave me hugs too, and then they all went upstairs to get some sleep. I have plenty of guest rooms on the second floor for them to use. It was kind of their home away from home, as this was not the first time they had all crashed here.

I sat down after they left and looked back into the fire. Closing my eyes, I reached out as strongly as I could. *"Alex?"* I couldn't feel him, couldn't feel anything. What if he was dead? Wouldn't I have felt something else if he died? I think I would have known deep in my soul if something terrible had happened to him. Somehow, the thought did not comfort me.

I stared at the fire for a long time, thinking about what I told my friends. About what they would want to know tomorrow when they'd had a chance to let it sink in. I knew there would be a million more questions.

Again, even though I knew it was futile, I tried to reach out to Alex. Nothing. Not a thing; not a buzz, a dull feeling...nothing.

A crushing weight was closing down on me, and I felt tears rolling down my face as memories of the short time we had had together ran through my mind.

"Kristin, for forty years I have loved you. From that night I met you in Night Crawlers, with your joke about the beer label, I have been in love with you." He leaned in slowly and kissed my jaw, sliding slow, hot kisses down my neck.

My skin was on fire, my body pressed tightly against him as we lay in our bed in the VMF house. "Alex, make love to me...take me as yours." I pulled his head down tighter to my neck as I felt his teeth graze the vein under the skin that was throbbing, calling for him, aching for him to pull my life from my body and join it with his.

I felt his body shudder as his mouth opened wider and his canine teeth slid through my soft tissue. Gently, he pulled the blood from my body and I melted into him. His blood was still burning through my veins from when he healed me. I was engulfed in fire now as my blood mingled with his. Both our bodies calling to each other, drawing each other into a bond so tightly, that it would carry us through our lives together.

As Alex kept pulling from my vein, I pushed my hips up and felt his hard sex enter my body. I needed him in every way. He moaned as I moved under him, and I turned my mouth into his neck and licked his pulse. I felt goose bumps break out on his body, and I could not help myself as I bit into his neck hard enough to draw his blood.

Our bodies were together, in every way possible, as we exploded into one being and bonded into mates. Slowly we came down from floating on air together and he rolled slowly off me to pull me into his arms from behind. Spooning up to him, I snuggled as tightly as I could. "I will always be yours, Alex, always now."

A NOISE behind me broke me out of my memory, and I turned to find Olivia walking in. I wiped at my eyes to remove the rest of the tears from my face.

"Kris, you okay?" she said quietly as she came to sit next to me.

"I thought you went to sleep," I said just as quietly.

She shook her head. "No, I was worried about you. You have gone through so much by yourself, and now you're worrying about Alex. I figured I would sleep when you did. I'm off the next two days, so I'll catch up tomorrow after the party." She climbed up in the leather wingback chair next to me, pulling her legs up under her. She had changed into a large T-shirt of mine, or actually, Julian's. I laughed and shook my head at that.

"What's so funny?" she said, resting her head back against one of the wings of the chair.

"That T-shirt belongs to Julian. I kind of stole it from him before he left." It was a navy blue T-shirt with no design, no words, nothing. Just a simple blue T-shirt, and looking at it made me wish I could talk to him.

"Tell me about Julian," Livy said, holding back a yawn.

Olivia was a wild spirit, but she was also an incredible friend. Sometimes she surprised me with how caring she could actually be.

I shook my head and chuckled softly. "Wow...Jules..." I sighed. "Jules was amazing, well, he is amazing, not was. He has the most amazing eyes. They are dark blue around the outside, and aqua in the middle. I would get lost looking into his eyes." I stopped and pictured him in my mind, instantly feeling the pull I had always felt for him.

She laughed. "You should see your face right now. You look all dreamy and gaga. You would think that if you felt that way about him, you would be with him. Why aren't you?"

"Too funny...Well, I used to be with him, forty years ago. I was mated to him, although I was supposed to be with Alex. I mated with Julian the night after I met him. It wasn't planned, it just happened. It was like our souls touched the moment our eyes met. When we kissed, we lost all control, and basically"—I shrugged—"we didn't think about the consequences."

She squinted her eyes. "What exactly is mating? It sounds rather animalistic."

I leaned my head back on the chair. "You crack me up." I shook my head as I laughed at her. "Mating is the sharing of blood at the same time you have sex. You bond your bodies in all ways, and your minds connect in a new way. That's the first step. After that is complete, in order to finish the full mating, you need to...well, you need to get pregnant." I picked at the cuticle of my thumb. I was trying to keep from clenching my hands into fists.

"So that's what you've been arguing with Alex about. He wants to complete the mating, but you don't?" She laughed. "Sounds just like you, little Miss Independent."

"Ha! Look who's calling the kettle black," I retorted. "But you're right. He wanted to complete it, but I just wasn't ready to leave my job yet."

"How long were you with Julian?" She pulled her legs in tighter under her, and I figured she was probably cold. I grabbed a blanket off the couch and gently tossed it over to her.

"I was with Julian for over five years. We had a daughter, Anastasia. She was killed at the same time as I was." I tried to say that without feeling the pain I knew would come along with it. I didn't like to think about how she died, but rather tried to remember that, like me, she was reborn and was out there living a full, hopefully happy, life.

Her eyes got wide, and her jaw dropped open. "You had a daughter?"

"Yep." I really didn't want to talk about that. "Look, I'll be right back. You need anything? I gotta get something to eat."

"Yeah, I could use a bite. I'll come with you." She got up and wrapped the blanket around herself. "What are you going to have?"

"Um…Not sure you want what I'm going to have," I said with a lopsided smile on my face.

She froze mid-step, looking at me with wide eyes. "It's not going be mine, is it?"

I burst out laughing at the way she stood there with wide eyes and a pale face. "No, I told you, I've never fed from a human vein, and I'm not going to try it out on you. From what I hear, it's pretty intense, and I'm not quite ready for that. Come on, let's find you a snack."

CHAPTER EIGHT

ALEX

J had no idea how long I was unconscious. Time meant nothing to me as I lay there in the dark, although it must have been hours, could have been days. When I was finally able to think clearly, I concentrated on my body.

I still had pain in my chest, but it was slowly healing. The titanium and platinum alloy stake had done a lot of damage, and the combination of being drugged and not being able to feed was making the healing slower than normal. I winced as I tried to move to make it easier to breathe.

How long had it been since I fed? Two days? Three? I knew it had been almost two weeks since I last fed from Kristin. Damn...two weeks...Kristin was going to start feeling the effects of not feeding from me. She would start feeling weak, and the bloodlust would be harder for her to control. She needed to feed from vampire blood soon to keep her transition moving along.

I lay still with my eyes closed; there was no reason to open them as the cell I was in was pitch-black and didn't contain anything other than the bed. Who had Burke been talking to on the phone? I heard enough to know it was a woman's voice on the other end, Angelina, but I didn't know who she was.

What did the woman say? "Yeah, she got the message."

Kristin...They had to be talking about Kristin. If they knew she felt the pain, then that meant they had someone watching her. Someone close enough to see her. Would they kill her? Would they bring her here? Why did they think she was involved with this?

Kristin would have felt my pain, would have known something was wrong. Somehow, I needed to let her know I was okay. I took a deep breath and tried to reach out to her, but I could feel nothing. I tried not to panic, thinking that it was because they hurt her. I knew it was really because of the cell they locked me in.

I knew enough time passed for Julian to get back to Poughkeepsie. Hopefully, he figured out what had happened. He was smart; he would have looked at the camera footage and been able to see the people who came after me. Did he find the letters I left tucked into the calendar on my desk? If he did, he would do as I asked? I knew he would not let anything happen to Kristin, which meant he would feed her, too.

A surge of rage and jealousy poured through my veins as I thought about Julian bonding with Kristin. I tried to calm my breathing, knowing that I needed to save my strength and not waste it on emotions. I reminded myself that I was the one who told him to do anything to protect her.

I allowed my mind to float away so that the pain would subside a bit. I thought back to two months ago when Kristin said she needed to go back to work.

"ALEX, I got an e-mail from my chief today. He wants to know when I'm coming back to work." We were sitting on the back porch of our house in Poughkeepsie, looking up at the stars.

"How about never?" I knew that wasn't what she wanted to hear, but I couldn't resist saying it. I didn't want her to go back to Pennsylvania. I wanted her to stay in New York, with me.

"Really, Alex?" she whined. "You know that's not happening. I really need to get back to work. I miss my job."

"Why can't you work for the VMF? You could work out of the office here. The job's not that different." It was not the first time I'd brought this up.

She pushed her head off my chest, and looked up into my face. "We've been through this before. I don't want to be stuck in an office. I want to be out on the streets doing what I love. God knows you wouldn't want me out in the field. You'd rather I stay locked up in the office with you. I would hate that!"

I tried to pull her back down to my chest, but she resisted. "Fine, I know. I know you would hate to be stuck in the office. Fine..." I closed my eyes and took a deep breath. "Go back to work, but you have to promise me that you will come back on your days off. I don't want you to go back to work and forget about me."

She watched me closely. "Are you serious, Alex? You aren't going to fight me on this anymore?" she asked quietly.

I looked deep into her eyes. "No. I know it makes you happy. Go back to work, but you know that in a few years you will have to leave. People will start to notice that you haven't aged."

She smiled. "Yeah, I know, I know. You know you can always come down and ride along with me, see what I do."

I laughed. "No, there is no reason to do that. That's your thing. I'm not interested in that, and besides, I have too much to do here."

I felt a small moment of pain wash over her. I'm sure it was because of me not being interested in her job, but she knew I was busy.

She looked away, and then turned back. "You're sure you're okay with this?"

"I want you to be happy, Kristin, safe and happy. That's all I want." We exchanged smiles and I watched her eyes lighten to a bright blue. She leaned in and kissed me, slowly, softly. With her eyes communicating her longing for me, she climbed up onto my lap to straddle my legs.

THE SOUND of the lock turning on the cell door brought me out of the memory I was lost in. That was probably a good thing, since I didn't need to be aroused now. I had enough issues to contend with. I kept my eyes closed this time to protect them from the harsh light that would come spilling in through the door.

"Time to wake up, Master," a rough voice said to me as I was grabbed by the arm and yanked off the bed.

I staggered a bit as I tried to get my balance and keep my eyes closed as well. Someone else grabbed my other arm, pulling me out of the cell and putting me back in the same chair I had been in earlier. I could feel the heat from the lights shining down on me, and I blinked my eyes rapidly to adjust to the brightness.

The human who had been on the floor before was gone, but I could still smell the scent of his dried blood in the air. I tried hard to hold down the hunger that was rising in me. At the same time, I had to keep the wall up to Kristin. I didn't want her to know how hungry I was.

I not only heard Burke walk up behind me, but I could feel him, too. His presence was almost familiar. I kept my eyes mostly closed. I was looking down at the ground when I saw his feet come into view in front of me. I wanted to jump up and rage at him, tear him limb from limb. I wanted to rip his throat out, but I knew that I needed to wait. Needed to bide my time.

"So, Master Alexander, how are you making out today?" Burke laughed. "Are the accommodations okay with you?"

I took a slow breath, raised my eyes, and blinked a couple of times to correct my vision as I looked at Burke from the tips of his black leather designer shoes up to the shoulders of his navy suit. He was a big man, but I had heard he was. Probably close to six foot six.

His shoulders were wide and solid. It was obvious that he was strong, fought hard, and took no prisoners—well, no prisoners except for me, that is. As I took in his height, his size, his clothes, I finally made contact with his face. His face was easier to see today. Not so many lights shining on it right now.

His cheekbones were not as angular as most vampires. They had a softer look to them, but they were still defined, still solid and forbidding. He was watching me with amusement, and I remembered that he'd asked me a question. I couldn't see the details of his eyes. There was too much light behind him causing shadows.

"Yeah, they're just peachy," I said with a sneer.

He cackled. "I'm so glad to hear that. Speaking of peachy, I thought you might be ready for a snack. Why don't we start off with you answering some questions for me, and if you give me the information I want, you'll get a reward." He stopped for a second and lowered his voice. "You don't tell me what I want, and we will just have to send Kristin another message."

At the mention of her name, rage boiled over in my body and I wanted to lash out at him, wanted to rip him apart. I was fighting so hard to keep my wall up, and I knew I was growing weaker; I needed to keep my strength for later when I would have a chance to fight. I took a couple of ragged breaths and kept my chin up, looking at Burke.

"I have nothing to say to you, Burke," I seethed.

He raised an eyebrow with a smirk. "Still being feisty, huh? Well, let's see how feisty you can be, shall we, Alex?" He reached into his jacket pocket and pulled out a knife. I knew by the look of it that it was probably a custom-made blade of titanium and platinum. A small ripple of fear ran through me as I thought of what it would feel like when it entered my body, and what it would cause me to send over the bond to Kristin.

He walked closer to me. "How did you figure it out, Alex? Did someone give you information about what we were doing?" He stepped behind me.

I said nothing.

"Come on, Alex, you can answer that one. Did someone give you information about what we were doing?" He was leaning down over my shoulder talking quietly into my ear.

I felt the tip of the blade on my shoulder. Felt the slight pressure of it cutting into my shirt. I could feel the blade nip my skin, and I tensed.

"Who told you, Alex? This is an easy question. They only get harder after this." He stood back up, still behind me.

I said nothing. I stared straight ahead, not giving him anything. The next moment, I felt the blade dig deeper into the top of my shoulder. I bit back the pain, the metal burning through my muscle tissue.

"Who, Alex?" he said, anger tingeing his voice now.

"You're not getting anything out of me, Burke," I said, knowing it would only piss him off, but not willing to tell him anything. I braced myself for what I knew was coming.

The anger rolled off him. He dug the blade into my shoulder, and I bit back the searing pain as it tried to escape my mouth. The wall I was holding up against the bond was falling. I fought to keep it up, but it was about to be a lost cause.

"Who told you, Alex?" he said loudly as he walked around in front of me.

"I'm not telling you anything, Burke. You might as well kill me now, because I'm not telling you shit." The last word barely got out of my mouth when his knife crossed over my chest, from my right shoulder down across my pecs and over my heart.

Searing pain raced through me, and I knew the wall had fallen. I could not hold it up, as much as I wanted to protect Kristin. It fell, crashing around me as the pain tore through my chest. My head hung back, the muscles in my neck and face taunt from the pain, and I clenched my teeth together to keep from making a sound.

"Who, Alex?" he yelled in my face, spittle landing on my cheeks.

I found cold steel-gray eyes boring into me. I spit into his face, and he dragged the knife blade back across my chest in the other direction, making a large X over my body.

The pain staggered me. I bit back the rage that I wanted to unleash. Groaning, I allowed my head to fall forward. I tried to take slow, even breaths, tried to pick up the wall that had fallen. It was no use.

"You do know that you are going to die, right, Alex? It's going to be a slow death, with a lot of pain. Pain that will be sent directly to your sweet little mate each and every time you refuse to talk to me." He was still right in front of me, but I didn't look up at him.

I continued fighting to control the pain. Fighting to keep as much of it in as I could. I was weak, and the pain was pulling me down into the darkness of my mind.

"Bring in the bitch," I heard Burke say quietly to someone.

The bitch? For a brief second, I thought he might have Kristin. I froze, trying not to panic. But the scent that came to me was from a human. A human who was very afraid.

They dragged her over to me, her hands tied behind her back, her mouth gagged with a black cloth of some kind. Her eyes were huge as they threw her to the hard cement in front of me.

She looked up at me. There was dried blood on her face and neck, a bruise around her right eye. Her dark brown hair was matted on the side from more dried blood. I could feel the fear radiating off of her as she looked around, not moving anything more than her eyes.

Burke squatted next to her and licked at the dried blood on her face, putting the knife blade under her chin. Her eyes grew bigger, and she raised her chin up trying to keep the blade away from her skin. Her breaths were coming in hard pants, moisture welling up in her brown eyes. She closed them and the tears spilled over the edges, running down her dirty cheeks.

"Hungry, Alex?" he taunted me. The woman looked at me pleadingly. I wish I could reach out and try to relax her, but I didn't have the strength to move. I looked away, trying to avoid the pain shining in her eyes.

"I bet you're hungry. How long has it been since you drank straight from a human's vein? Years, I bet. So long, you probably forgot how wonderful it can be. We made sure we found you a nice, tasty, fresh one."

I glanced at the woman as tears streamed down her face in an endless river, small sobs caught in her throat.

"I don't want her," I said, and glanced back to see a quick moment of relief as she thought she might survive this.

"Oh, come on, Alex, I know you do." The blade slowly pierced her skin and a small bead of blood came to the surface. That little bead of blood was enough to make my mouth salivate and my fangs start to extend. The pain I had endured had burned through my blood supply, and I needed it—wanted it—but I refused to take it.

The woman's scream was muffled by the gag in her mouth. Burke grabbed her around the back of the neck and held her still. "Come on,

Alex, you want this. I know you do. Tell me who told you, and you can have her all to yourself."

I watched the bead of blood slowly slide down the woman's throat, her pulse racing in her neck, and my fangs lengthened even more, the intense need expanding. I stared at the blood as my mouth watered. Yet, I said nothing.

The fangs in Burke's mouth popped out quickly, and he struck into the woman's neck like a cobra. She screamed for only a moment before her eyes rolled back into her head and she shivered. The endorphins he was injecting into her body made her feel good, so good that she moaned in ecstasy.

My body responded to what was in front of me. Deep inside, the thirst was raging and the lust was building. Yeah, I wanted to sink my teeth into her neck, wanted to suck long and hard on her. I also wanted to bury myself into her deep and sate my sexual hunger as I devoured her life force.

My bloodlust was engulfing me. I tried to fight it, to block out the scene in front of me, but the sounds of Burke drinking from her and the soft moans she was putting out caused me to open my eyes again.

He was watching me with an evil look in his green eyes. He pulled his fangs out of her neck and very slowly licked the holes he had made in her soft tissue, closing the area. "You can have the other side, Alex. What do you say?" he spoke quietly, almost sensually, as you would to a lover; only I wasn't a lover, I was his hostage.

By now, the bloodlust was raging in me, and I wanted nothing more than to give him an answer and dig my teeth into her neck. The pain from wanting to feed and needing to be sated was overwhelming, more so than the pain of the knife that had dug into me.

It took the last of my strength to speak. "I do not want her." And I closed my eyes, because I knew what he would do next.

I was not wrong. In one quick move, he pulled the knife across her throat, and the smell of her blood permeated the air around us instantly. A small gurgling sound came from her neck as she tried to breathe, and then she was silent.

My body shook with need, with wanting to dive onto her and lap up the last of her warm blood. The pain was so intense I couldn't control it. I broke out in a cold sweat and watched as she fell back to the ground when Burke stood up. Her blood pooled around her, her eyes no longer begging for mercy, but dead and flat.

The bloodlust raged in me as I felt two people grab my arms and drag me back to the cell. I couldn't think, couldn't move from the need to drink. I was dropped onto the bed in the cell and the door slammed closed, putting me back into total darkness.

The last of the energy I had raced through me as I threw myself back on the bed and roared.

CHAPTER NINE

KRISTIN

I didn't sleep much during the hours of the sun. I tossed and turned as dreams and nightmares devoured my mind. Several times when I woke I tried to reach out to Alex, but I could never feel anything from him.

Was he dead now? I knew he was hurt, but how bad was it?

Finally, I gave up trying to sleep and took a shower. I was hoping the hot water would calm my nerves and ease the tension in my body. As I stood under the hot water, I let it run over my head and down my shoulders. My thoughts drifted back to Alex again.

Alex said that he needed to talk to me about something, something other than our mating. Did that conversation have to do with what was happening now? I had so many questions, and I had no one to ask. If I didn't hear from him today, I would head up to Poughkeepsie to see what I could find out from the office. Someone there would know how to reach Julian. Maybe he would know what was going on.

I stood with my hands on the tile wall and let the hot water cascade down my back. My head hung low as I watched the water drip off my body. The steam swirling around me made me feel as if I was lost in the fog. Being in a fog would explain what I felt like now— lost, bewildered, looking for direction.

Eventually, I decided that the shower was not helping. I turned it off and stepped out. I wiped the towel across the mirror; there were deep shadowy circles under my eyes from the lack of sleep. My eyes were light gray today, reflecting the worry I felt for Alex.

I quickly dressed in black jeans and a deep navy silk blouse and pulled on a pair of black boots. I did a quick hair dry and put on the barest of makeup. I was not a fancy dresser and only wore makeup to add a bit of color, something Livy and Izzy had tried to change about me many times.

I didn't feel like going to the party, but my friends would force me to go. I knew they wouldn't leave me alone right now because they were too worried, especially after the shocking explanation I gave them last night.

I left my room and headed downstairs. I didn't expect anyone to be here. I figured they would have left during the day while I was sleeping. When I got down to the first floor, I found Kat sitting in the kitchen reading a book and drinking iced tea. The coffee pot was gurgling as it finished brewing.

"Hey. I didn't think anyone would be here," I said as I entered the kitchen. "Thanks for making coffee."

She looked at me over her book. A feeling of nervousness rushed off her. "We didn't want to leave you alone in case you heard something," she said with a lopsided grin.

"Katherine, you can relax. I'm still the same person even though my body has changed. I'm not going to hurt you." I watched as the tension fell out of her shoulders. "You guys don't need to babysit me, you know."

I grabbed a mug and poured my coffee as the dog door burst open and Garda came barreling through.

"Well, hello there, buddy!" I pet him for a minute and grabbed him a treat from his jar. He took it happily and went to lie down next to Kat.

"We aren't babysitting; we are friend sitting."

"Friend sitting, huh?" I shook my head and chuckled.

"Yep! I ran home when I got up and changed. Then Izzy took off when I got back. Livy just got up a few minutes ago and stumbled out of here. She said you guys stayed up late and talked."

"Wasn't that late for me, but, yeah, we did." I sipped my coffee and sat down next to her. "Did she fill you in on all the details of our talk?" I looked at her over the rim of my mug as I inhaled the rich smell of my coffee.

She rolled her eyes. "Did she ever! She told me she watched you drink blood too; said it wasn't gross at all."

Figures Livy would tell her that. I laughed.

"How often do you need to uh...drink that stuff?" She folded back the corner of the page where she was reading and laid the book down.

"Normally? Well, normally, I only need to drink once every day or two, but lately, I have been craving it a lot more. I think that has to do with the fact that I haven't fed from Alex recently. His blood makes me stronger, and when I don't drink from him regularly, I crave blood a lot more." I put my mug down and watched her. I wondered absently when I would get to feed from Alex again, and a foreboding feeling filled me.

"Okay, so that is just totally gross." She shook her head.

"Yeah, I know. I was grossed out at first too, but you do what you gotta do, and believe it or not, drinking from a guy's neck is freaking hot! It really is!"

"I'll take your word for it." She sat back in her seat and looked at me with humor in her eyes.

"Hey, let's go do some shopping. I need to do something to keep myself busy until I hear from Alex. I can't keep sitting around waiting."

"Sounds good. I could use some retail therapy myself!"

A couple of hours later, Kat and I met up with Izzy and Livy and headed over to the party. When we got to the restaurant, we found it was already filling up fast. Mick's wife had planned a heck of a party for his thirty-fifth birthday celebration.

As we entered, I felt the presence of a couple of vampires in the room. I immediately scanned the area, my hackles up, and found one on the other side of the bar. He was a tall male with a high and tight haircut. Even from the dimly lit distance that separated us, I could tell he had bright green eyes as they met mine and he raised his chin slightly in a nod. Another time, another place, and I might have wanted to see why the way he looked at me warmed me from the inside out. My arm was yanked as Livy pulled me away toward the bar and I broke eye contact with him.

We threaded our way through the group to the bar. First things first—alcohol, then chatting. After grabbing our signature chocolate martinis, we split up to mingle with the other guests.

Mick showed up shortly after we did, and he was thrilled to have been surprised—even though he wasn't—to have all his friends there to celebrate with him. I watched as he made his way around to everyone, laughing and joking. I couldn't help but be happy for him. He was a great guy, and someone I enjoyed having as a partner and friend.

While watching him, I felt a strong presence behind me. I turned and found the tall vampire standing there. He was clearly over six feet and was built like a stone wall. I had to tilt my head back to see into his face as he was jostled closer to me by the crowd. He was probably a foot taller than my five-foot-five frame.

"Hey, beautiful," he drawled with a slight Southern accent, emerald eyes sparkling.

I laughed. "Hey, right back at you." He seemed to study every inch of my face and I felt a warmth spread through my body again as I gazed into his eyes.

"You're Mick's partner, aren't you?" he asked quietly. Although it was noisy in the room, we didn't need to speak loudly to hear each other. I glanced over my shoulder to find Kat engaged in a conversation with one of our friends before giving the man in front of me my attention again. The strong hard features of his face seemed to soften the longer he gazed down into my eyes.

"Yep. How'd you know that?" There was something familiar about him. When he spoke, I caught his scent and inhaled it a bit deeper than necessary. A unique scent of chocolate and spices mixed together in an almost exotic combination, and I felt a shiver on the verge of running up my spine. Hold it together, Kristin. You are not out on the prowl tonight.

"I hear things." He shrugged. "I met Mick at the gym. I spot for him some nights when he's not working."

Yeah, he worked out, that was for sure. My eyes flicked down to his wide chest and took in his muscular arms. There was something about him, other than the rocking body, that reminded me of someone. I watched him, wondering where I may have met him before. His scent was different, but so insanely appealing I had to force myself not to lean forward and put my nose against his chest to fill my senses.

A magnetic pull seemed to bring me closer to him and, with only six inches between us, Livy shoved her way between us, shooting him a flirtatious grin over her shoulder before glaring at me. I stepped back, just then realizing how damn close I had been standing to him.

"What's doing?" I asked her, and peeked over her shoulder to watch the guy check Livy out from behind. I raised an eyebrow at him, and as his appraisal ended, he actually looked somewhat ashamed to have been caught. Although, the shy, sexy smile only added to his appeal. Down, girl, down!

"Have you been able to reach *Alex* yet?" She stressed his name while glancing over her shoulder again at the guy.

His expression shifted instantly, and he looked at me intently. *What was up with that?* He took a step away and searched my features harder, his face becoming more intense. Before I could ask him why the name Alex peaked his interest, I felt another presence walk up behind me.

"Hey, Kristin," I heard someone call from behind, and I broke off my eye contact with the hot blond guy. Thomas walked toward me, his arm wrapped around a woman's waist. It wasn't really a woman. It was a vampire; the same one I saw last night in the bar. I immediately shifted back a step.

"Kristin, I wanted you to meet Angie." Tom looked like a proud rooster, crowing over his escort, his chest all puffed up, his cheeks flushed with excitement. I gawked at her open-mouthed, and almost grabbed her by the throat and threw her up against the wall to find out what she knew about Alex.

She smirked at me and it looked beyond evil. "So, you are Kristin. I have heard so much about you." She reached out to shake my hand, and I stepped further away from her, avoiding her touch.

Olivia joined us and stood on my left side, while Izzy was on my right. When I stepped back, I ran right into the hot blond guy. His hands landed on my shoulders. For an instant I felt trapped, but I realized that he was only trying to steady me and, in some strange way, I knew he was being protective and wasn't a threat to me.

At that moment, I welcomed the strength of his hands on my shoulders as that was the moment that I felt Alex again.

Alex! He was alive!

My knees nearly gave out as I felt the rush of anger and pain swallow me. I felt the man pull me tighter to him. I knew he was holding me up. Was I in trouble? Was this guy part of what was going on with Alex? I couldn't think.

My breathing was coming out in small, staggered breaths as I continued to look at the woman next to Thomas. Tom leaned toward me, his date forgotten. "Hey, Kris, you okay?" The woman peered around him, watching me closely.

I felt the guy tense against my back. The air around me was shimmering, and I tried to gain some control over everything that was happening.

Olivia grabbed my hand. "Kris...Kris...What's going on?"

Pain pierced my body, and I squeezed Livy's hand. The guy tore my hand from hers. If he hadn't, I would have shattered the bones in her hand. I heard Olivia gasp and could only imagine the way she would be staring daggers at him.

Vaguely, I heard him say, "She would have broken your hand." She shifted away from us, probably realizing what this man really was.

A new pain raced through my body and my knees finally went out from beneath me. I felt the man's strong arms pick me up, and I realized even as my body raged in pain, that he had me cradled against his chest and we were moving. Oh God, who was he? Was he taking me away?

I heard voices behind me and thought I heard a woman laughing, but I was so overcome by the pain that was hammering at me through my bond with Alex that I couldn't comprehend what was going on around me.

I grabbed on to the guy's arm and squeezed. He didn't make a sound as he carried me outside into the cool night air, but I heard footsteps following us. I couldn't make out the words that were spoken as I tried to control the continual pain that burned through my veins.

The man set me on top of a car and spread my legs so that he could step between them. He wrapped his arms around me and pulled me close to him. With my head against his chest, I tried to focus on his heartbeat to calm down. His scent filled me.

I felt his hands softly rubbing my back, and he whispered in my ear, "What are you feeling, Kristin?"

"Pain..." was all I could get out as I fought to control my breathing and hold on to what sanity I had left. I focused on his hands rubbing down my back and on the sound of his heart, steady under my ear. His scent of spices and chocolate entered my body and almost made me high while slowing my racing heart.

Eventually I relaxed, and the pain ebbed away from me enough to understand what was going on. I tried to pull my head off the guy's chest. I was so lost in trying to deal with the last parts of the pain slithering through my body that I failed to notice someone walking toward us.

I closed my eyes and gathered enough energy to separate my body from the guy's.

"Kristin, are you okay?" Olivia asked from beside me. She didn't touch me. I think she was afraid after what happened inside.

"Yeah, I'm okay." I inhaled again, holding it deep in my lungs; the spices and chocolate scent made my mouth water.

I tilted my head back to speak to him, but a new feeling clawed its way into my chest. It wound quickly through my veins, and my fangs emerged. I grabbed at the man's arms. I was so hungry—no, I was starved—but not for food. My throat was burning, Jesus, it felt so dry. Other parts of my body burned inside, and I found myself panting again. Lust was building in me, and I tugged the guy closer, my legs locking around his waist, holding him prisoner.

I heard his gasp, felt him grab for my arms. I could feel his instant arousal as I locked him against me; it pulsed against me, and I wanted more.

"Kristin...You need to fight this," he said tensely.

I heard gasps around us. I had no idea who was standing out here watching me, but at that moment, I didn't care. At that moment, I wanted the man in front of me, this hot male vampire, with eyes like Alex, who was locked in my grasp. I wanted his blood running down my throat, and I wanted his sex deep inside of me.

"Kristin, stop! Damn, girl...You gotta get a hold of yourself!" The guy was practically yelling. He was trying to get out of my leg hold, but at the same time, he was holding on to me to keep me off his neck.

"What the hell is wrong with her?" I heard Izzy say shakily, and somewhere in my mind I knew she was scared, knew I should stop, but I didn't care. All I wanted was his blood, and his dick deep inside of me now.

"Bloodlust...She's in bloodlust," he blurted out.

"What the hell is that?" Livy asked.

So this is bloodlust. Oh yes, yes, it is. Bring it on. I clawed at the man, trying to get to his throat.

"Whoever she is bonded with just went into bloodlust, and she is feeling exactly what he is." He was struggling with me now, but I fought as hard as I could, trying to pull him closer, trying desperately to sink my teeth into his neck.

"Trent, I'm going to grab her from behind. Unlock her legs from you as soon as I tell you, and push her away." I knew that voice. Deep in my mind I knew that voice, but I was so far gone that I couldn't connect it.

A moment later, a strong arm grasped me around the chest, while another locked around my throat and I was yanked back across the hood of the car. I landed on the ground, the strong arms still wrapped tightly around me. As my head cleared, a new scent intruded my senses, and the bloodlust struck me again.

I jerked and spun around in my captor's arms and went directly for his neck. He put his hand on the back of my head and held it against his neck as my canine teeth dug in. After the first strong pull from his vein, I shivered. I knew this blood. It tasted familiar to me. I was so far gone into bloodlust that I couldn't figure out who it was though, and I didn't really give a damn anyway.

After a couple more satisfying pulls, my body rubbed up against the person underneath me. I wanted to rip his clothes off and take him right there on the ground. My body was so hot, so in need. The blood was good, but I wanted more. I wanted to feel his sex deep inside of me, wanted to feel my hot skin slipping against his. I felt his hard arousal pushing against my lower stomach, and I ground my hips down against him.

Words surrounded me, but I couldn't comprehend them. Someone grabbed me around the neck again and yanked me off the vein that I had attached myself to. I fought back. This man was mine...but the other person was stronger, and eventually they had me off the ground and away from my meal.

Part of me felt drunk from the blood; the rest of me felt raw with the lust that rushed through me. I watched the man in front of me, not seeing his face, only seeing the blood run from his neck where I had been feeding.

When he spoke again, I blinked, and as he started to talk, recognition slowly came to me and my eyes opened wide.

"Man, Kristin, I hope you forgive me for this," Julian said right before he punched me in the face and everything went black.

CHAPTER TEN

TRENT

J wandered around the bar talking to people I had never met. I was the proverbial social butterfly. I enjoyed human company and found them entertaining. I'd met Mick at the gym where we both worked out, and he told me that some people were supposed to be surprising him for his birthday tonight. Of course, he wasn't supposed to know about it, but he did. He invited me to come on down, and I was glad that I'd accepted the invite.

I didn't know too many people in the area since I just recently moved here, and I was enjoying the conversations. A lot of the people I'd met were police officers and their mind-sets went right along with mine; they were entertained by the things humans did. I found myself laughing along with them during their stories of recent calls and funny things they had witnessed.

I felt her before I saw her. She felt me too, because when she walked into the door, her eyes began searching immediately. Not a casual glance around, but on a mission. When we made eye contact, I tried to be casual. I lifted my head in a small nod to let her know I recognized her for what she was.

I didn't know who she was, just what she was. Or rather, what she was becoming. She gave me a tight-lipped smile and continued into the crowd with several of her friends. I observed her from a distance for a while. She knew a lot of the people here, and I leaned over to the guy next to me and asked him who she was.

"The strawberry blonde over there? That's Kristin, Mick's partner from work." He laughed and continued. "Good luck with that. She is one hardheaded woman, and from what I hear, off the market." He patted me on the shoulder and turned back to the conversation he was having with a couple other people.

So she was a cop. That was interesting.

I walked over to her shortly after that, and she turned to me after feeling my presence, I was sure. I smiled down at her. "Hey, beautiful," I said slowly, while drinking in her face. Her eyes were a light blue, and she stared at me intently with a smirk on her face.

I liked her lips, and almost instantly, I wanted to reach down and pull her close to feel them on mine. I was drawn to her, which was strange because normally I didn't much like the half-breeds. I was generally more attracted to humans.

I listened to her talk, her voice was soft and it fit well with the soft light blue of her eyes and the sweet scent that flowed around her. I closed in on her without even thinking. Her eyes changed from blue to green as we somehow got closer. They were fascinating.

I got another whiff of her sweet sugary scent mixed with a small amount of creamy butter. There was something about her, something almost familiar. She was examining me as I was her, her eyes warm on my body as they explored.

She was just about to speak when a short, dark-haired human woman injected herself between us. Kristin took a step back, looking up at me over the woman's shoulder. I gave her a shy smile. Once her friend was gone, I'd swoop back in. My thoughts shifted track when I heard her friend ask, "Have you been able to reach Alex yet?"

Alex? What! It dawned on me just then—this was Alex's Kristin. Of course! That is why I was drawn to her. I could smell Alex in her blood. Time to back off, there was no way I was crossing that line. Hell, no!

She gave me a confused look, and I felt the presence of the other female vampire just as she did. We both oriented ourselves toward her at the same time. As Kristin made eye contact with the other woman, she tensed. I felt her anger and confusion all at once. She reared back when the woman smiled at her.

Instinct kicked in and I stepped directly behind her, putting my hands protectively on her arms. Something was wrong here. I felt it coming from Kristin. I didn't know her, but I knew Alex, and if this was Alex's woman, then I needed to defend her as if she was mine.

Just as I steadied her, I felt her pain grip me. It was so strong coming over her, she swayed under my hands. I looked at the woman to see if she was somehow causing the pain, but she only smiled at Kristin. Slowly, the woman looked up at me, and her smile turned lopsided, in an evil way.

Kristin was having trouble breathing. The pain came off her in waves. As my hands gripped her arms, I felt each wave pass over her into me. Where the hell were they coming from? Alex? Her body shook, and her friend grabbed her hand. Kristin pretty much collapsed in my arms and I lifted her up against my chest and headed straight for the door.

She was squeezing my arm so hard that if I were human I would have had trouble containing the pain. Instead, I dismissed the pressure and made a bee-line for the parking lot, holding her tightly to my chest as we walked out into the cool air. I needed to get her calmed.

I set Kristin down on the hood of my car and pushed her legs open so that I could get her close to me. If I could get her head on my chest, she would be able to calm herself with the beating of my heart. I held her closely, trying not to think of her body pushed up against me so intimately. Her scent was flooding my mind and making it hard not to be aroused.

"What are you feeling, Kristin?" I whispered in her ear. Her tantalizing aroma filled my senses and made my mouth water.

"Pain..." was all she got out before she shuddered against me. I rubbed her back, trying to soothe her.

I felt another presence approaching from behind, but it was

different from the woman inside the bar and I didn't have time to pay much attention to it.

"Kristin, are you okay?" her friend asked from a safe distance away.

Kristin let the air out of her lungs and replied, "Yeah, I'm okay."

Right after she answered, Kristin's entire body surged. I could smell and feel the hot waves of bloodlust take over her. She looked up at me wildly, her eyes glowing green, her fangs coming down from her upper jaw. Before I could pin her down, she locked her legs around my waist and pulled me tightly against her.

Immediately, my own bloodlust peaked. It burned deep within me. She pushed against my arousal and went for my neck. I couldn't allow it to happen, no matter what. I pushed against her to hold her back. Jesus this woman was strong!

"Kristin...You need to fight this." I was telling myself this just as much as her.

Her friends were screaming around us. They were freaked out by what they were witnessing. I wondered if they even knew that she was a vampire. If they didn't before, they were figuring it out now.

"Kristin, stop! Damn, girl...You gotta get a hold of yourself!" I tried to pry myself from the leg-lock, but it was no use.

"What the hell is wrong with her?" one of her friends asked hysterically.

"Bloodlust...She's in bloodlust," I said through clenched teeth as I fought my own. My fangs were throbbing in my jaw even as I spoke.

"What the hell is that?" the woman asked.

"Whoever she is bonded with just went into bloodlust, and she is feeling exactly what he is." My God, if she was Alex's, then it must be him who was feeling this. What the hell was going on?

Just then, Julian appeared on the other side of the car. I almost sighed in relief as our eyes met.

"Trent, I'm going to grab her from behind. Unlock her legs from you as soon as I tell you, and push her away." Julian reached over the hood of the car and put one arm around her chest and the other around her neck.

"Now!" Julian yelled, and I unhooked her legs as he jerked her off of me and over the hood of the car. He did it with such force that they both ended up tumbling several feet away. I ran around the car as Kristin flipped in his arms.

I couldn't believe what I was seeing when Julian grabbed the back of her head and pulled it down to his throat. She instantly latched on, and I heard her sucking from his neck.

Fury burned through me. What was he doing? This was my woman—I mean, Alex's woman. Why was he letting her drink from him?

My woman? Where did that come from?

"Julian! What the fuck are you doing?" I reached down and grabbed her around the throat to stop her from drinking. I yanked her back while Julian shoved her off. "You can't let her do that! Especially not here!"

Julian stood casually as I held Kristin in a headlock. He shook his head and clenched his jaw momentarily before he focused on Kristin. "Man, Kristin, I hope you'll forgive me for this." Before I knew what he was going to do, his arm snapped back and he punched her square in the face. Her body went limp in my arms.

If I wasn't holding her up, I would have gone after him. A low growl came out of my chest.

"Trent, relax. She was too agitated to be calmed down with words. We need to get her back to the house. I'll explain when we get there."

I was shaking so damn hard, that I could only nod. I scooped up her limp body and went toward Julian's car. I heard him talking to her friends, but my mind was in such turmoil that I couldn't listen. Why the hell would Julian allow her to drink from him, and then knock her out? What did Alex have to do with this? I knew she was Alex's. I could clearly smell him on her now.

Julian caught up to us as I laid her down in the backseat. I was about to climb in with her, when Julian tossed me the keys and told me to drive. I locked ferocious eyes with him. The need to protect her was so intense that I almost didn't understand it. "Trent, I'm not going to hurt her." He slowly raised his hand and put it on my arm. He knew that by touching me, I knew he spoke the truth. "I need you to drive us back to the house before she wakes up."

"Wait, Julian, I need to close your neck." I leaned into him and slid my tongue over the bite marks from Kristin, quickly sealing them up. There was nothing sexual about it. It was a survival mechanism.

"Thanks, yeah, that probably wouldn't be a great thing to have open while I'm sitting with her in the car," Julian said, climbing into the backseat.

I hurried to the driver's seat, looked in the rearview mirror, and watched Julian gently caress her face, pushing some hair off her forehead. He looked at me in the mirror. I knew my eyes were serious, but as I looked into his eyes, I saw the love and pain in his. Mine softened slightly. Julian loved this woman. It was obvious by the emotion in his bright blue eyes.

I broke eye contact and, with a shake of my head, drove us to the VMF house. I was so confused.

CHAPTER ELEVEN

JULIAN

*B*y the time I checked around the offices and the video feed for anything further, it was way too late to drive to Fawn Hollow. The sun would be up soon, so I headed to my loft apartment and tried to get some sleep; "tried" being the operative word, because it was useless.

I lay in my bed and stared up at the ceiling in the dark of my room. Yes, it was daylight, and the sun was probably shining outside, but I had shutters on the windows to hold it out. I looked at the clock next to my bed—it read 1:16. I still had several hours before I could comfortably get in the car and head south.

I wasn't sure if there were any agents in that area. I assumed that if Alex mentioned Trent, then he was probably somewhere around there. I spent so much time over the last three months trying to not think about Kristin that I had blocked out any information about who might be working in that area. I wouldn't put it past Alex to keep someone around to make sure Kristin was safe and to also let him know if I showed up in the area. Maybe that's why he mentioned Trent.

I had respected Kristin's decision about going to Alex. As much as I loved her, and wanted her to be mine, I knew that giving her up for her own happiness was the right thing to do. Alex was right when he told me that Kristin wasn't Calista anymore. She had changed. That thought did not take the pain away; it still felt like a knife in the heart.

What was she going to do when she saw me again? How would she feel? Would the chemistry that we always shared still be there? I closed my eyes as I thought about how good she'd always felt in my arms. How amazing her eyes were as they looked into mine and changed color as they filled up with passion. I felt my body heat rise and my arousal coming on hard and strong at just the mere thought of her.

I closed my eyes and tried to block those thoughts out. I couldn't go to her and think like that. I had to protect her. The words that Alex had written played in my mind over and over again. *"Go to her...protect her. You and Trent are the only ones I can truly trust. Do not let Burke get to her. Do what you have to do to protect her, Jules. If she is in a lot of pain because of me, either you or Trent break the bond. Do not allow her to suffer because I am. Do whatever it takes to protect her...I trust you to do the right thing."*

Finally, I got up and started to get things ready for the trip. I called Gabe and told him to get on the first flight north and head straight to Fawn Hollow. I called a couple of our other guys and told them to get down and take over for Gabe in Florida. I knew Burke had headquarters there, but I doubted that was where they were keeping Alex. That would've been too far to take him, so he had to be someplace local.

As soon as I knew the sun was setting, I climbed into my Mustang and started the drive to Fawn Hollow. I needed to find out where Kristin was, but I didn't want to call the house and alert her to the fact that I was coming. So I ended up calling her station and talking to the officer on duty. So that he would tell me where she might be, I told him I was Alex and coming down to surprise her. He said she was off and that there was a party tonight for her partner at a local restaurant. I knew the place and headed straight there.

As I pulled into the parking lot, I saw Trent walking out the front door with Kristin in his arms. My first thought was one of possessiveness and a small growl rolled out of my chest. As I watched, I saw several women running them. Something was wrong.

I parked the Mustang and kept an eye out for anything out of the ordinary. Slowly, I headed toward the group and noticed the way Trent was protectively holding her against his body. A pang of jealousy stabbed my heart, but I tamped it down and picked up the pace.

As I got closer, I watched as Kristin transformed from calmness to increasing bloodlust. She latched onto Trent with her legs and tried to pull him toward her so she could reach his neck. Astonishment raced through me as I watched her lose control. What the hell was going on?

Trent was fighting to keep Kristin off his neck as I came up on the other side of the car. When Trent looked up and saw me, I saw a moment of relief flash through his eyes.

I reached over the top of the small car.

"Now!" I yelled as I pulled her back and over the car. Trent pushed her so hard that we both fell back onto the ground. Kristin froze in my arms, caught by surprise, but it lasted only a second before she spun around and went for my throat.

The words Alex wrote ran through my mind again. *"Whatever it takes...protect her."* I put my hand on the back of her head and held her to my throat as her canine teeth broke the skin and I felt the first pulls of blood leaving my body. I knew she had no idea who I was or what she was doing, but that didn't stop me from taking this moment.

She greedily pulled from my neck, and I felt the lust rising in her as she pushed her body hard against mine. My body reacted immediately, and it took every ounce of strength to not bite down on her neck and take her right there. Trent broke through my pull at the lust when he shouted at me.

"Julian! What the fuck are you doing?" I felt him grab Kristin, and thought about fighting him, but stopped myself. His next words rang true in my ears. "You can't let her do that! Especially not here!"

I pushed up on Kristin as Trent pulled her from behind, quickly removing her from our position on the ground. Three startled women gawked at me with their jaws dropped, probably all friends of

Kristin's. I wasn't sure who was going to be madder at me for what I was going to do next—the friends, Trent, or Kristin.

"Man, Kristin, I hope you forgive me for this." As I pulled my arm back, I saw a flash of recognition in her eyes. Trent scooped her up as soon as she went unconscious. I not only felt the anger in Trent, but saw it flash across his face.

"Trent, relax. She was too agitated to be calmed down with words. We need to get her back to the house. I'll explain when we get there." He answered with a nod and took off for my car with Kristin cradled to his chest. I felt the groan welling inside and held it back.

I faced the three women; two of them looked shocked, fear clearly etched in their eyes. The third appeared to be getting ready to throw her own punch my way.

"I assume you are all friends of hers. I'm Julian." I noticed the dark-haired one relax her hands when she heard my name. The other two only nodded. "Come back to the house and I'll explain what's going on. I'm sorry you had to see that." I didn't wait for an answer. They could come or not, I didn't care. My concern was standing beside my car in the arms of another man.

Trent was a good guy. I knew that he was being protective, and I knew he didn't understand what was going on. My touching his arm was to show him that I meant what I said. Trent could feel emotions when you touched him, could tell if you were being serious or lying. He seemed satisfied with my intentions, and even took a moment to close the bite mark on my neck. I had forgotten about that even though I still had blood running down it.

I gathered Kristin in my arms as I climbed into the backseat and looked down into the face of the woman I loved. The circles under her eyes stood out against her pale skin. I gently pushed some of her bangs off her forehead and wanted to run my fingers through her hair, but I stopped myself.

I looked up and found Trent's eyes intent on me in the mirror; it was as if Alex was looking back at me. I realized I had a lot to explain to Trent, and to Kristin.

Trent pulled his focus away and started to drive while I watched

Kristin, cradled to my chest. She didn't move at all for the entire ride. I would have been worried except her breathing was calm and relaxed and she seemed content to be where she was. I knew I was more content now than I had been in a very long time. I never thought I would ever get the chance to hold her this close again.

When we arrived at the house, another set of headlights pulled in behind us. Trent got out, and I handed Kristin to him through the door. He held her tightly and immediately went into the house.

The women got out of a big black Hummer and walked cautiously toward me. I wondered if they knew what I was, and I figured that with how carefully they were approaching, they probably did.

"Neither Trent nor I are going to hurt any of you. We are here to protect Kristin, so please relax and come inside." I smiled gently and turned to walk in. I'd let them take their time coming in.

Trent had laid Kristin down on the living room sofa. I heard Garda come running in, and he immediately growled at us before he put his nose up in the air and sniffed. A quick look between us and he seemed to be satisfied that we were not going to hurt her. He went directly to Kristin and sniffed her all over. Turning around, he sat down near her head and turned to watch us. He whined quietly as he looked at me.

"It's all right, Garda. She'll wake up soon." I watched him as he looked at me for a second longer, and then lay down next to the couch to take up guard duty.

I turned to encompass the group with a look. "Why don't we go talk in the kitchen?" I left without waiting for a reply.

In the fridge, I grabbed several bottles of beer and handed one to everybody. I didn't know if her friends drank, but I could bet they would all welcome something right this second.

"I already introduced myself, and by the way you all reacted, you seem to know who I am already, correct?" I studied each of them for a moment.

The one with the dark hair watched me closely. "You would be Jules. Yes, Kristin told us *all* about you." She smiled and tipped her head to the side as she looked at me. "I'm Olivia, but everyone calls me Livy. This is Katherine, or Kat, and that is Isabell, or Izzy." She pointed each of them out, and they each smiled or nodded as they were introduced.

"We not only know who you are, but what you are too. I'm assuming that he is like you?" She pointed toward Trent.

"Yes, he is. This is Trent. He works with me, and speaking of which, why are you here in Fawn Hollow? I thought you were still out west."

"I was until about a month ago. Two months ago, I told Alex that I wanted a change of scenery. He suggested I come here. I wasn't sure why, but I think I just figured it out." He nodded toward the hallway. "What's going on, Julian, and why are you here?"

Trent stood on the other side of the kitchen, back straight, leaning against the counter with his arms crossed over his chest. He didn't seem angry, but he looked rather intense. He was eyeing me up just as I was eyeing him up. Neither one of us heard the sound of someone entering the room until the voice rang out, but the first word spoken was a silent one meant just for me.

"Jules..." I heard softly in my head on the catch of a sigh before she spoke out loud. "Yeah, Julian, why are you here?" It was said softly, but the voice caused goose bumps on my arms. I spun to find Kristin in the doorway, watching me with soft gray eyes. Three steps and I could have her in my arms.

Garda stood protectively against her legs, and she absently petted his head as she waited for my reply.

Before I could answer, her friend Isabell crushed her in a hug. Garda moved out of the way so that he wouldn't get trampled on. That dog was too damn smart. "Kris, are you all right? What the hell happened out there?" Kristin hugged her friend, but she kept her eyes on mine. The intensity of them caused my blood to warm. Finally, she broke the vision lock so she could look at her friends one at a time.

"Well, if what I told you last night didn't convince you, I guess tonight did, huh?" She gave them a sad smile.

"Girl, you freaked the hell out of us!" Olivia said as she threw her arms around Kristin, holding her tightly.

"Oh, I'm sure I did. I kind of freaked myself out a bit, too." She hugged Kat before walking over to stand in front of Trent.

"First, let me say, I'm sorry for what I did, or tried to do to you earlier." She smiled into his eyes and a jealous twinge electrified my nerve endings when he smiled back.

"It's okay, Kristin, I understand," Trent replied.

She paused as she watched him. "Well, I'm glad someone understands because I sure as hell don't. Do you or Jules want to fill me in here? Who are you anyway?"

I spoke up before he could answer. "Kristin, that's Trent. He works for the VMF. He's one of our agents." I looked pointedly at him. *"Don't tell her the rest yet,"* I sent silently to his mind.

"Why not?" He replied back to me in the same manner without taking his eyes off Kristin.

I growled back, *"I'll explain it later, but now is not the time."*

"Kristin, what do you remember about what happened tonight?" I queried to change the subject. She was still studying him closely and turned slowly toward me, but only as her neck hit ninety degrees did she pull herself away from viewing Trent and focus on me.

"Julian, where's Alex? What's going on?"

Alex's words ran through my mind again. *"Do not allow her to suffer because I am. Do whatever it takes to protect her...I trust you to do the right thing."* I had to tell her the truth.

I stood a bit taller and looked her in the eye before I spoke. "I don't know where he is, Kristin, not yet. All I know is that he was kidnapped last night."

As she took the information in, her eyes turned from a light gray to a dark, stormy gray, anger and pain evident on her features. For about five seconds she didn't move, then she flew into my arms and wrapped them around me. She buried her face in my neck and I felt her body quivering, but it was the words that she spoke as I held her that had my blood stopping in my veins.

"They're killing him, Jules. I can feel it."

CHAPTER TWELVE

KRISTIN

"They're killing him, Jules. I can feel it." I spoke the words against Julian's neck as I clung to him.

His body tensed against mine, and he whispered into my ear, "We'll find him, Kristin. I promise, we will find him."

I knew he was trying to make me feel better, but his words didn't. It was the feel of his arms around me that comforted me at that moment.

"Kristin, what did you feel earlier? I need to know everything that's happened in the last couple of days." Julian pushed me back so that he could look into my face.

Man, those eyes...How much I had missed his eyes. I wanted to wrap my arms around him again and forget about everything else, but I knew that was wrong. I turned away and went over to one of the stools at the counter.

Izzy, Livy, and Kat had already taken seats there, and I was glad they were here with me. I didn't want to deal with this alone. I needed my friends with me right now.

Kat pushed her beer over in front of me. "I think you need this more than me."

I spun the bottle around in my fingers for a moment, and then took a long pull from it. After, I swallowed and scanned around the room again.

"A couple of days ago, Alex called me and insisted I come up to see him." I shrugged as if it was no big deal. "I had things going on and told him I couldn't." I didn't want to tell Julian or Trent what I thought the conversation would have been about. "He seemed tense and told me he really needed to see me, so he said he would come down last night. He never got here." I waited for Julian to respond.

Julian rolled his hand in front of him as though he wanted me to continue.

"After work last night, since he wasn't here, I went and met these guys for a drink at Joe's Bar." I waived my hand toward the ladies. "We were there for a while when I got this intense feeling from Alex. It was more intense than I had ever felt before over our bond. It was incredibly painful, angry..." I shook my head as I remembered the exact way it had felt and knew that my words did not do it justice.

Livy spoke up then. "It was like she was in physical pain that came out of nowhere. One second she's calmly talking, the next she was grabbing the edge of the table and trying not to scream."

Julian crossed his arms over his chest, leaning back against the counter in a similar position as Trent. I eyed Trent again; his bright green eyes were watching me intently. There was something about him that I felt drawn to. God, I had enough to deal with. I didn't need my hormones getting out of control with another man.

"It stopped almost as quickly as it began. I called Alex on his cellphone and tried to reach out to him so many times, but didn't get anything from him again—until tonight." I examined the beer bottle in front of me and began to pull the label off it, momentarily lost in the memory of the first night I met Alex and how he was peeling the label off his bottle when I sat down beside him. I clenched my eyes to pull myself back to the present.

I couldn't remember all that happened tonight, and part of me was very grateful for that. I did remember throwing myself at Trent and trying to bite his neck. It had felt incredible to be in his arms. I peered up at him and felt a blush color my face. I went back to staring at my bottle.

Julian cleared his throat to get my attention. I saw possessiveness in his eyes. "So what happened tonight?"

"Stop, Julian." I said to him silently. He shrugged and waited for me to go on with the story. I had to be extremely careful to watch what my thoughts were. Julian had always been able to read my mind quickly and completely even if I was being careful. I could put up the wall, but I needed to keep it down incase Alex tried to contact me again. Leaving my mind this open just made it easier for Julian to step into it.

Pulling a large piece of the label off my bottle, I continued. "I was talking to Trent at the party, and all of a sudden, I could feel Alex again. It wasn't as bad as last night, but it was a similar pain that ran across my chest like an X. Last night, yes, it did feel as if someone stabbed me right in the chest, but this was different. It was like I was being sliced." I noticed my hands shook, and Kat, who was sitting next to me, put her arm around my shoulders.

"I remember Trent picking me up and taking me outside. Then I remember listening to his heartbeat and starting to relax, but then things got kind of crazy and I don't remember much more than throwing myself at him and being so thirsty." As I thought more about the night, I suddenly remembered what else happened. My head snapped up from where I was sitting on the stool looking down at my beer bottle. "I fed off you," I said quietly, staring at Julian with wide eyes.

Oh no! I remembered sinking my teeth into his neck, the aroma of cinnamon rising up in my nose and filling my mouth with his blood. The sensation of that warm blood taking the thirst away as it ran down my throat. I put my hand up to the front of my throat as I recalled the intensity of it. Oh, man...Alex was going to be pissed!

"Tell me again why you let her feed from you, Julian." Trent's voice was tense. I wondered why he might be upset. What difference did it make to Trent if I fed off Julian?

"She's had my blood before, Trent." Julian eyed him carefully and seemed to say something to him silently. Trent gave him a tight nod back that confirmed my suspicion.

"Yes, Kris...You fed from me, but like I just said, you've fed from me before so it's no big deal." He shrugged his shoulders again, but didn't look me in the eye as he answered. He was avoiding something.

Izzy spoke up then. "Why is it a big freaking deal who she feeds from? I thought that's what you all did." She looked around the room.

I exhaled loudly and looked at her. "I'm Alex's mate for all intents and purposes. I shouldn't be feeding from other vampires, because it can break our bond." I peered at Julian. "That wasn't enough to break the bond, was it?"

"What do you mean 'for all intents and purposes'? You didn't finish the mating process with Alex yet?" Julian asked me.

"Julian, don't go there," I warned quietly. I did not want to get into this with him. "Was that enough to break the bond with Alex?"

"We need to talk," Julian said to me silently.

"Not now...okay? I can't do this right now," I replied back, trying not to be irritated by his intrusion.

Trent rescued me then and answered the question that Julian was supposed to have answered. "Kristin, don't worry, that wasn't enough. Just feeding from someone isn't enough; you need to exchange blood. That's what breaks the bond. Drinking from another person just confuses your scent and will probably piss off Alex." Trent threw Julian a nasty look.

The two of them stared each other down. *Damn men and their testosterone!* I shook my head.

I heard Livy laugh. She caught it too. "Okay, boys, stop the pissing match." I couldn't help but laugh at the way they both looked at her with innocent "who, me?" looks on their faces. "Why did she get all freaking crazy and shit tonight?" Livy asked.

"Since she is bonded to Alex, she feels his emotions when he doesn't protect them from her." Trent stopped talking and everyone turned to Julian, each of us knowing that if Alex couldn't stop those emotions from coming through, then he was in really bad shape.

"What about that woman, Angie, from the party? You didn't seem too happy to see her, and I got the feeling that something was wrong with her," Trent asked me.

"What woman?" Julian questioned immediately.

It took me a second to remember the woman who had been with Thomas. "Angie...Yeah, there is something wrong with her, all right. I think she has something to do with Alex being missing." As I thought back, I remembered the night before and how she had taken off from the bar right after I felt Alex, and then just as she came to me tonight, I felt him again.

"I was getting bad vibes off her too, but I have no idea who she is." Trent focused his next question on Julian. "Do you know an Angie? She is about Kristin's height with long hair about the same color as hers, too."

Everyone watched Julian again. He clamped his eye lids shut and inhaled through his nose. Damn, this wasn't good.

"Angelina. Yeah, I know who she is. She's Burke's daughter. Burke is the one who kidnapped Alex."

"I'm gonna kill that bitch!" I said through gritted teeth.

Trent looked at me. "Stand in line, honey," he drawled with his soft Southern accent.

"Are you sure Alex was kidnapped? Did you get a ransom note or something?" Kat asked when we had all gotten quiet, thinking about the painful things we wanted to do to Angelina.

Julian replied, "No, no ransom note, but I saw some of it on video at the headquarters."

"What was on the video, Julian? Anything we can use?" Trent queried as I opened my mouth to ask the same question. Trent and I exchanged a quick look but both of us looked away quickly.

"Not much. They had blacked out the cameras in the garage. I only got a few seconds of video feed from the camera in the elevator. The only thing I could see was that Alex stopped quickly, then he fell to the ground, and I saw a black boot just as the elevator doors closed."

"What did they do to him? Unless they were using platinum and titanium bullets, a bullet wouldn't hurt him." As I waited for him to reply, I was trying to hold down the panic I felt at Alex being hurt. I saw Trent glance my way.

"A normal bullet, no, you're correct; that wouldn't hurt him. I don't think it was a PT bullet. I think it was a tranquilizer. I found only a drop of his blood on the ground, and it had a chemical smell to it. If he had been shot with a PT bullet, there would have been a lot more blood." He reached around and grabbed the beer bottle he'd set on the counter, taking a long drink from it.

I felt a little bit better knowing that it was probably a tranquilizer that had put him down, and that he hadn't been shot. A little better, but not much.

"So how do you know it was this guy Burke who took him?" Izzy asked Julian.

He exhaled slowly and met my gaze head on. "Alex left me a note." He pulled a white envelope out of the back pocket of his jeans and tossed it across the granite countertop to land in front of me. "He left you one, too."

The ordinary white office envelope stopped when it hit my hand that was wrapped around the beer bottle. I reached out slowly, unfolding the envelope, smoothing it out as I read my name written in Alex's handwriting. My heart sped up as I slowly lifted the envelope.

I didn't look at anyone as I slid off the stool and left the room. The sight of his handwriting brought tears to my eyes as it brought Alex's face to my mind.

I heard Julian speak behind me quietly to someone. "No, give her some time." I didn't care who he was talking to.

I went into the living room and sank down in one of the wingback chairs. I was so afraid to open the letter, but I needed to know what he had written. Carefully, I tore open the top and pulled out the single piece of paper.

Kristin ~

I know that you are probably scared, but you have to be strong right now. There is a man named Burke whom we have been investigating for a while, and he recently made some serious threats. I would not have been concerned about those threats if they had just been made against me, but they were against you, too. I will not allow him to hurt you, and will do everything in my power to stop him and protect you.

I hope that Julian has gotten to you quickly to help you deal with what is happening. I can only assume it has been confusing, painful, and scary for you. He will be able to explain all of this to you and help you through the pain of it. I am so very sorry. I want—no, I need—you to do me a favor, and do as Julian or Trent asks of you. I know you hate to take orders, but I need to know that you are safe.

I realize that you don't know Trent, but you can trust him, and he will be good for you. I know you have a history with Julian, but Trent will provide for you, too. He is very close to me and will do everything he can to protect you.

I have already told Julian to do whatever is necessary to protect you... whatever needs to be done, he has my permission. There is a good chance I will not make it out of this alive, and I will do everything I can to protect you up to the last second of my life. If I do not make it, go on with your life, Kristin. Make yourself happy, for me...I have only ever wanted you to be happy. Please...Be strong. I love you.

~ Alexander

BY THE TIME I had read the letter three times, the page was so wet that the ink was starting to smudge. I rested my head back against the chair and let the tears continue to fall. This letter was a good-bye. He was asking me to stay with Trent and Julian so that they could protect me. He was talking as if he knew he would not make it back alive.

He said he was close to Trent. How was he close to him? In the three months we were together, I had never heard of him. I knew it must have been very hard for him to ask Julian to come to me and protect me after everything that had happened before. Maybe he thought that if he was gone, then Julian would take me as his mate.

I mulled over what he had written. The longer I sat there, the angrier I got—at the letter, and at Alex. I wanted to scream, but I closed my eyes and tried to calm down. Alex was making decisions for me again, telling me what to do. I hated that. I tried to stay calm, until I heard footsteps coming down the hall. Then the anger swooped in again. I stood and glared at Julian and Trent as they walked in the door.

My heart slammed against my chest. Scared and angry, I kept flipping my gaze between the two of them. They stood silent as Livy walked around them and over to me.

"Kristin...Are you all right?" Julian asked me quietly, mind to mind. I ignored him.

I turned to Livy in a near panic. "Livy, get me out of here."

"What? What's wrong?" She reached out for my arm, but I pulled it back from her.

"Just get me out of here. I need to get out of here." I twirled around to get to the front door.

"Kristin, wait!" I heard Julian shout.

"No! You wait!" I spun and glared at him from across the room. "I'm not ready to discuss this...this...this letter with you. I need to get out of here." I turned the corner out of the room before he could say anything else, and ran to the front door.

I heard Isabell and Kat asking what was going on, and then heard three pairs of feet running behind me. I prayed they were my friends' feet and not those of Trent or Julian.

Right before I heard the door slam shut, I heard Trent say to Julian, "What the hell was in that letter, Julian?"

CHAPTER THIRTEEN

TRENT

*N*o one heard her as she entered the kitchen, but I saw Julian's face as he turned toward the entrance. Kristin stood in the threshold, her focus trained on him. Her eyes darkened, while his lightened, and a flair of something roared through my blood.

My heart skipped a beat as she approached me, and I fought to breathe normally.

"First, let me just say I'm sorry for what I did, or tried to do to your earlier." Her eyes changed from blue to a light shade of green.

"It's okay, Kristin, I understand." Although, I couldn't understand the way I was reacting to her. The way her eyes changed color mesmerized me. It had to be her blood that was causing me to want to pull her to my chest and hold her, there could be no other reason, I told myself.

I don't know why Julian didn't want me to tell Kristin about my relationship with Alex, and I shrugged it off; it really didn't matter to me. If it didn't matter to me, then why did I tense up when she launched herself into Julian's arms and took comfort against his chest?

The words she said rocked me on my feet as if I had been slugged. "They're killing him, Jules. I can feel it." Julian gave Kristin the note that Alex had left for her. Her entire demeanor changed as she slid off the stool and left the room. Her buzzing energy evaporated from the air. It was some time later when Julian and I looked up at one another. We could smell her tears, and they had been a heavy presence in the room for a while now. As if verbally decided, we headed toward the hallway together and entered into the living room to find Kristin standing upright, board-stiff, the note clenched in her hands. Her eyes a dark, stormy gray, and tears streaking her pale cheeks. Her chest heaved with anger as she sneered at us.

She fled the room, her friends in tow, before I had any clue what the hell was going on. "What the hell was in that letter, Julian?" I asked right before the door slammed behind her friends. Julian didn't answer me, so I dropped down onto the couch, throwing my arm along the back and resting my head on the cushion. "What was in that letter, Julian?" I asked again.

"Damn it!" Julian grunted as he sat down in one of the wingback chairs.

The emotions flickered over his features. I knew there was a huge, messy history with Julian and Alex, but I didn't know the details. For some reason, I felt as though I was about to have story time and I wasn't sure I wanted to hear it.

"Do you remember my mate, Calista?" Julian asked quietly.

Yep, there was a story here.

"Yeah, I remember hearing about her, but I don't think I ever met her. Wasn't she killed by Damon?" He flinched slightly.

"Yes, she was. What you probably don't know is that Alex was going to mate with her, but when I met her it didn't quite end up the way it was supposed to. We had this bizarre chemistry, and Calista and I ended up mating on our first night together. Alex was furious, of course."

I laughed. Of course, he would have been angry. I would have been too if someone took the woman I wanted.

"Well, after that, Calista and I were together and we had a daughter named Anastasia. Both of them were killed by Damon five years later. When we found out Damon was back in this area, we found Kristin.

We also found out that Kristin was actually Calista, reborn." He peered up at me under low brows.

"Wow...Kristin is your mate?" Why did I not like the sound of that?

"No, not really. Calista was, but when she was reborn, of course that part of the bond did not hold. Although strangely enough, we do still share the same kind of intense chemistry that we had back then, and a strange bond none-the-less."

Why did that bother me? I didn't want to contemplate the thought and brushed it off as just wanting to protect her because she was Alex's mate.

"When Damon was killed, Kristin decided that it was Alex whom she wanted and not me," he said softly.

I didn't know what how to respond, so I stayed quiet for a while until I couldn't take the silence anymore. "So, why are you telling me this?"

He cleared his throat and leaned back. "Remember I said that Alex left me a note? Well, in that note he said he wanted us, you and me, to protect her. He told us to break the bond with her if she was in pain."

"No way! He wants you to mate with her?" I was stunned, and a very large part of me did not like the idea of him mating with her.

"He didn't say that. He said he wants either *you or me* to break the bond." Julian stressed the "you or me" part, which I tried like hell to ignore.

I didn't know what to say. Why the hell would Alex tell us to do that? "Why us?" was all I could get out without showing my nervousness at the thought.

"I assume he picked you because of your blood, and picked me, well, because of the bond I have with her already. I told you I drank from her before, although that was a long time ago." He looked away.

I let that latter part slide for now. "So why do you think Kristin was so upset by her letter? It was clearly obvious that she was pissed." I sat forward and rested my elbows on my knees, staring at the pattern on the wood floor.

"I have no idea. I didn't look at her letter." His gaze traveled over the room as if he was looking for something.

Just then, the front door opened and in walked a tall, dark-haired guy wearing a black leather jacket and whistling some tune that sounded country.

"Gabe, hey, man, glad you made it. That was pretty quick." Julian stood up.

"Yep, got on an early flight and made it here in good time. Is Alex here? Where's my girl, Kristin?" He smiled wide. I caught the "my girl, Kristin" part, too. Why did everyone have such a connection with her, and why did I even care? I'd known her what, two hours now?

I had heard of Gabe, although I'd never met him. I quickly realized why everyone said they liked him. He came across as the boy next door, easygoing and friendly.

"Neither one of them are here right now. You just missed Kristin, and, well...we have no idea where Alex is," I told him as I went over to the bar.

"What do you mean no one knows where Alex is? And who is he?" Gabe asked Julian.

"That's Trent," I heard Julian say as I pulled some glasses out of the cabinet. I glanced over in time to see Gabe nod as recognition of the name came to mind.

"Come on in and sit down," Julian told him while I put three glasses on the bar and poured a good amount of whiskey in each. Gabe dropped the garment bag he was carrying and took my abandoned seat. I passed out the glasses before I took residence in the wingback chair next to Julian, taking a long, slow drink from my glass.

"Alex was kidnapped by Burke last night," Julian explained to Gabe. The glass stopped a half inch from his lips as he turned angry eyes on Julian. Damn, he might look like the kid next door, but I wouldn't want to be on the receiving end of that anger. He looked downright villainous.

"How do you know it was Burke?" Gabe asked, his voice deep and strong, the Southern charm gone now.

"He left me a note, said that Burke was on to him and that we were to come here and protect Kristin," Julian replied as he swirled the brown liquid inside the crystal.

"So, where's Kristin?" Gabe looked between us.

"She took off when she read the letter that Alex had left for her," I responded, and then kind of half-laughed. But when I started to think about what Alex said in Julian's note, the humor faded, fast.

The last thing I wanted to think about was bonding to someone, especially someone who belonged to Alex. Kristin might be one fine woman, but I knew I didn't want to get tied down just because Alex volunteered me. We were so going to have a chat when we got him back from Burke.

Gabe was watching us, and Julian continued to swirl the whiskey in his glass, watching it spin around and around.

"Damn...What the hell did Alex write in his note to you?" Gabe asked quietly.

Julian and I sighed at the same time, and then looked at each other. I think we would have laughed if the subject wasn't so serious.

When Julian didn't say anything, I spoke up. "It seems that the Master has decided he wants to protect Kristin by breaking the bond, and he wants either Julian or I to do that."

Gabe's jaw went slack for a good twenty seconds before he cleared his throat. He looked as if he was going to speak, but instead, he emptied his glass in one large gulp.

A long silence followed, as Gabe contemplated a spot on the wall over my head. Julian continued to swirl his drink, and I waited for someone to say something, anything. Finally, Gabe went to the bar and poured himself another whiskey.

I watched as he filled his glass, spun the cap back on, and rested his hands on the cherry-wood bar. He shook his head back and forth slowly before he finally looked up at us.

"So which one of you is going to do it?" he asked.

I didn't hesitate. I pointed to Julian, just as I saw Julian—out of the corner of my eye—point at me.

"What? Wait! Julian, you two have a history! It would be easier for you to bond with her. Besides, it's obvious that you're in love with her." I spoke quickly, trying to figure out what he was doing. The thought of bonding with any female freaked me the hell out.

Julian grunted. "That's exactly why I shouldn't do it." He took a drink. I made eye contact with Gabe, and his eyes seemed to examine me as if he was trying to see if I would measure up. Oh, hell no!

"What do you mean, that's exactly why you shouldn't do it?" I asked angrily. Panic was tickling the back of my brain.

Julian huffed loudly. "Trent, when Alex gets back, whose bond do you think will be easier to break? You don't think he's going to allow the bond to continue, do you? He's going to want her back. I don't think I would be able to let her go if I had her again. No, I know I won't be able to."

I gaped at him. Gabe was frowning at Julian. Okay, the panic was grabbing my chest like a vice around my lungs and it was getting tighter. Damn...I put my glass to my lips and finished my drink in one quick gulp.

Gabe brought the bottle over to me and I held it out without a word. "Sorry, man, but he has a point," Gabe said as he filled my glass higher than it had originally been filled. I took another long gulp.

"Shit!" I closed my eyes and bounced my head off the cushion behind me a few times. Yeah, he was probably right. Seeing how Julian was so head-over-heels in love with Kristin, he probably wouldn't let her go, but I wouldn't bat an eye at giving her back to Alex. Being bonded with anyone was not something I ever wanted to do.

I sat forward and put my forearms on my knees, hanging my head down and staring into the light brown liquid that pooled in the bottom of the glass.

"What if he doesn't come back? What then?" I didn't need to look up to see the distress in either of their eyes. I didn't need to touch them to know what they were thinking or what emotions they were feeling. We were all feeling the same thing.

Damn, Alex...We have to get you back.

Gabe changed the subject. "So, aren't we supposed to be protecting her? Where is she anyway?"

"I have no idea where she went. She just took off with her three friends," I said.

Julian threw back the rest of his drink, and stood. "I know where she is. She's at Eagle Glen Lake. That's where she always goes when she's upset."

"I know where that is. I'll go find her and bring her back." Gabe went to the bar and set the glass and bottle down.

Julian was about to leave the room when he stopped. "Take Trent with you. He needs to start working on Kristin."

"Great. Just great," I muttered under my breath as he left. He looked back at me. "The sooner the better; try to get it done tonight." He spun back around, but not before I saw the pain in his eyes.

Gabe put his hand on my shoulder. I felt the tension begin to relax. "Come on, Trent, I've got an idea."

CHAPTER FOURTEEN

KRISTIN

When I ran out of the house, all I could think about was that I needed space, I needed air, and I needed to think. I knew I shouldn't be driving, and I didn't want so many people with me. I turned to Izzy and Kat and smiled tightly.

"Do you guys mind if I send you home? I need some quiet time, and I think your husband's probably miss you guys by now. I'm surprised they haven't put out a police bulletin to try to locate you."

Izzy gave me a hug. "If that's what you want us to do. I'll stay if you need me."

"I know you will, but right now, I just need some downtime," I said quietly as we continued to hug.

Kat immediately hugged me when Izzy stepped back. "You know where to find us if you need us."

"I do. Thank you, guys! I love you two!" I said good-bye to them.

"Livy, let's go down to the lake. You don't mind, do you?" I asked, but I knew she was in for the long haul; she always was.

"Oh, hell no! This has been one of the most interesting weekends of my life. I'm not leaving you alone for a second!" She laughed to lighten the mood as we climbed into her Hummer.

Livy immediately cranked up the music, and I stared out the

window. She knew if I wanted to talk, I would. Right now, she gave me the space I needed.

Although thinking wasn't what I really wanted to do, I wanted to back up. To rewind a couple of days and forget my extra shift and Mick's party. I wish I had gone up to see Alex as he had practically begged me to. Maybe if I had been there, he would be safe. Or maybe we would be together, wherever he was.

Hindsight is always 20/20.

Olivia pulled into the dirt parking lot near the lake. Funny, the last time I was here was when the memory came back of my life as Calista, and I told Julian that I needed to be with Alex. It was the last time I had seen Julian, and now, three months later, as he re-enters my life, I find myself here.

We walked through the woods and exited the other side to see a long T-shaped dock. During the day, a lot of people fished from there; but since it was really early in the morning, it was empty. We walked quietly, and I listened to the sound of our feet on the boards. I could hear the wind blowing through the trees and some animals walking in the woods behind us. I knew that Livy couldn't hear them with her mortal ears. I wish I could share this with her. It was a different kind of peace, the life that surrounds us, that so few even know exists.

When we got to the end, I braced my forearms on the metal railing and looked out across the water. A light breeze blew, and the air smelled crisp. It would be getting very cold soon. Winter was coming.

"So what did the letter say?" Olivia finally asked me quietly.

The dark sky above me held millions of sparkling stars, reminding me of Julian's eyes. I took a deep breath and held it for a second, not sure if I could say the words. Why couldn't the sky be green so that it reminded me of Alex's eyes?

"He said good-bye."

I heard her gasp. She stepped closer to me and put her hand on my back between my shoulder blades. "No! He did *not!*"

I turned my head to her. A tear ran down my face. She saw it.

"He did..." She threw her arms around me and rested her cheek against my back. I leaned my head back to rest on hers. I stared up at the sky, the stars blurring as tears filled my eyes and slipped over.

"He doesn't think that he's going to make it through this. He said that he sent Julian and Trent to protect me from this Burke guy. Told me to do what Julian and Trent asked me to, and told me that if he didn't make it back to stay with them, basically." The words all came out slowly and painfully. More tears rolled down my cheeks as I spoke.

"Oh, Kristin...I'm so sorry." She pulled back and grabbed my arm, spinning me around. "Look, we'll find him. He'll be okay." She pulled me into her arms, and I held on to her and cried.

She knew that I didn't cry often, so for me to break down like this, she knew I was hurting. She held me until the sobs stopped and I gathered myself. We eventually ended up lying on the dock, gazing up at the galaxy of stars above us. I'm not sure how long we lay there before I heard footsteps in the woods. They were not the footfalls of an animal; they were the footsteps of a person, mortal or immortal, I was not sure. I tensed immediately.

Olivia felt the change in my demeanor and immediately began to sit up.

"No, don't move," I whispered. I didn't know if this was going to be Julian and Trent or the people they were sent here to protect me from. She stopped trying to sit up and lay still. I could hear her heart beating faster.

I continued to listen, and when I heard the two sets of footsteps break through the woods, I heard another sound that made my heart want to sing out in relief. One of them was whistling quietly, a Garth Brooks tune. I sprang up and confirmed what I thought.

"What? What's going on?"

I took off running a little faster than an average person could. Gabe's face broke out into a huge grin when he saw me coming, and I leaped up into the air as I reached him, throwing my arms and legs around him.

"Gabriel! You're here!" I hugged him so tightly I was surprised he could breathe. I wanted to start sobbing all over again. Gabe was like a brother to me. He knew when I was stressed or scared. He had a way of calming me completely, and he was just plain ol' fun to be around.

"Krissy! Man, it's good to see you, sweet potato!" He spun me around and hugged me tightly.

I laughed. "Sweet potato? Where did that come from?" I looked into his smiling brown eyes while still holding on to him tightly.

He laughed again. "I don't know. It just popped into my head. Girl, it's so good to see you!" He hugged me tightly again, and I was just about to say something else when I heard someone speak next to us very quietly.

"Maybe it should be you," Trent said under his breath.

I glanced at Trent and was going to ask him what he meant, but I heard Livy's footsteps coming closer on the dock. I pulled out of Gabe's hold and slid to the ground.

"Olivia, this is Gabriel." I was holding Gabe's hand, still smiling. Having Gabe here was like having fresh air to breathe after being stuck in a moldy room for hours.

Livy held her hand out to Gabe. "You're the one she's been telling me was like her brother," she said, and laughed.

I heard Trent hiss under his breath, and Gabe chuckled.

"Yep, this is my adopted little sister, sweet potato." He grinned and pulled me close to his chest.

I laughed. "We need to discuss this whole sweet potato thing, bro."

"Speaking of sweet potatoes, we wanted to make sure you guys were here. We brought a snack with us, but we left it back at the car. Olivia, why don't you and I walk back and get it. We'll have a picnic under the stars before the sun starts to come up."

"Please tell me you brought more than bagged blood with you." She laughed as she followed him toward the parking lot. I heard his deep mellow laugh as he turned toward the woods.

I watched them disappear up the trail before turning to Trent. He seemed extremely tense. Shadows lined his face, and I couldn't get a good look at his eyes. Eyes told me so much about a person. If I couldn't see their eyes, it made me nervous. I went back down the dock to avoid what I didn't know.

He followed me, and when I reached the end, I leaned on the rail again, tilting my head back and giving my attention to the night sky. Trent stood next to me and watched me for a long moment.

"Take a picture. It lasts longer," I said, being snarky. I didn't like being watched.

I heard him chuckle. "Maybe I like the real thing better," he replied softly.

I looked at him slowly, as if it was hard to pull my eyes away from the stars above. His green eyes were so deep in color. Even in the dark I could see how intense of a green they were. He held my gaze for a few moments, and it reminded me of when I'd stood in the bar talking to him. I had wanted to be closer to him then. With the way he was watching me, I found myself wanting to lean over his way now.

I broke the eye contact, clenched my jaw, and glared at the water. Why did looking into his eyes mess with my mind? It had to be because they were so similar to Alex's, although I don't remember Alex having this same effect on me when I looked in his eyes.

I was surprised that the quiet between us didn't feel full of tension. It was actually relaxing after he stopped staring at me and turned to focus on the lake.

"This place is nice. Do you come here often?" Trent asked, still scanning out over the water.

"I used to come here all the time, but I haven't been here for several months. I like to be near water when I'm upset. It soothes me."

"Yeah, me too. I just moved from out west; had a house on a really nice lake there. Loved to sit on my deck and look out over it at night. My favorite part was sitting out until dawn started to creep over the horizon. The sky would turn all kinds of wild colors and glow off the water."

I smiled. "That sounds pretty wonderful. I like to look at the stars and feel the breeze as it caresses my skin." I chuckled to myself. That was probably more than he wanted to know, especially when I heard his loud swallow. "See that area over there?" I pointed across the lake to the shore on the other side where the ground gently slopped up from the water bank, up onto a hill.

His eyes followed in the direction I pointed. "Yeah, I see it."

"I want to build my dream house right there," I said quietly.

"Then why don't you?" Trent was no longer leaning on the rail beside me.

"Alex doesn't want me to." I'm not sure why I told him that, but I should have kept my mouth shut. Before he could say anything, I decided to change the subject. "Alex says you two are close. How come I've never heard about you?" I pulled my eyes from the scenery and checked out his profile.

The tips of his blond hair were bright in the moonlight. I had the urge to run my fingers over it and feel the tickle of the soft short locks on my palm and fingertips. I decided that probably wouldn't be a good idea and turned my attention elsewhere.

"Oh, I've worked for him for a while on the West Coast. We stayed in close contact while I was gone." He glanced at me.

I couldn't help but look back at him. Our eyes locked, and I had this unbelievable urge to step closer to him and touch his face. Sharp, angular cheekbones, narrow chin, perfectly full nose, they were all begging to be touched. I mentally shook myself and looked down at the railing. I squeezed it with my hands, and then turned around to rest my back against it, bracing my elbows on it behind me.

I heard Trent inhale deeply as he stood next to me.

"How old are you, Trent?"

When I peered at him sideways, he was standing up straight and facing me. I had to tilt my head back a bit to see up into his face. His eyes look brighter.

"I was thirty-four when I was changed. That was forty-two years ago," he said in a low voice, and stepped closer to me. I tilted my head back a little bit further. I felt my breath still in my chest.

Trent reached out and touched my chin, tipping it up higher and looking deep into my eyes. I was getting lost in the deep green; felt myself being pulled into him. He lowered his face to mine and, for a moment, I thought he was going to touch his lips to mine. In that moment, I very much wanted him to kiss me.

Instead, he turned my chin to the side and brought his lips to my neck, not quite touching, but so close that I could feel the heat from his breath across my skin. My pulse jumped. I knew he could hear it.

"Is it wrong for me to want to lick your neck?" he murmured against my ear. I closed my eyes at the sound of his sweet Southern accent caressing my ear. My body was reacting to him, wanting to lean closer, wanting to feel his body against mine. I wanted him to lick my neck—wanted him to lick more than that at this moment.

"Is it?" he asked me again. I couldn't answer. I was still holding the air in my lungs; maybe that was why I was starting to feel dizzy. I let the air out on a sigh, still not answering the question.

"If you aren't going to answer me, then I guess that's a no." I felt the tip of his tongue run along the edge of my ear and down my throat along a sensitive vein. My pulse kicked up even higher, and I knew he would feel it in the tip of his tongue as he traveled down to the collar of my shirt. I shivered with need, with the lust that was building in my body.

I was about to reach out and touch his chest when I heard laughter coming from the edge of the tree line that led to the parking lot. Reality check! I jumped back from Trent and moved a few feet away. That's when I heard him chuckle.

What the hell was that? I was a freaking mess. This whole thing with Alex, and then the bloodlust earlier, and now Trent's green eyes —it was all turning me into a crazy person. Please tell me I just imagined that and it didn't really happen. I saw the lust in his eyes. Damn... I didn't imagine it. I gave him my back.

"Don't do that again, Trent, you hear me?" I said as I sat down to wait for Olivia and Gabe to join us.

Trent chuckled louder and sat down on the wood planks across from me. He put his long muscular legs out straight between my knees as I sat with my back up against one of the metal railings, my arms resting over my bent knees. I narrowed my gaze at him, and he just laughed. I'm glad someone was enjoying themselves.

Gabe and Livy joined us then, and I ignored Trent the best I could as we ate roast beef sandwiches out of plastic lunch baggies. I made sure I didn't make eye contact with Trent again, and I kept shifting every time he moved one of his legs to touch mine.

About halfway through the sandwiches, Gabe opened the cooler and took out some bottles of water. "Hey, Kris, I brought you a flavored water. I figured that's what you liked to drink since your fridge was full of it." He loosened the cap and handed me the bottle. Everyone else drank plain water.

Gabe and Livy kept conversation light, but I know Livy noticed Trent's legs and my agitation. I saw her look at us several times, and I knew she wanted to ask me what was going on. By the time we were done eating, I didn't know whether I wanted to scream at Trent or crawl up his legs and have my way with him.

As we cleaned up our sandwich baggies and water bottles, Trent glanced up, noticing the color changes in the sky. "Time for us to get home. It's been a long night. I think we could all use some rest." Livy yawned at the mere mention of it and agreed. I felt the drain of the day myself as I stood.

With the thought of climbing in bed, I tried not to imagine what Trent would look like lying in mine with his eyes closed. Oh, damn... This man was bad to be around, almost worse than Julian. I started walking down the dock and Trent caught up to me.

"You're riding with me."

"Thanks, but I'll ride with Liv," I shot back at him.

"Nope. Our note, and I'm sure your note too, said that either Julian or I were to be with you and protect you. Last I looked, Olivia was not a vampire and can't quite do that."

"It's a ten-minute ride back. What's going to happen?" I was tired, and I was getting snarky with him because of that and the lustful hormones raging in me.

He leaned close as we walked and whispered in my ear, "I know a lot that can happen in ten minutes."

I thought my knees would go out from under me, but I kept myself standing upright and moving forward, tripping slightly.

"Seriously, though," he said as he stepped away, "consider yourself locked to one of us until we figure out how to stop Burke."

I was too tired to argue, so I groaned and kept moving. I heard Gabe tell Olivia that he was going to ride back in her Hummer, and she told him only if he sang to her on the way. It was obvious they had made friends quickly.

When we got to the cars, I noticed that Trent had Julian's Mustang. The thought of getting into that car made my knees weak. Oh, the stories that car could tell. It was a piece of my past, and after everything that had happened, I wasn't sure I could handle one more thing to haunt me tonight.

I stopped short of the car and watched as Olivia and Gabe pulled out in the Hummer. I should have told them to drive this instead.

Trent opened the door for me. I stood and stared at the car.

"What are you waiting for? Me to show you what I can do in ten minutes?" he said with a very sexy smile.

Maybe it was seeing the Mustang again, maybe it was because I was so exhausted, or maybe it was because I wanted to wipe that sexy smile off his face, but whatever it was, I couldn't help exploring every inch of his body as I approached the car. As I started to climb into the passenger seat, I stopped and looked him straight in the eye.

"Been there, done that, lover boy. If you think that you could satisfy a woman like me in ten minutes, well then, you're even more of a boy than I thought." His eyes enlarged, and he rasped in a rough breath. Then I smirked and sat down in the seat, letting his spices and chocolate scent wash over me as he closed the door.

CHAPTER FIFTEEN

ALEX

*J*t felt like days, but could have been merely hours since I was last out of the cell. I hoped that by now, Julian had gotten to Kristin. Hopefully, Trent would be there, too.

I knew Julian would hate the note that I left him, but I knew that I could trust him to make sure Kristin was protected. Breaking the bond with me would be the best way to quickly protect her. If I knew the bond was broken, I wouldn't worry so much about feeling the pain. I'd take as much as Burke could dish out and not care. As long as she wasn't feeling it, I could do it.

What would happen once the bond was broken? Who would she choose to break it? I would have preferred Trent, but I kind of figured with the history of Julian, that he would jump at the chance to have her again.

If Julian broke the bond, I was sure that he would not only exchange blood, but he would fully mate with her. Would he let her go if I survived this? Somehow, I doubted it. I realized that I might have another fight on my hands when this was over. I would not give her up to Julian again, that I knew for sure.

Now, if Trent broke the bond, I knew he would be more than happy to hand her back over. He never was one for commitments. He actually preferred human females to vampires and half-breeds because of the commitment issue. He didn't want to get stuck with someone in that moment of bloodlust. I trusted him to do it.

I lay there on the bed thinking back to one of the conversations that Kristin and I had the last time we were together. We were lying in bed after making love, and it seemed as if that was the only time I could get her calm enough to talk about things. Any other time, she was too hyper or busy to stop and really listen. Sometimes, I felt as if our roles were reversed, me wanting to talk and her avoiding the conversations.

"KRISTIN, I'm not trying to take you away from your job. I know it means something to you, but don't I mean something to you, too? I mean, we barely get to see each other, and it always seems like you are taking extra shifts which takes away from us."

She started to pull away, but I held on to her tight.

"Alex, how many times do we have to go over this? I love my job! It's who I am, not just what I do. I want to keep doing this as long as I possibly can. Our department is shorthanded right now with Cole out on his injury. I know it's not the ideal situation, but we have to make do right now."

I ran my hand up her arm. "I know...I know. I just wish I knew why you were fighting the rest of our mating. Why is it that you don't want to have a child? Is it me you don't want a child with, or what?"

"Alex, I'm not a very maternal person, as you can see. I want to have children, but right now, my career is more important."

"Kris, you are going to have career after career in your lifetime. Did you forget that you are going to live for a long time?"

"You're right, I am going to live for a long time, so why do we have to have a child right now?" She raised an eyebrow.

"I want a child with you, Kristin. I want you to finish your change so you can be the strongest you can be." I ran my fingers through her short hair.

"I'm already stronger than most female vampires. Your blood is changing me quickly. If I keep feeding from you, then the change will be complete soon."

"For once, can't you just do it my way?" I was serious, but trying to be lighthearted at the same time.

"I like to make my own choices, Alex. Having a child is a choice, and it's one I don't want to choose right now. Can't you just be happy with us for now?" she asked softly.

Like I normally did, I gave in to her. I always gave in to her to make her happy. We didn't speak about it anymore before she had to leave and head back to Fawn Hollow.

CHOICES...I didn't give her much of a choice in this, did I? Man, how angry would she be when she found out I had told Julian or Trent to break the bond?

I tried not to think about it, letting my mind drift off into a dreamless sleep again to try to conserve my strength.

CHAPTER SIXTEEN

TRENT

*G*abe and I pulled into the dirt parking lot, and walked through the trees to where the dock was located. I felt myself growing tense, and Gabe put his hand on my shoulder. I immediately started to calm down. What a gift Gabe had, being able to calm someone with just a touch.

"Thanks," I muttered, feeling like a kid going to meet his prom date for the first time.

When we walked out through the tree line, I didn't see them at first, although I knew Olivia's Hummer had been in the parking lot. A brief moment of panic rushed through me, but then I caught sight of them lying on the dock. When neither of them moved, I felt the panic start to rise again quickly.

Gabe started to whistle a country tune, and it wasn't long before Kristin jumped up and rushed down the dock toward him. When she threw herself into his arms, I was both surprised and a little jealous, which surprised me even more.

Judging by the way she hugged him, she cared a great deal about him. "Maybe it should be you," I commented quietly, and Kristin noticed I was there for the first time.

When Olivia spoke about Gabe being like a brother to Kristin, I couldn't help but hiss. Yeah, if they had a brother-sister relationship, they sure didn't want a blood-bond connection. That would just be weird. Gabe chuckled, understanding the noise I made.

Gabe and Olivia went back to get the coolers we left in the car. We'd left them there for just this reason, to allow me a few minutes alone with Kristin where she was relaxed.

I followed her out onto the dock and watched as she stood at the railing and looked up at the sky. She had a beautiful face. Her soft skin glowed under the stars, her mouth was slightly open, her neck long and thin. I watched as her pulse beat in her neck and wondered what it would feel like on my tongue.

She was snarky and I loved it. She slowly turned her head. Her eyes were a smoky blue, bright and clear, but I could see pain and confusion in them. I felt her emotions changing as she watched me. She looked away, and I almost said something, but decided to allow her to be in control for the moment.

I looked out around the lake. There were trees over on the far side, and the lake appeared to be very long, as I couldn't see the ends on either side from where we were. The breeze was slight and a bit cool as the weather was really starting to change. The sky was clear tonight, and the stars twinkled brightly above us. It was peaceful, serene. I liked it here. It reminded me of my home out west.

She was wistful as she talked about the dream house she wanted. Why would Alex tell her no? He had more money than he knew what to do with, he could afford to build her a new house.

The more she relaxed, the bluer her eyes became. I loved the way they changed so dramatically with her moods. She turned around to lean her back against the railing, and the way she was standing caught my attention. Her shoulders were back and her elbows rested on the railing, causing her chest to stand out; I was taken in by their round- ness of her breasts and the long line of her neck. I held myself still as temptation tickled my fingers to reach out and touch her.

She asked me how old I was, and my voice sounded husky when I answered her. "I was thirty-four when I was changed. That was forty- two years ago." I approached her without even thinking. Putting my finger under her chin, I tipped it back to see into her eyes more, and to see the veins in her throat. The bloodlust that we had both felt earlier was coming back to me, and I began to think that breaking this bond might just be kind of fun.

As I lowered my face to hers, I saw her mouth open slightly, and she licked her bottom lip. I wanted to kiss her, but I wanted to feel her pulse on the tip of my tongue even more. I turned her lips away and put my face close to her skin. I could smell the blood running through her veins, could feel her pulse picking up. Her sweet-scented blood was intoxicating me.

"Is it wrong for me to want to lick your neck?" I murmured against her ear. I heard her pulse beating faster.

"Is it?" I asked her again. Even if she had said, yes, it was wrong, I would have done it anyway. When she didn't answer, it was like getting a personal invitation.

"If you aren't going to answer me, then I guess that's a no." I slowly touched the tip of my tongue to her ear and trailed it down. The sweet sugar scent of her rolled over me and caused my canines to pound in my gums. I continued down from her ear to trace a vein in her neck, feeling it throb under my wet touch. My cock throbbed in time with her pulse. I felt her shiver as my tongue stopped at the edge of her shirt collar. I could feel her need matching mine.

I knew that she wanted me and realized that this was going to be easier than I had originally thought. I heard Gabe and Olivia coming out of the woods before she did and watched as Kristin jumped away from me. I couldn't help laughing softly.

"Don't do that again, Trent, you hear me?" she spat. She could say that all she wanted to, but I knew she wanted my touch. I felt it, and I had every intention of doing it again, and there wasn't going to be much she could do about it. I intentionally sat across from her and extended my long legs so that they were right between her bent knees. Every once in a while, I "accidentally" touched her with them, and she practically jumped away. Each time I touched her, I felt her mounting sexual tension. She was very aware of me.

I watched as Gabe pulled a water bottle out of the cooler and pretended to crack the lid, handing it to Kristin. She didn't seem to notice and drank from the bottle. Gabe and I glanced at each other. This was going to be so easy.

When we were done eating, I saw Kristin was looking very tired. The sleeping pill we put in her water was working nicely. It probably helped that she was already worn out from tonight's earlier events.

She had groaned when I told her she was now attached to me or Julian until this matter was settled. The sound that rumbled from her throat made me wonder what noises she would make in bed. She stopped ten feet from Julian's Mustang and stared at the car. What, she didn't like Mustangs? Everyone liked Mustangs.

I opened the door and waited. She watched Gabe and her friend pull out of the parking lot with a wistful look on her face.

"What are you waiting for? Me to show you what I can do in ten minutes?"

An array of emotions crossed over her face, and then she sauntered toward the car.

"Been there, done that, lover boy. If you think that you could satisfy a woman like me in ten minutes, well then, you're even more of a boy than I thought."

Her comment caught me unprepared, and it zipped through my mind. My body wanted to show her just how well I could please her, and, yes, it would definitely take longer than ten minutes. I didn't say anything as I closed her door, but I had to take a few deep breaths before I got in on the other side.

We didn't speak on the ride back, and as we pulled in, I noticed her head resting against the window and that her eyes were closed. If she wasn't asleep, she would be very soon.

I went around to the other side and opened the door. I caught her before she fell out of the seat and lifted her easily into my arms. Was it really only earlier tonight that I had carried her like this out of the party?

Gabe stood at the door and held it open. He put his finger to his lips to tell Olivia to stay quiet, and whispered, "She's sleeping."

I carried her upstairs and laid her on her bed. She snuggled down into her pillow and sank into a deeper sleep. For a few minutes, I stood over her, watching. She was a strong, beautiful woman. I could see what Alex saw in her.

When I went downstairs, I found Julian and Gabe in the kitchen. "Her friend went to bed," Gabe said as I glanced around the room.

Julian watched me tensely, and I tried not to look back at him. His emotions were strong and all over the place. "Julian, are you going to be all right with me doing this?" I pulled a beer out of the fridge and leaned back against it, popping the lip off with the thumb on my hand. I watched it flip up in the air, and I caught it.

Julian stiffened. "Like I told you before, it will be easier for Alex to break your bond than it would be for him to break mine. It's the right thing to do."

I nodded. After taking a long pull from my beer, I started to leave the kitchen.

"Trent," Julian called from behind me, "you *bond* with her. Don't you dare *mate* with her—do you understand?" He glared, and at that moment, I could only return it. What did he think I was? I wasn't going to mate with her; she was Alex's.

I turned and walked out of the room. "Understood, Master Julian," I said in a clipped tone as I left.

I walked hesitantly up the stairs. I know I was acting as if this was no big deal, but to me, this was huge. This would be the first time I bonded with a female vampire. I had never allowed one to take my blood, and had only drunk from a handful of them myself.

No big deal. She's out like a light. I drink some of hers, and then I'll cut my wrist and get her to drink some of mine while she still groggy. Done deal, I thought as I walked into her room and closed the door.

I stopped at the edge of the bed and studied her. Her strawberry blond hair looked so soft against the side of her face, and I pushed a few strands back. Her lips were slightly open, and her breathing was calm and relaxed. I reached up and pulled my shirt off and dropped it onto the floor, thinking that I would get on my knees there and do it, but then I decided to walk to the other side of the bed and climb on.

I got up behind her and put my hand on her hip. I could feel the calmness running through her in her sleep. No other part of my body was touching her, but at the moment, it felt as if we were pressed up against each other as my body began to respond.

My teeth started to punch down, and I felt the first stirrings of lust wash over me as my cock hardened in my jeans. *Don't think about it; just lean down and take her neck. It's wide open for you.*

As I leaned in to put my teeth to her neck, she barely stirred, but it was enough to swirl her scent around me. My teeth throbbed. I realized as I started to sink my teeth into her neck that I was doing this for more than my job. For the first time in my life, I wanted to taste someone for pleasure, not for need.

My teeth gently tore through her tissue and latched onto her vein, I felt her pulse begin to race and her breathing changed. She moaned in her sleep, and I moved my body automatically closer.

My hand held her hip tightly, and her body pushed back against mine, grinding her hips into my arousal. The feelings flowing up my arm from where we were connected were lustful. It took everything in me not to stroke her body. My fingers twitched with the sudden need to feel her skin.

She was rotating her ass against me, her moans growing deeper, more passionate as I sipped from her neck. I could have swallowed a few mouthfuls and been done, yet she was like a fine wine that I wanted to enjoy slowly. Her blood was so sweet, so damn thick and warm as it ran down my throat. I didn't want to stop. I wanted to drink forever.

I was holding myself in check—just barely—when my name came out of her mouth on a sigh. She did *not* just say my name! My eyes flashed open, her head was thrown back, her lips wet as she licked them. My control was gone. I pulled my teeth from her neck, licking it closed, and proceeded to kiss up the column of her neck, under her chin, and right to her mouth. She rolled toward me, still asleep, but moving as if she were wide awake. Her small hand wrapped around my neck and she held me against her mouth.

Jesus, I was done. I couldn't resist. She'd called out my name. She was sleeping, and she'd said my name. I claimed her mouth, my tongue darting past her lips, and I pulled her closer as she slid her leg over my hips, dragging her foot along my calf and up the back of my thigh. Her shift put my groin right between her legs and she ground against me in a tantalizing movement. She was so fucking hot, and her tongue was sliding over mine. She ran it over my fangs, and I almost came unglued. Her hands dug into my back, pulling and kneading the muscles that were holding her tightly.

I pulled my chest off hers long enough to grab the front of her silk blouse and rip it open, her breasts heaving under her bra with each panting breath that she took. I ran my hands over them, squeezing them and plucking at her hardened nipples. She moaned into my mouth as I pinched one harder.

One of her hands was on the back of my head; her fingers splayed and kept me from pulling back. Her other hand traveled over the heated skin of my back, waking every nerve ending in its path to my waist. Her fingers dipped under the waistband of my jeans. I shifted, and she brought her hand around to the front, teasing me with her palm. She began to work on the snap and zipper of my jeans, and I almost stopped her. Almost.

The thought of what was happening spun once through my mind. I was supposed to bond with her. I needed her to take my blood, and then I needed to get the hell away from her. But then her hand slipped into my jeans and around my hard shaft, and as quickly as the thought had formed, it was gone.

Her emotions were intense. She needed me, but more importantly, I could feel that she *wanted* me. Me, not just any man—me. I felt her emotions, heard her moans. I'd heard her say my name.

I tore at the zipper of her jeans, and she lifted her hips to allow me to push them off of her body. In a frenzy, she took her hand off the back of my head and grabbed the waistband of my jeans, trying to push them down. I helped her and was back against her hot, smooth body in an instant.

She kissed my neck, licked my shoulder, teased me with her hands, and I ripped her bra off in another quick movement. She scored my back with her nails and I heard her inhale as the scent of my blood permeated the air. Jesus, I'd never felt such amazing pain.

I caressed the soft skin on her stomach and slid it lower. I reached the edge of her panties and I could barely contain myself. In a primal move, I tore them from her body.

"Yes…" she whispered from her parted lips.

My mouth and tongue did little circles on her breast, while my hand covered her mound. The small triangle of soft hair tickled my palm, and she arched toward me. I could not keep myself from groaning as I ran my fingers through her soft wet folds. My God, she was so wet.

She pulled my head from her breast and tilted it to kiss me deeply. I was drowning in the feelings she was offering me. She was in constant motion, every part of her body sliding against mine, the friction was igniting my skin. My fingers got lost in the moisture of her folds, caressing her, loving her, feeling her as I had never felt another woman before. It wasn't just her body I felt, her blood was flowing rapidly through my veins, making me know how good I was making her feel.

She whispered my name again.

It was as if I was in a dream, my mind floated through a dense fog. I pulled my hand away from her and she whimpered once before I lifted myself over her, our mouths still locked in a ferocious kiss. I entered her with a fast thrust. She seemed to anticipate it and met me half way. She arched her back to deepen the entry, and I shook from head to toe with the intensity of it. The insides of her body were stroking me softly, clenching me tightly as I moved in and out.

I slowed down, wanting to enjoy every single movement, every inch of her body as she moved right along with me, in perfect time. It was as if we were of one mind. Her moans vibrated on my tongue and I knew I wasn't going to be able to last much longer. The fog was thickening inside my head. I started to move faster within her, when she broke off the kiss and trailed her tongue down my neck. It felt so good that I mimicked her movements to reciprocate the feeling.

As if by some unspoken word, we both latched on to each other's neck at the same moment. My fangs slid into her vein as her sharp-pointed canines entered mine. When I felt her pull the first draw of my blood, my entire body spasmed and my mind exploded. A few seconds later, our bodies followed into the most earth-shattering climax I had ever felt.

As we came down from the explosion, we each took one last pull from the veins we fed from and licked the openings almost simultane-ously. I shifted off of her slightly, wondering why I felt so tired, but knowing that I also felt more sated than I had in forever. I pulled her to me, and she turned on her side, spooning back up to me.

"You belong to me," I said quietly as I kissed her neck below her ear.

"For life..." I heard her whisper in return. It was only a few seconds later that I fell into a deep sleep holding her body close to mine, hearing the words *for life* echoing through my mind.

CHAPTER SEVENTEEN

KRISTIN

*T*hat moment in time when you are between being asleep and being awake can be one of two things: It can be heaven, or it can be hell. And sometimes, it will be both.

I felt my mind coming around slowly. The dark edges of sleep still pulled at me, but were losing ground as my mind started to wake up and process what was around me. As I did every time that I woke, I turned inward and did a mental check. I felt good today, physically strong and sated as I hadn't felt in a long time. I must have really slept good to be feeling like this.

As my mind started to process more information, I stretched to get my muscles moving. Then I slowly rolled to my back and pushed my arm out to the side. My eyes snapped open as it made contact with hot tight skin, a flash of lust rushing to my mind.

Instantly, I looked to my left—and right into Trent's eyes. *Oh crap!* I jumped up and moved away from him.

"What the hell are you doing here?" I demanded shakily as I stared down into his dark green eyes. It wasn't until I saw his eyes slide down my body that I realized I had nothing on, and I grabbed the first thing I could find and pulled it over my head.

A lazy smile ran over his features. "My T-shirt looks good on you." His voice was so husky that it made my knees weak.

I glanced down and saw that, indeed, it was the black T-shirt he had been wearing last night. Of all things to pull on! Damn!

"What the hell are you doing in my bed?" I said a little bit louder, feeling my face heat as I imagined what must have happened. I was naked, and I assumed he was too, so there was only one logical explanation. He stretched and pulled the sheet back as he sat up.

I got a quick glimpse of his morning erection and my blood went on slow simmer. I was out of control all of a sudden. "What the hell are you doing in my bed?" I screamed. *Oh my God! Oh my God! What have I done?*

Just then, the door to my room burst open and Julian stood there holding the doorjamb with one hand and the doorknob with the other. With the fire running through his eyes, I suspected that I was about to buy a new doorknob because he was going to tear that one out of my door.

I watched as Julian sniffed the room, his eyes going wide and feral.

Gabe showed up behind Julian just in time to grab him around the chest as he was about to fling himself at Trent. Trent stood up nonchalantly and picked up his jeans, sliding them up his body. I had enough sense as a woman to check out his nice, tight ass, but also enough sense not to let it show on my face. Only my bright red cheeks and the rush of lust through my body were the telltale signs as my mind registered the fact that I had run my hands over that extremely fine skin just hours before. *Oh my God!*

"I told you to *bond* with her, not *mate* with her!" Julian said with steel in his voice.

"What!" I screamed.

He quickly flashed me a look as if forgetting I was even in the room, and then glared back at Trent.

Mated? Trent and I mated? I felt inside of myself and, yep, I felt the bond. Holy Shit! Wait…What did Julian just say?

"You told him to bond with me? Julian, what are you talking

about?" I gawked at him, my heart thudding against my chest wall, my legs feeling as if they would collapse right out from under me.

It was Trent who decided to answer that. "Yep. Julian wanted me to break Alex's bond." I watched Trent as he stood, still watching Julian. Julian was breathing heavy, and if it wasn't for Gabe holding him back, I think he would have torn Trent to shreds.

"Why?" *Why the hell would Julian of all people do that?* "Julian, what the hell is going on?" I watched him as he tried to calm down. I knew that Gabe was pushing calming vibes to him, but he was resisting them.

"Why? Because Alex told us to," he spat, then turned his death stare back to Trent. "I should kill you for what you just did, but you know what? I'm not going to because I'm going to have a front-row seat to watch when Alex does," Julian bellowed.

"Whatever, Julian," Trent said quietly.

As I watched them, I realized something. I couldn't remember much after leaving the lake. In fact, I didn't remember getting back to the house, and I could only remember some very intense moments from the mating with Trent. I felt my face turn red as I remembered calling out his name.

"You belong to me," ran through my mind. Did Trent say that? Did he *really* say that?

I took a deep breath. "Alex told you to break the bond between us?" I looked between the two of them, not sure who would answer.

It was Trent, although he didn't look at me when he did. "Yes, he told us to break it to spare you the pain he would be in."

I was so angry right this second. Angry at everything! Angry at the fact that I realized they must have drugged me last night. Furious about the fact that Trent had taken advantage of that and broke my mating bond with Alex, and that Julian and Trent had discussed this. Plus, I was livid and embarrassed at how I had so quickly fallen into bed with Trent and mated with him. None of this anger even came close to the fury I felt at Alex because he told them to break the bond!

"Get out," I said quietly. I encompassed them all with the most intense look I could, and it was the first time since Julian enter the room that Trent looked at me. "Get out of my room. All of you get out of my fucking room, now!" I ended up shouting and all three of them looked taken back by the extent of my fury.

I was shaking, and it took every ounce of my energy not to start freaking out. Gabe pulled Julian out of the room, and I heard him talking to him as they walked down the hall. My pulse beat so hard in my ears that I could not hear what they were saying. Trent considered me for a long time.

I didn't want to look at his eyes—the eyes that reminded me so much of Alex, and of what we had done—but I couldn't look away. Was that regret, pain, anger, or just annoyance that was flitting across his gaze? I didn't care.

I narrowed my gaze at him, and he took a deep breath and walked toward the door, not looking back as he pulled it closed behind him.

I immediately dropped to my knees and rested my head against the bed. *Are. You. Kidding. Me!*

I was so beside myself, I couldn't control my thoughts—and they were everywhere. The memories of last night finally started to trickle into my brain: Trent licking my neck at the lake, Gabe opening the water bottle for me, remembering the feel of Trent under my hands and in my throat as I drank his blood. *"You belong to me...for life..."* floated through my mind. I groaned into the quilt on my bed, wanting to forget the taste of his incredible blood and the feel of his God like body, but at the same time craving it.

If Alex came out of this alive, I would kill him myself! As I took a deep breath to calm down, I inhaled and caught Trent's scent coming off of his shirt. It intoxicated me immediately, and a shiver tore up my spine. I ripped it off and threw it across the room. That was when I noticed my bra and panties shredded beside the bed. Humiliation smacked me in the face.

I grabbed some workout clothes and knew that I needed to head into my gym down on the second floor. I had just a little bit of aggression to work off. Damn...I wish I was working tonight. That would be a good distraction. I really needed to get away from everyone right now.

I opened my bedroom door and made sure no one was in the hallway before I went to the stairs and ran down to the second floor. Olivia's door was still closed. I could hear her gentle heartbeat on the other side. She was still asleep. I walked past quietly. As least my outburst hadn't waken her up. I wasn't sure how I would explain all of this to her. I couldn't figure out how to explain it to myself.

I jumped onto the treadmill, cranked up the speed and the incline, and took off running. I didn't need to work out to keep my body in shape. It was natural now, but it felt good to do it. Today, I needed to do it to let out some of the pent-up anger.

I felt her before I saw her. Olivia walked into the room thirty minutes later, and I was drenched in sweat and still running hard. She shouted over the music that she was taking off. She had to work tonight and needed to get some things done.

She told me to call her later. I nodded, and she left. I decided I had run long enough and turned off the treadmill. After wiping the sweat off my brow and drinking half a bottle of water—that I had opened myself—I went over to the heavy bag and started punching and kicking like there was no tomorrow.

I knew someone else was approaching. I could feel a presence, but I wasn't sure who it was until he entered the room. Gabe watched me for a minute before turning down the stereo.

"Is that Julian, Trent, or Alex?" he said as he stood behind me.

"Hmmmphhhhh." I kicked the bag hard and watched it fight to stay in place with the upper and lower bands that secured it. "I'm done with Julian. This is Trent. Alex is next." I threw a roundhouse kick and turned to throw a couple of good punches. My hands were hurting from the force of my punches, but the pain felt good.

"Take a break, sweet potato. We need to talk," Gabe said, and tossed a towel at me.

I threw another kick and then a few punches before I scooped up the towel and wiped my face. I left the towel around my neck as I dropped down onto one of the weight benches.

Somewhere in the distance I heard the phone ring. I didn't care.

"I know you're pissed, Kristin. I would be, too. I wasn't happy about the idea when I heard it myself. You know how I feel about Alex," Gabe said quietly. His dark hair was shaved close to his head, making him look as if he could don any military uniform and fit right in. Today, he looked much more like a man than the boy he normally appeared to be.

"Yeah, I'm a little pissed, but I'm mostly hurt," I said as I leaned down to rest my elbows on my knees, watching the sweat drip off me and onto the floor. "What's messed up is I can understand Alex wanting to break the bond. I can see him doing that because he wants to protect me. It is so like him to do something and not give me a choice in the matter. It's Julian that I am most hurt by. I mean...come on! Why didn't he just tell me about it? I wouldn't have liked it, but I probably would have allowed him to break the bond. I trust him." I shook my head, took a long pull from my water bottle, and looked back down at the ground.

"Now I'm mated to Trent. I have no idea who Trent even is, and now I'm mated to him after he drugged me. Again, I was given no choice in the matter here." I shook my head. "Don't think I'm not upset with you too, Gabe. You're the one who pretended to open the water bottle."

"You didn't know Julian either when you mated with him."

"Touché," I retorted.

"Actually, the sleeping pill was my idea," he admitted quietly and had the decency to look embarrassed. "We figured you would fight us, and we wanted to help you, take the pain away, so we just did it. We did it to protect you, all of us did." He stopped for a second, then continued. "What we should have done was have Trent bond with you with us there. We didn't think it would get so out of control. If we had been there, then we could have stopped the rest. I'm sorry."

I considered his words. "It's okay, Gabe. I actually understand it, and strangely enough, I'm not mad at Trent for what happened. We all know the kind of feelings that go through you when you feed. Yesterday was a pretty high emotional roller coaster for all of us. I think that just intensified things. I know when Alex gets back we'll fix things, and it'll be okay." I wanted to believe what I was saying, but part of me knew I was lying.

"Kristin, can I ask you a question?"

"Sure." I shrugged and looked up at him. It took a few seconds before he spoke, and I was kind of worried about what he was about to ask me.

"Why didn't you finish your mating with Alex?" He looked me in the eyes, but I knew it was hard for him. This was very personal, and he didn't want to intrude.

I laughed once and muttered to myself, "I was wondering when someone was going to ask that." Slowly, I shook my head and drank the rest of the water from my bottle.

"Alex didn't want me to go back to work. He never understood how important my job was to me. He wanted me to have a child and come up to New York with him and put all of this life behind me, but I can't. I won't. This is me…This is who I am. Yeah, part of Calista is still in there, and it longs for Julian, and it cares deeply for Alex; but I'm me, Kristin, and I'm a cop. He wanted to take my choices away from me, and I feel like too many choices have been taken away already, especially after today." I laughed again, although it wasn't funny.

Just then I looked up and found Trent, a strange expression in his eyes as he looked at me and held the cordless phone out. "Sorry to bother you, but your chief is on the line."

I wondered how long he had been standing outside the door listening. "Thanks." I took the phone and turned around to put some distance between me and his amazing green eyes. My knees could get weak just looking into them for the slightest second.

"Hey, Chief, what's up?" I spoke into the phone when I had my back to them.

"Took you long enough to get on the phone."

So Trent must have been standing out there for a while. I glanced over my shoulder and he looked away from me quickly. "Mike was in a small car accident on his way into work. I need someone to cover his shift tonight."

"Is he all right?" I asked, and glanced up at the clock. It was almost five thirty.

"Yeah, he's going to be okay, but he's going to the hospital just to be sure. Can you cover?"

"Yeah, I can. Give me about forty-five minutes. I gotta take a shower and get ready." I felt the tension from Trent and Gabe fill the room.

When I hung up, I found them both staring at me. I raised an eyebrow. "What?"

Trent spoke up first. "You're not going to work."

My eyes flashed steel gray, I knew they did. I hated when someone told me what to do. "Oh really? And who's going to stop me?" I glared at him, my body tense, ready for a fight.

Gabe took my arm to get my attention. "Kristin, now is not a good time for you to be going to work. Not with Alex missing and this woman being in the area."

"Gabe, I appreciate the concern, but I have a job to do and people depend on me. I'm not going to sit around and wonder what they are doing to Alex." I pulled out of his grip and turned to walk out of the room. Trent stepped in front of me. He didn't touch me, but his dark green eyes stared down into mine, and I almost stepped back. Instead, I held my position and glared.

"Fine, then, I'm going to work with you," he stated firmly.

"What? No!" Then I thought for a second. *Why not?* "Fine. You want to come to work with me? Black BDUs, boots, and a dark shirt. Be ready in thirty minutes."

He opened his mouth as if he was going to argue, but realized he had nothing to argue about and closed it.

I gave him a fake smile and stalked out of the room to get dressed.

CHAPTER EIGHTEEN

JULIAN

$\mathcal{I}$ had been spending a lot of time on the phone trying to figure out where Burke might be hiding Alex. We had a couple of ideas, and I had a few more guys heading this way. Once we had a location, we were going to move in quickly.

What I was still trying to figure out was how Burke found out about us investigating him and how he connected Kristin and Alex together. No one seemed to have the answer to that.

I was just hanging up the phone with Brendon Taylor, telling him about what was going on, when Gabe and Trent returned from the lake. Gabe told me that Kristin fell asleep in the car and Trent was putting her in bed.

I was filling Gabe in on what I had done and learned when Trent entered the kitchen and took a beer out of the fridge. I watched him, trying to figure out if he would be able to pull it off, when he asked me if I would be able to handle it.

It took every single ounce of my willpower to hold back from saying anything. If I felt as though we wouldn't get Alex back, then I would have taken Kristin in a second. However, I wasn't sure I could stand to lose her a third time, so I had to let Trent do it.

"Trent," I called out to him as he started to leave, "you *bond* with her. Don't you dare *mate* with her—do you understand?" Trent glared back at me.

"Understood, Master Julian," he called out over his retreating shoulder.

How I would love to punch him in his face. He was a cocky ass.

I cringed as I heard him climb the stairs. I had to find something to do to keep my mind off what he was about to do.

I left the kitchen and went into the living room, making a beeline right for the bar. I poured myself a full glass, drinking back half of it in the first gulp. It burned as it went down, but I needed that. I finished the glass in two more gulps and refilled it.

There was no way I was going to go upstairs to bed now. I didn't want to be that close to them. I lay down on the couch and threw my arm over my eyes. I heard Gabe come in and sit down next to me.

"You sure you can handle this?" he asked me quietly.

"Gabe, I can't lose her a third time. I just spent the last three months thinking that she was alive and happy with Alex. Then I come here and find out she has barely seen him and they haven't finished their mating yet." I moved my arm off my face and took another drink.

We were quiet for a long time, each lost in our own thoughts. After I finished my second glass, I debated on a third, but realized it had been over an hour since Trent had gone upstairs. It would be done by now. I stood up slowly and told Gabe I was heading up to bed.

I walked cautiously up the stairs, listening hard to make sure I wasn't walking into something I didn't want to. At the top of the stairs I saw that Trent's door was closed, and I figured he had finished it and gone on to bed.

I went to my room and found that with the stress of the last two days and the amount of whiskey I had ingested, I was ready to fall sound asleep. I climbed into bed and was asleep within minutes.

I don't know how long I slept, but I woke up to a loud female voice. Oh, shit…she was awake, and she realized what had happened. I sat up in bed and threw my legs over the side. It was when I heard her yell again that I rushed out the door. *What did she just say?*

"What the hell are you doing in my bed?"

I grabbed the doorknob and nearly ripped it out as I opened the door. When I saw Trent sitting on the bed naked, I latched on to the doorjamb to steady myself.

Before I could do anything else, the scent of their mating slammed into me like a freight train and I couldn't believe that he had done it.

"I told you to *bond* with her, not *mate* with her!" The only thing holding me from tearing him to pieces was Gabe's strong arms that had come around me.

"What!" Kristin screamed from the other side of the room. Damn...I forgot she was even there.

Oh Jesus, this was not going well. Gabe started to pull me back when I realized that I just made things so much worse than they had been. Kristin's eyes were a glowing silver that almost scared me. I let Gabe drag me out of the room, and we started down the hall.

"She'll calm down in a little while. I'll go talk to her and make her understand," Gabe said as we walked toward the stairs.

Trent came down shortly after. It was obvious that he had showered as he walked into the kitchen; the scent of Kristin was milder now. Gabe immediately got up off the stool and prepared to do what was needed if we started to fight. I just shook my head.

"Gabe, sit down. I'm not going to go after him." I pulled three coffee mugs out of the cabinet and poured for us all. When I turned around and handed a mug to Gabe and Trent, both of them had eyebrows raised and shared a quick look.

I grabbed the third mug and sat down. "What happened, Trent?" I said as I studied my coffee.

Trent sighed and went to the fridge, pulling out the coffee creamer. I knew he was stalling, but I gave him some time to figure out what to say. After he sat back down, he stirred his coffee and finally looked at me.

"I fucked up." He shrugged and went back to contemplating the steam coming off his coffee.

I tensed and thought about diving over the counter at him, but I held myself still. "Obviously," was all I said back to him.

"Shit, Julian, I swear to you that I didn't mean for it to happen. So much happened yesterday, and when I got that close to her, I just couldn't control myself. Her scent just took over. The feeling of bloodlust she'd had felt slammed into both of us. You know that I feel everything that someone else feels when I am touching them. It was overwhelming."

He hung his head, and at that moment, I felt sorry for him. How many times had I been that close to her and almost lost control? Two? Three? A hundred? Something like that.

"Ironically, I know exactly what you mean." I took a gulp of my coffee and watched him over my mug. He winced as he made eye contact with me.

"You know, that's what I always heard, but I wasn't sure if it was true or not. That's how you took her from Alex before." He said it quietly. I nodded. The memory of that night all those years ago, the night that I had met her at Night Crawlers—and we had come back to this very house—was still clear in my mind. On the hood of my Mustang, right out front under the stars, we shared that same reaction —immediate chemistry and mating. Yeah, I understood too damn well.

"Look, I'm not going to say I'm not pissed, but really, it's your problem now, and you are going to have to deal with her—and with Alex." I watched him.

Gabe chuckled and punched him in the arm.

At least I wasn't the one who was going to hurt Alex this time. I wondered how Trent was going to deal with him, but even more, I wondered how he was going to deal with Kristin.

CHAPTER NINETEEN

KRISTIN

J'm not sure why I said Trent could come to work with me. Maybe it was because I wanted to prove something to him, or maybe I needed to prove something to myself. I don't know, but once I made the decision, I was actually kinda glad.

I got ready for work quickly, grabbing my shoulder bag and heading downstairs. Trent was standing in the foyer as I came down. He was dressed exactly as I told him to: black BDU pants, a black shirt, and boots. I was a sucker for a man in a tactical uniform and I slowed as I reached the last few steps so that I could absorb his appearance. A craving for something struck me, but it wasn't food. His eyes were hidden behind thick lashes, and I wondered what he was thinking. I'd been careful to keep my wall up. I had yet to try to reach out to him mentally, and had no clue if he had tried it with me.

I walked past him without a word and went straight out to the garage, where I jumped into my Dodge Challenger. It was a present I bought myself after my human husband Trevor was killed a couple of years ago. He had been a police officer too, and while trying to apprehend a dangerous subject during a firefight, he had stood up at the wrong time and was shot in the back of the head by one of his own officers. It was an accident, but many of us paid dearly for that brief moment.

Trent climbed into the passenger seat and smiled as I started up the Challenger. The deep rumble from the exhaust made the car vibrate as we backed out of the garage and headed to my station. I called my chief on the way to let him know I would have someone riding along. He didn't care as long as I got the paperwork signed saying he wasn't responsible for the person. I didn't think he had anything to worry about.

When we got to the station, the first thing I did was get my uniform on. Trent stood against the wall watching, and I tried very hard to ignore him. As I pulled my vest out of my locker and put it over my head, he finally spoke.

"Why are you wearing that?"

I peered at him, then turned my back on him to pull my shirt out of my locker. "Everyone knows I am religious about wearing my vest. It saves lives, and it would seem kind of strange if all of a sudden I stopped wearing it now."

"Makes sense," was all he said in return.

John walked into the back door of the station and stopped dead in his tracks when he saw Trent. Trent stood up straighter and inspected John over from head to toe. I almost laughed as I felt the testosterone filling up the room.

"Hey, John, this is Trent. He works for Alex and wanted to see how the big boys do it." I grinned at John, and he seemed to relax and shook Trent's hand.

I heard Trent make a gruff sound at my explanation. I'm sure he loved my use of "big boys." I bit back a smile.

John filled me in on his day. Not much going on—some alarms and ambulance calls, nothing major. Trent followed me out of the station as I went to get my patrol vehicle out. He was lucky that I drove an Expedition as his large frame would have been a tight squeeze in the Chargers that we had.

As I logged on to the computer, a car pulled up into the driveway. I saw that it was an elderly woman, and she stopped next to me and rolled down her window. I beamed down at her. I knew who she was and what this was going to be about. Perfect.

"Officer Greene, I'm so glad you are on duty. Buffy has taken off again. Do you mind?" I knew exactly what she wanted me to do. Her little dog had taken off into the park woods again and with her bad hip, she couldn't venture over the terrain to bring her in.

"Mrs. Valero, I would be more than happy to bring Buffy home." I gave her my sweetest smile.

"Oh, thanks, dear. She's getting restless again. I think they are back," she said quietly in an awe-filled expression.

I laughed. If she only knew. "No problem. I'll bring her home in a little while." I drove off toward the park, typing a message to my dispatcher over the MDC that we had in the car. Our Mobile Dispatch Computers connected us with a lot of information, from our direct connection with our dispatchers and other officers to information on stolen items, cars, and driver information.

"Who is back again?" Trent queried as I pulled off the roadway to drive through the grass along the trees.

I couldn't help but laugh. "Oh, just wait."

I pulled up along the tree line and hit my air horn twice. Then I climbed out of the truck and whistled loudly in the air. "Buffy, come here!" I shouted and could hear fast little feet tramping over brush and sticks back in the woods. Buffy always came to me.

The little dog wasn't more than twelve pounds soaking wet and she came bounding out of the brush and right into my waiting arms. She was always happy to see me.

I walked around the truck and opened the passenger door. Trent gave me a funny look as I handed over the fuzzy little dog. "Trent, meet Buffy. Buffy, the vampire slayer." His eyes widened as he stared down at the little dog in his lap.

Buffy, in turn, growled at him and pulled her front lip up, baring her sharp canine teeth. Her entire body vibrated with the growl as she stared him down. The look on Trent's face was so priceless that I burst out laughing.

"Are you kidding me?" he asked as I closed the door and started back for the driver's side of the truck. I was still laughing when I got into the seat, and Buffy was still staring Trent down and growling low at him.

"Nope. Buffy knows when the vampires are here." I put the car in drive and started heading out of the park to take the dog home. Trent sat stiffly, holding the dog as she continued to growl at him. I snickered from the driver's seat. This was such a perfect call.

When we pulled up in front of Mrs. Valero's house, Trent was very happy to pass the dog right over to me. I handed her off to Mrs. Valero, and my dispatcher informed me that they had a phone assignment waiting for me. I told them to clear me from my animal complaint and send it down.

As I drove away from Mrs. Valero's house, I looked at the incident that had been sent to my MDC. *Really? Michelle Elgins wants me to call her about a custody issue.* I shook my head and picked up my cellphone to make the call.

Trent sat next to me and watched, not saying anything, just watching and reading my computer screen. I dialed Michelle's phone number. I practically knew it by heart. When she answered, I pulled over on the side of the road to listen to her. Putting my head back against the headrest, I sat patiently as she went on and on about the same things I had heard her talk about many times before. I was humoring her by listening.

As she spoke, I heard my call number coming over the speaker behind me. "Thirty-One-Paul-One." I put my hand over the mouthpiece of my cellphone and answered my dispatcher.

"Thirty-One-Paul-One," I said clearly into the car mic.

"Thirty-One-Paul-One, I know you're busy. You have an accident with injuries pending at fourteen fifty-seven Saddle Springs Road. One vehicle into a tree, two occupants with injuries. Fire and EMS are en route."

Michelle was still talking, and I was still ignoring her. I answered my dispatcher. "Thirty-One-Paul-One, clear the phone and send it down. I'm en route."

I pulled out from the side of the road and flipped on my lights and siren. "Michelle, stop talking." I waited until she stopped. "First of all, Michelle, this is a custody issue, a civil issue. The police do not deal with civil issues. You need to speak to your attorney and call domestic relations. Second, you are not a resident of my township, and you need to call your own police jurisdiction to report these things. Third, hold on a sec." I stopped talking and looked at the window as I passed a group of houses.

"Third, your kids are fine. I just drove past, and they are outside playing with a glow-in-the-dark Frisbee with your ex-husband. Fourth, do you hear all that noise behind me on the phone? That's my siren, and that means I'm going to a call where someone actually really needs my help. Call your attorney and go to domestic relations. I'm hanging up now. Bye-bye, Michelle." I disconnected the call and clicked it back into the belt holster.

Trent chuckled, but I was getting close to the accident and didn't take my eyes off the roadway or ask him what was so funny. I needed to focus on what was in front of me. When I pulled up to the scene, I pushed a button on my computer that recorded that I had arrived. Immediately, I jumped out and only slightly realized that Trent had exited the vehicle behind me.

As I got to the car, I saw one person leaning next to the vehicle and one person sitting in the passenger seat. The female that was in the passenger seat had a laceration on her forehead and appeared to be trying to focus since she kept blinking. *Head wound,* I thought. The male standing outside of the car was holding his arm but appeared otherwise not hurt.

"Thirty-One-Paul-One," I called out on my lapel mic.

"Thirty-One-Paul-One, proceed," came the male voice of my dispatcher.

"Thirty-One-Paul-One, make sure I have a medic unit en route for a possible head injury and call my on-call tow for one Ford sedan, heavy front-end damage," I replied back, and then put my attention on the female occupant.

"Hey there," I said as I squatted down to talk to her. "How are you feeling?" I asked as I put my hand out and touched her arm. Physical touch during a time of trauma was an important thing. People who were scared or hurt needed to feel someone near them. Sometimes the only thing you could do was be that person.

As my hand made contact with her arm, a flash of pain ran up my arm, but it wasn't like it was in my bond with Alex. This was different. I could feel what she was feeling. I pulled my hand back and it stopped. I reached over to her again and made note that her pulse was erratic and she blinked at me several times before she answered.

"My head hurts. I keep seeing spots." She kept blinking, but I knew that. I had felt that. Weird.

"What's your name?" I glanced up at the male who appeared to be the driver. I heard several cars pull up to the scene then, and I knew someone would check him out pretty soon. He seemed a lot better off than the woman who was trying to focus on me.

"Melanie," she said, and blinked again.

"Okay, Melanie, this is what we are going to do." I gently slid my hands onto the sides of her face to brace her neck, slowly moving her head back to a straight position. Once I had her head back to that position, I stood up and bent over to look her in the eye. "I'm going to hold your neck very still. You appear to have struck your head, and we need to make sure there is no damage to your spine. I need you to stay as still as you possibly can. Do you understand?"

The automatic reaction for anyone is to start to nod when they say yes, and she tried to do just that. "Don't move your neck, Melanie. You need to speak out loud."

"I think I'm going to be sick," she said quietly, but I already knew that. I could feel the nausea building in her through my hands on her face. This was something new and different, and I wasn't quite sure what to make of it yet.

"Okay, this is what we're going to do. You need to turn in your seat, straight, stiffly, and put your legs between mine, got it?"

"Yes," she answered, and she started to turn toward me. I held her neck straight and made sure she moved slowly as she turned to put her feet out of the car. As soon as she had her feet planted on the ground, I spoke again.

"We are going to lean over to your left and you can get sick. You ready?" I spoke slowly.

"Yes." I could feel her body getting ready to throw up. Head injuries were funny like that. They made you puke.

I held her neck straight and allowed her to bend over to the left. She instantly threw up, and I watched as it splashed all over my pant leg and boots. Lovely...

As she continued to throw up, one of the EMTs came to my side, and I explained what I knew. He quickly grabbed a stabilization collar and explained to Melanie what they were about to do. Once he had the collar on, a medic showed up and I stepped back out of the way to allow them to do their job.

One of the EMTs was standing behind me and threw me a towel. I bent down and wiped my pant leg and boot. Talk about a spit shine. *Not the first time, won't be the last time either,* I thought as I tossed the towel into the back of the damaged car.

I glanced around and found Trent standing off to the side watching me, his legs spread wide, his arms crossed over his wide chest. I had forgotten that he was even with me. I got so wrapped up in doing my job that the small things around me seemed to disappear.

I made eye contact for a second and wondered what he was thinking. The fire chief was standing next to him, and they appeared to be talking. I watched as Trent answered something the fire chief said, and the two of them looked in my direction. With all of the ambulances and fire trucks around, there was too much noise to hear what they were saying. I nodded to Trent and turned back to look at the scene.

I still had a lot to do before I could clear this incident, so I walked around the truck and pulled out my notebook to take notes. Pictures were taken, and I interviewed the driver who stated he had been driving too quickly and lost control. The fact that he admitted that dropped his citation down from Reckless Driving to a simple Careless Driving citation. I was being nice.

Once the scene was cleaned up, the injured were transported out, and the car was on the bed of the tow truck, I turned to thank the guys from the fire department and went back to my truck. Trent was standing by the driver's door, leaning back casually, watching me. His arms were crossed in front of him again and it made his biceps pop. I shivered as I remembered that they had been wrapped around my body last night.

He watched me approach the truck, and our eyes were locked together. There was a warmth coming from his that I assumed was lust. I stopped in front of him and continued to stare at him. *"You belong to me,"* ran through my mind, and I had to catch myself before I gasped for air. He searched my face for a second and I thought he was going to reach out and touch me, but he dropped his arms to his side. "We done here?" he asked in a husky voice.

It took a second to find my voice after hearing his husky tone. "Yeah, we're done at the scene."

He nodded and walked around the truck. I couldn't resist watching him as he moved around to the back of the vehicle. My words, *"for life,"* rang through my mind. Damn…I was in so much trouble.

CHAPTER TWENTY

TRENT

I couldn't figure out what had happened after I'd taken Kristin. It was all a fuzzy blur. I remembered drinking from her, and then making love to her. The feelings were more intense than I had ever known. Holding her to my body had felt so good, so very right somehow.

When I felt her move in bed the next morning, I became wide awake and the memories of the night before rushed back. Had the sleeping pill we gave her affected me when I took her blood? That was the only thing I could think of that might have happened.

The words that I'd spoken, *"you belong to me,"* echoed through my mind. Had I really said that? Did she really say *"for life"* back? Or was it the sleeping pill that had caused those fuzzy memories to surface in my mind.

She stretched, and her hand came up against my thigh. She instantly turned to me with huge blue eyes. It took only a second before she jumped out of bed and demanded to know what I was doing there.

She stood naked by the side of the bed, and I allowed my eyes to travel over her beautiful body, instantly becoming aroused. She realized then that she had nothing on and grabbed my T-shirt, pulling it over her head quickly.

Damn, it looked so good on her. It hung down to her mid-thigh, and I wanted to slide my hands up under it. She continued to ask me what I was doing there, and each time she did, her voice rose a little bit. I sat up, knowing that she was about to get an eyeful. I think that seeing me alarmed her even more, and she screamed.

The door flashed open, and Julian stood there barely contained as he took in my naked appearance and the fact that I was climbing out of Kristin's bed. I knew there was about to be a fight, so I picked up my jeans and slid them on. I could feel a rush of heat coming from Kristin, and then Julian was yelling at me.

Kristin was angry, but more than that, I could feel the hurt coming off of her. We should have told her. I knew that now. As Kristin asked questions, I answered them pointedly. I knew that each one of my answers only hurt her more, but I wasn't going to lie to her.

When she yelled for us to get out, I contemplated what I should do. I wanted to tell her I was sorry. I wanted to make her understand that we had only wanted to break the bond to protect her, and I hadn't meant to do what I did. I had hurt her, and I never meant to do that.

I saw the pain in her eyes and wanted to comfort her, but I knew that I should leave and allow her to deal with this her own way. I left without saying a word.

I needed to face Julian, but not before I showered. As soon as I walked into the kitchen, Gabe stood, alert for whatever would happen. I never expected Julian to pour me coffee.

"What happened, Trent?" Julian asked as he sat there looking at his coffee.

"I fucked up." What else could I say? It was the truth. I never meant for that to happen. I had never wanted to mate with anyone, and I had been feeling weird and her scent just pulled me in. It didn't help that she'd said my name in her sleep or that I could feel every little thing that she was feeling.

Julian and I talked for a while about what he had learned and about what ideas we might have in order to find Alex and Burke. Gabe left us to go talk to Kristin, seeing as she had been in her gym for over an hour. We could all hear the loud music and feel the vibration in the house from her kicking the weight bag.

The phone rang next to me and I reached over and picked it up. "Hello," I said into the receiver.

"Hello, this is Chief Henderson. I'm looking for Kristin."

"Okay, hold on. I need to find her," I said as I headed for the stairs. As I got to the top of the second floor, I heard Gabe and Kristin talking quietly. I made my way to the door slowly, listening to what was being said.

"Kristin, can I ask you a question?" I heard Gabe ask her quietly.

"Sure," she replied.

"Why didn't you finish your mating with Alex?" I heard her laugh and say something to Gabe under her breath.

"Alex didn't want me to go back to work. He never understood how important my job was to me. He wanted me to have a child and come up to New York with him and put all of this life behind me, but I can't. I won't. This is me...This is who I am. Yeah, part of Calista is still in there, and it longs for Julian, and it cares deeply for Alex; but I'm me, Kristin, and I'm a cop. He wanted to take my choices away from me, and I feel like too many choices have been taken away from me already, especially after today." She laughed quietly again.

As she was speaking, I'd stepped into the doorway and she saw me. I had taken her choice away, and for that I was sorry. I had hurt her. I wanted again to tell her I was sorry, but all I could do was hand her the phone and tell her it was her chief.

Gabe and I both heard her say she was going to work, and neither of us was happy about that. She shouldn't be working right now with all that was going on. She all but demanded she was going, so the only thing I could think to say was that I was going with her.

If I couldn't tell her I was sorry, I could at least be there to protect her if she needed it. I went to get dressed and was waiting for her downstairs thirty minutes later when she joined me looking fresh and smelling sweet and clean. She had her uniform pants on and work boots along with a tight-fitting Under Armour T-shirt. Seeing her in this was almost better than the T-shirt she'd worn earlier. I liked this look on her.

I watched her from behind hooded eyes. She appeared so sure of herself, so competent and solid. I liked that about her. She wasn't a soft woman; she showed you that she was strong. She walked right past me, and I followed behind her like a puppy. Her Challenger was even more fitting as she turned over the engine and it rumbled to life. I couldn't hide the grin as I thought it fit her so well.

When we got to her station, I glanced around at the modest setting. It wasn't a police station by any means. It was a house turned into something for police officers to use. No bulletproof glass or safety features. I was glad I had come with her.

I watched as she put on her vest, thinking it was strange that she was wearing one. Bullets wouldn't kill her. I couldn't fault her logic for wearing it, though. I watched as she took out her shirt and pulled it over her head; her hands slid over the front of her shirt as she worked out the wrinkles and flattened it to her vest. She had a fierce look of pride on her face, and I felt myself responding to her.

That was probably why when John walked into the station, I felt territorial toward Kristin, but I calmed slowly as I realized she had picked up on it. I watched as they spoke to one another and found myself a bit jealous over how she interacted with this human male. I knew she wasn't attracted to him, but it was the friendship that they shared that I envied.

The whole incident with Buffy would eventually be funny; Kristin sure found humor in it. We had just barely gotten the little vampire dog back to its owner when Kristin received another call. She unclipped her cellphone from her belt and I sat back in my seat and listened to the woman chatter, all while Kristin sat silently and allowed her to go on and on. Apparently, Kristin knew the history and was only humoring the woman. How she kept her patience was beyond me; I would have told her to shut up already.

As the dispatcher announced she had another call, Kristin flipped into a totally different person. She immediately took charge of the phone call and flipped on the lights and sirens of the vehicle. She spoke in direct, no-nonsense sentences and when she told the woman to hold on, she darted a look out the window at a house where two kids were playing glow-in-the-dark Frisbee and appeared to be having a good time. I was totally taken by how she could do so many things at one time, being professional, straight forward, and very forceful. When she hung up the phone I grinned to myself. I loved the way she handled that.

When we pulled up to the accident scene I watched her become even more intense as she jumped out of the truck, taking everything in and going for the female who appeared to be the most injured. Kristin immediately bent down and started to render aid to her. I watched her reach out to the woman and snatch her hand back. She reached for her again and held her face gently between her hands this time. Kristin had a puzzled look on her face and it dawned on me that she had no idea what I was able to do, what she was now able to do.

Damn, I had never shared that with anyone. It was a heady feeling to know that I had given her a gift.

The scene filled up with more emergency vehicles. I watched from the sidelines, careful to stay out of the way, but also keeping a close eye on anyone who got close to Kristin. I turned back to watch the female passenger throw up all over the ground next to Kristin. Gross...

Kristin rolled her eyes, but other than that, didn't seem bothered by it.

A tall man joined me as I stood next to her patrol vehicle. He gave me a curt nod, which I returned, and we both turned in unison to watch Kristin.

"She's pretty fun to watch, isn't she?" the guy said to me.

I eyed him carefully. He was an older man who looked rather weathered from the job. I was trying to figure out if he said that because he was interested in her as a man would be to a woman, or if it was just a fatherly respect. When he turned to look out at her, I realized that it was a fatherly respect that he had for her.

"Fun isn't the word for it," I said. "She seems so intense when she does her job. Is she always like this?" It was his turn to measure me up, trying to decide whether or not he could trust me. I guess he decided he could because he chortled. "She's not being intense at all right now. This is her normal self. It would scare the hell out of you if you saw the intense version of her."

I turned back in her direction as she met my gaze. Our eyes held for a moment and I drank her in. She gave me a small smile and nodded my way. Turning back to the scene, I watched as she took notes, pictures, and talked to the driver. As the scene was being cleaned up, I watched her say good-bye to everyone and thank them for helping. Everyone she spoke with smiled back and made friendly small talk with her. It was obvious that not only the fire chief liked her, but the rest of the guys she was dealing with respected her, too.

I waited next to the truck for her to finish. As she approached me, our gazes collided. I was so glad I had come to work with her tonight. I was seeing the real person, seeing who Kristin actually was. I found that I liked who this person was, and right at this moment, I was glad that I was bonded to her. She was someone to be proud of, someone who seemed to care more about others than herself.

Our eyes were still intent on each other as she returned to her truck. I wanted to pull her into my arms and kiss her. I wanted to hold her and tell her how incredible I thought she was, but I held back.

"We done here?" I asked, and knew my voice sounded lower than it normally was. She kept studying me, and I wished that I knew what she was thinking.

"Yeah, we're done at the scene."

I nodded abruptly and turned away, needing to put some distance between us before I lost control and pulled her into my arms.

She stayed quiet as we left the area and headed back to the station. I watched as she took a rag and wiped off her boots and pants again. Just after she finished, her phone rang and a guy asked her if she was ready for coffee. She told him yes and to double the order.

"Come on, we're gonna go have coffee hour." She put her hand on my arm as she walked by me, giving me a gentle squeeze that caused a sizzle in my skin. I reached out and stopped her. I couldn't help it.

When she turned to face me, I stepped in close to her and she had to bend her head back to look into my face. I was holding her arm around her bicep, not tightly, but hard enough that she couldn't step away from me easily. I could feel confusion washing over her mixed with a tingle of pleasure.

"I'm sorry, Kristin. I'm so very sorry. You didn't deserve to be treated like you were." I spoke quietly as she stared up. Her eyes went from blue to gray, and then started to turn a light green. I continued to feel the confusion, pain, and sadness as it shifted over to a moment of wanting.

It took a while for her to answer. "I understand why you did it, Trent. I wish that you had talked to me, though." She replied just as softly, looking at me with wide bright green eyes. "I'm sorry for what you have to deal with, though." She looked away.

"What do you mean?" I asked her, and put my finger under her chin to turn her head back to me. Why would she apologize to me? Why was she feeling sympathy for me? I wanted so badly to kiss her, and I was just about to when she stepped away and put her hand to her lapel mic.

"Thirty-One-Paul-One," she said, still looking at me.

Man, I don't know how she even heard that. I was so intent on her eyes that I didn't even notice the radio had made any noise.

"Thirty-One-Paul-One, you have a disabled vehicle in the two hundred block of Ridgeview Drive." She started to turn away and told the dispatcher she was on her way.

"Kristin, what did you mean?" I called out to her as we went to her truck.

"Alex. You're going to have to explain it to Alex. Hopefully, that good relationship you have with him will keep him from killing you." She climbed into her truck, and I went around to the other side to get in.

I wasn't too worried about that right now. I was more worried about how I was going to deal with it when Alex came back and claimed what was his again. After seeing her tonight in her element, I wasn't sure I wanted to give her back. *"You belong to me...for life"* was bouncing around in my mind, and judging by the feelings I'd just gotten from her, she wasn't too sure she didn't want the same.

CHAPTER TWENTY-ONE

KRISTIN

J had to focus on the road in front of me so I could clear my head. Trent had been so close to me in the station, and I'd wanted to kiss him so badly that my lips tingled at the mere thought of it happening. I felt his sincerity when he apologized, and the desire that filled him. It scared me, because at that moment, I didn't want to say it was a mistake. What the hell was wrong with me? How could I want him the way I did? I knew that once Alex was back, I would go back to him, and he would keep Trent away from me as he did Julian. I knew that Trent only bonded to me because Alex asked him to, and the mating had been accidental due to the bloodlust that rose between us at the heat of the moment.

While I worked out earlier, I'd remembered more of what I originally thought of as a dream. I remembered the feel of Trent's hands on my body, how he touched me and kissed me and made love to me in a way I had never known. Although to him, it had just been sex, I was sure. To me, it was more; it was a joining of body and mind. It was a joining that felt strong and solid, and right to me in a way that neither Alex nor Julian ever had. I didn't understand it.

I enjoyed having Trent with me tonight; it was something that Alex was never interested in doing. Why not make the best of the time we had together? What could it hurt? I would relax and just get to know him. "What's your last name, Trent?" I asked.

I saw him peer at me quickly. "Myers, why?"

I shrugged. "No reason. Just trying to get to know you. I figured it couldn't hurt seeing as we have no idea how long we are going to be in this position." I gave him a lopsided smile. I couldn't help but think to myself: *Kristin Myers.* I laughed out loud.

"What's so funny?" he asked as he continued to look at me.

"Nothing. Was trying on the name for size. Kristin Myers. Funny, huh?" I chuckled, and then glanced at the look on his face and outright laughed. "Oh, relax, I was just joking. Oh, damn...it's Mr. Albertson. Looks like he's got a flat tire." I pulled up behind Mr. Albertson, whose sedan definitely had a flat tire. "Mr. Albertson is a nice man. His wife recently passed away, and I stop by every once in a while to check on him."

I parked my truck and flipped my overhead red and blue lights on to alert other motorists to be cautious. Mr. Albertson was surprised to see the flashing lights around him and turned to squint at my truck.

"Mr. Albertson, are you okay?" I called out. While I approached him, I heard Trent get out of the passenger seat and shut the door.

"Ah...Kristin. I'm so glad to see you. Seems my tire flattened on my way home. I was trying to figure out how to get the spare out of the trunk." He scratched the side of his balding head.

"Let me do that, Mr. Albertson. I don't want you to hurt your back." I reached in to grab the spare and felt Trent's hand on my shoulder.

"Let me do that." I felt a wave of emotion pass through me—kindness, maybe?

"What? You don't think I can handle changing a tire?" I laughed at Trent but backed up out of the way. Changing a tire was not my favorite thing to do, so if Trent wanted to do it, that was fine with me.

He pulled the tire out easily, taking it over to the shoulder of the road. "I wouldn't want you to break a nail." He threw me a smirk.

I laughed and looked down at my hands. "I don't have nails."

"Oh yes you do. I have the marks on my back to prove it." He grinned, and his eyes were so bright that my body began to melt. I a blush crept up my face as fast as Mr. Albertson looked at me.

"I take it this very fine specimen of a man is your boyfriend." Mr. Albertson winked at me and smiled.

I got my blush under control and figured Trent wanted to play, so two could play at this game. "No, he's not my boyfriend; he's my fiancé." I grinned and batted my eyelashes at him. His eyes were smoking hot, but not with anger as he met my playful gaze.

"Yeah, we were just trying out her new last name in the car as we pulled up." He was still grinning as he looked at me, and I snickered, feeling silly. Silly? When the hell was the last time I felt silly?

"Well, that's mighty fine! How exciting!" Mr. Albertson seemed ecstatic with the news. "You two make a wonderful couple. I can only imagine how beautiful your children will be with both of your looks." He smiled broadly between the two of us.

My smile stuck on my face, and I saw Trent glance away and focus on the tire. Luckily, Trent was able to talk, because I wasn't sure if my voice would work. "I'm sure they will be," he said to Mr. Albertson before starting to loosen the lug nuts.

Did he just say "will"? No, I must have misheard him.

The light conversation had taken a very heavy turn when the mention of kids came up. Kids I had never really wanted. Trevor and I never wanted them, and I wasn't ready to have one with Alex; but suddenly, the thought of having a child with Trent almost warmed my heart. Almost. It was obvious by the look on his face that it was the last thing he wanted to talk about.

I found my voice and changed the subject quickly. Mr. Albertson and I chatted while Trent finished with the tire, and then we said our good-byes. I promised him I would come to visit soon, and Trent and I climbed back into the truck. Both of us were purposely avoiding eye contact with one another.

We drove down to my park, where we were meeting officers from the next area over. I was happy to have someone else around to break the tension that hung between us. I introduced Trent to Ian and

Stefan and grabbed the two coffee cups that were still in the card-board carry holder on the hood of their patrol car.

I handed Trent one of the cups. "Hope you like it sweet and flavored. I had them make it like mine." My eyes didn't quite make it to his, but I flashed a quick smile and turned around to talk to the guys.

The three of us joked and talked about recent incidents. Trent seemed to hang on to every word. Eventually, Ian and Trent got into a conversation about guns and Trent seemed to open up a bit. I could see him visually relax. Thank you, Ian, for your love of firearms!

I watched them out of the corner of my eye as I talked to Stefan about some seminar that was coming up that he was going to. We had almost finished our coffees, and I knew that both Trent and I had calmed down and gotten over the strange air that had been surrounding us, when my radio called out for me.

"Thirty-One-Paul-One."

"Thirty-One-Paul-One," I answered back, as Trent downed the rest of his coffee and pushed off the car where he was leaning. Look at him—he was already up and moving toward my truck. I bit back a smile.

"Thirty-One-Paul-One, ten fifteen Blue Bird Road for a cardiac arrest. Ambulance and medics are en route."

"Paul-One, I'll be en route." I was already jumping into my truck, and knew that Trent had picked up on my adrenaline spike as he rushed into the passenger seat. I flipped on the lights and siren imme-diately and stepped on the gas.

"When we get there, open the back of the truck and grab the red bag and bring it to me," I said as we raced down the road. I knew that Ian and Stefan were following us. You could never have too many hands that were quick enough during an incident like this.

It took just a few minutes to arrive at the location. "Thirty-One-Paul-One , on scene." I spoke quickly into the mic as I rolled to a fast stop and jumped out of the truck, running for the door. The dispatcher told me it was a forty-five-year-old male, too damn young to be having a heart attack.

I heard Trent open the back of the truck as I ran to the front door. Inside were four people, all in different states of mind. Two small kids were scared and softly crying, holding on to a woman who was possibly a grandmother. The wife was leaning over the man who was on the floor, and she was holding the phone to her ear with her shoulder as the dispatcher walked her through doing CPR.

I ran to the man on the floor. "Step back. I'll take it from here." She looked at me with shock in her eyes and fell back from her kneeling position, dropping the phone to the ground beside her. The scent of her tears filled the room as they fell freely now. I instantly found the spot on his chest that would best compress his heart to get the blood moving, and I started to push while counting out loud, "One, two, three, four, five…" Ian sat down next to me, and he grabbed a pocket mask out of the bag that he brought with him. He took it out and got it ready. I felt Trent behind me.

"Trent, open up the bag and pull out the pads. Plug them in and have them ready for me. Twenty-four, twenty-five, twenty-six, twenty-seven, twenty-eight, twenty-nine, thirty." I stopped pumping as Ian leaned down and pushed two deep breaths through the pocket mask covering his mouth.

As soon as he was done with the second breath, I started to compress again, counting out loud once more. I looked up and saw that Trent had the pads out and was plugging them in.

I heard Stefan trying to herd the kids and the grandmother out of the room, and I looked over to where the woman sat observing us with silent tears rolling down her cheeks. I finished with my set of compressions, and Ian started on the breathing.

I grabbed the edges of the man's T-shirt and ripped it wide open, exposing his chest. I put one hand out to Trent, and he handed me one of the pads. I placed it down on the man's chest and reached for the other. As soon as I had them both on, I pushed the button that would analyze the man to see if there was any cardiac rhythm.

"Clear," I called out to make sure everyone knew to step back. I heard more people coming in and knew it would be EMS and the medics.

"Shock advised; stand clear," the machine called out.

Three seconds clicked off and the man's body jerked as the AED shocked the man. We all sat still waiting to see what the machine would tell us. Finally the automated voice spoke. "Continue CPR."

Damn it!! I immediately began another round of compressions as the medics around me opened boxes of equipment and started an IV on the patient. Ian pushed more breaths into the man's chest, and we allowed the AED to run another check on the man. Another shock was advised, and we all stood clear as it delivered the second shock.

"Pulse detected," the male voice on the AED spoke after the shock. There was an almost collective sigh that crossed over the room. The woman sobbed, and Trent stood up and moved away from where he had been sitting to make room for more medical personnel.

I stood up too and looked around the modest living room with toys spread around in little piles. A small stuffed bunny was lying near the woman. I moved to her side and helped her stand up. Then I bent down to pick up the bunny, took the woman's arm, and led her to the other room where her children had stopped crying and were looking at Stefan, who was down on one knee talking to them. I handed the small bunny to the little girl, and she hugged it tightly to her chest.

The ambulance crew now had the man on the stretcher, and they were wheeling him out to the ambulance. I heard them say as they went out the door, "His pulse is strong."

A few minutes later, after I made sure all of the medical supplies had been picked up and disposed of properly, I walked to the door. Trent held it open and came up on my side as we walked back to the truck.

I threw the AED in the back of the truck, making a mental note to pull out a new pair of pads after we got back to the station. I closed the hatch door and turned to find Trent standing there watching me intently.

"What?" I said, cocking my head to the side. I was surprised to see him standing so close to me.

"I could feel your adrenaline. It was so strong, and then I felt all of your thoughts. I knew everything you were about to do before your hands were moving. You were worried about the man and the woman who was crying. You were fighting for that man's life because he had small children and he was too young to die. I heard them. I felt them. That was incredible." He finished it on a quick, hushed note.

I was startled by his words; he looked almost as if he was in awe. Before I could say anything or move, he backed me up against the truck and put his thumb under my chin. He tilted my face. "That was one of the most beautiful things I have ever seen," he said just before he put his lips to mine.

It was a small kiss, but it was full of so much passion that I wanted to throw my arms around his neck before I melted to the ground. He pulled away slowly. I didn't know what to say. I knew what was possible to feel over a bond, so it didn't surprise me to know he felt my adrenaline. Strong emotions were easily passed over the bond without trying. Before I could think to say anything else, my radio once again came to life. "Thirty-One-Paul-One."

I sighed, closed my eyes, and grabbed my mic. "Thirty-One-Paul-One."

"Thirty-One-Paul-One, when you are clear, we have a phone assignment holding for you."

I sighed. "I'm clear. Send it down." Then I turned from Trent and walked away to get into the truck. I heard Trent chuckling as he opened his door.

CHAPTER TWENTY-TWO

ALEX

I was living in a constant pattern of waiting. There was nothing else to do. I tried to keep my thoughts quiet and not dwell on what was going on outside of here. I had to hope that Julian and Trent were figuring out where I was and how to get to me.

I prayed that the bond with Kristin was broken. I didn't want to imagine what she was thinking about all of that. It was the right thing to have done. Our bond was strong, and her ability to pick up on my pain and hunger would have been too intense for her, especially with how young she was.

The key rattled in the lock and the door swung open quickly, the bright light once again blinding me after hours of darkness. Two men entered and pulled me up roughly by the arms, dragging me to the room outside of my cell.

I was pushed roughly down into wooden chair again, and while my eyes were adjusting, I took the moment to test the bond. I could feel Kristin, but it was weak, distant, as it should be after having been broken. My heart ached at the same time that my mind told me it was better this way.

I could tell that Kristin was dealing with something that would cause a lot of adrenaline to course through her body. It was strong and easy for me to pick up on. I could only hope it had nothing to do with me. I held on to that feeling of adrenaline for a few moments until it started to ebb.

The men who put me in the chair stood sentry behind me and said nothing. My eyes finally accepted the lighting conditions, and I took a second to inspect my surroundings. The lights were still bright so it was hard to see beyond them, but I could finally make out unfinished wooden steps off to the left, the kind you'd find in the average house-hold. I was in a basement as I'd originally thought.

As I scanned the area, I reached out a bit longer to see what else I could feel from Kristin. It was hard to feel anything since her emotions had calmed down. I heard the door at the top of the steps open and heavy feet moving down them. Burke.

Since I could still feel Kristin slightly, I thought it would be best to close off my wall to her. She might still be able to feel some things from me, so I'd do the best I could to keep as much away as possible. Just before I put the wall up, I felt this incredible warmth start to flow through the connection. It was strong, rolling over me with a crash. It was an intense feeling of desire. Something I would not have thought she would feel with just being bonded to someone else. It would take a mating to cause that kind of an emotional reaction.

Mating...My heart beat harder and my breathing increased, and I realized that our bond wasn't just broken—it was ripped wide open. She had mated with someone else. Julian...It had to be Julian. He had taken her back, but wait...I felt around inside of my mind and realized I was picking up someone else. Someone else was feeling that same desire, too.

I wanted to rage, but I sat still, trying to get my breathing under control. Burke stood in front of me.

"Something the matter, Alex?" he asked, as a concerned friend might.

I kept looking at the ground. I threw up my wall because I knew what was about to happen.

"Come on, Alex, you can talk to me," Burke said again quietly as he bent down to look me in the eye.

As he did, I used the strength that I had been storing in my body, and the anger of what I just learned, and pulled myself up out of the chair in a quick movement. I smashed Burke in the face with my knee. I knew it would not kill him. Knew that it would only enrage him, but right then, I wanted to be angry; needed to feel the fury.

I caught Burke squarely in the face and he was thrown back. As his body slammed against some of the lights behind him, I was grabbed from behind by the two men. Both of them threw punches, one to my face, and one to my gut. I bunched over from the pain.

I heard Burke from behind me. His laughter only made me seethe, and I began to struggle with my two captors.

"About time you show your stuff, Alex. Although that little outburst probably had more to do with what Kristin is doing rather than me." He stood.

One of the men held me, his arm wrapped tightly around my neck. I didn't have the strength to fight him. I had used up what little strength I'd managed to salvage. I glared at Burke as he came closer. His eyes turned from a steel gray to a light blue. He was smiling even as he wiped the blood from his nose with the back of his hand.

"You feel like talking to me now?" He came closer and I watched his eyes to see what color they might turn next.

"I have nothing to tell you, Burke," I said slowly. His eyes flashed a light gray color. Son of a bitch...

"Okay, fine. Bring her in here, will you?" he said to one of his men.

The door upstairs opened again and I heard two sets of feet coming down. As they got to the bottom of the steps, I saw a guy push a woman forward. She fell to her knees in front of me, trying not to sob. Her arms were tied behind her back and I couldn't see her face, although I could feel her fear.

Burke grabbed her light blond hair and yanked her face up, pulling her up so that she had to rise onto her knees to keep from having her hair ripped out. Her face was bloodied and bruised, pain radiating over her features, and fresh anger bloomed in me.

I knew she was a half-breed; could tell that she had not fully turned. She didn't open her eyes, but kept them tightly closed, tears sliding down the sides of her face from the corners of her eyes. Some women might have cried out, might have begged to be let go, but she was tough and kept her torment and pain locked inside.

"Tell me who told you what I was doing, Alex." He looked up from her and into my eyes. "Tell me or I kill this woman." He looked down at the woman and pulled her hair tighter. She whimpered, but didn't scream out. Her eyes stayed clamped shut, tears slipping from the corners.

He knew how I was bound to protect the innocent. How it was my job to keep vampires and half-breeds safe to continue on with our breed. I was being pulled in two directions. Did I try to protect this woman, or did I protect those I knew and worked with?

When it came down to it, the choice was taken out of my hands. I didn't say anything, and I watched as Burke pulled a knife out of his pocket, flipped it open, and stabbed her in the chest. She let out a scream and sobbed. I felt the pain in the air, and the scent of her blood hit me like a wall.

I could see the blood running down her chest, it was coming out fast. I wasn't sure how long she would live being a half-breed. My anger was rampant now, but I did not have the strength to do anything. The metal bracelets around my arms kept me from fighting out against the men who were holding me.

"Put them in the cell." Burke turned and walked away then, dropping the knife on a bench as he stalked out of the room. The man who was holding me by the neck pulled me to the cell and threw me in. A second later, the woman was tossed in behind me and fell to the ground, sobbing in pain. The cell door slammed shut.

I realized then that this was a bad situation. She was a half-breed; she would die from the injury, but it would take her a long time. During that time, the sweet scent of her blood would invade my senses. I was hungry; I needed to feed, and I could go to her and take her. Feed myself to become stronger. She would die faster, of course, and that was where I hesitated. Could I cause the death of an innocent one when I could help to heal her instead?

She sobbed softly on the ground, and I heard her breathing

starting to become labored. Her heart was beating slower now that the adrenaline had run down from being stabbed.

Damn it! I couldn't let her die. I knew I needed my strength, but I couldn't allow her to die here in front of me. I moved down to the floor to where she was lying. Her heart picked up as I got closer, probably afraid of what I was going to do.

My fangs were out, throbbing with the need and the taste for her blood. As I touched her, I felt her fear, and I dragged her up to me. One quick bite to her neck and I could feed myself and gather my strength. I pulled her up into my lap, bracing her back against my chest. I moved her hair off her neck and she whimpered. I could feel her pulse rising, and I knew that it was pumping more of that precious blood out of her body away from me. Her scent rising to meet me was slightly sweet with a mint flavor, making my mouth water and my teeth throb harder.

As I got closer to her neck, I pulled her tightly to me. My arousal was pushed up against her back. My breathing was labored. I opened my mouth and got ready to bite down. I stopped just as my breath caressed her neck, and I felt her body tense and push back against me. I stopped and groaned.

Pulling my arm up from around her chest where I had been holding her, I bit down into my wrist. I pulled my wrist away from my mouth and pushed it against hers, forcing her to open her jaws. It didn't take much to get her on board with the idea, and she immediately sucked on my wrist. My other arm came up to the hole in her chest and put pressure on it to stop the bleeding.

What was I doing? I needed my blood, needed my strength, yet as I sat there feeding this woman, I felt good about my decision. Her sweet minty scent cascaded over me causing my arousal to grow harder, and I felt her shudder as she swallowed and pushed back against me.

I allowed her a few more pulls from my wrist, and then removed it gently but forcefully from her mouth. I licked the holes in my wrist and pushed her away from me. I was able to untie the ropes they had around her wrists. I could hear her heart beating more steadily, could tell she had stopped bleeding. She would live.

"There's a bed to your right. Go lie down. You will need time to heal." I pushed myself away from her and up against the wall. I was dizzy and tired, and I just wanted to sleep.

I heard her start to crawl around and opened my eyes to watch her. Her long hair hung around her face and over her shoulders, almost touching the floor as she crawled. She had one hand out in front of her, feeling for the bed. When she got there, she weakly pulled herself up. She was barely on the bed when she lay down, and I knew she had passed out instantly.

I closed my eyes and hoped that I hadn't just made a terrible mistake. I fell asleep after that thought crossed my mind.

CHAPTER TWENTY-THREE

KRISTIN

*I*n the truck I flipped up the cover to my MDC. I didn't want to look at Trent and I sure didn't want to think about what he just said. I groaned as I looked over the phone assignment.

It was a death notification. Man, my night was going south fast. The text in the incident told me to call a Sergeant Caldwell about a twenty-year-old kid who was killed in a traffic crash. I put my head back against my seat and groaned louder.

Trent read the information on the computer and hissed. Humans were so fragile, and I hated having to tell someone that a loved one had died. I picked up my cell phone and called the sergeant to get the details.

When he came on the line, he sounded about as good as I felt. "Sorry to ask you to do this," he said softly, "but, we think it's important to give them notification in person."

"I understand. What kind of an accident?" I asked, so that I could have the facts.

"It was a DUI. He wasn't intoxicated, the driver of the other car was." Isn't that the way it always was? The innocent people were the ones who got hurt, not the drunks and druggies who were doing wrong. I sighed loudly into the phone.

"I know, it's not fair, is it?" he said.

"No, it's not. Do you want me to tell the parents about this or just pass along your information?" Sometimes they wanted us to tell it all; sometimes they wanted us to only pass along their information so that they could speak to them in full later.

"If you could tell them about it and tell them the guy is in custody I would appreciate it. Give them my phone number, and they can call with any other questions. The kid's body was taken to Mercy." I nodded, even though he couldn't see me.

"Okay, will do." We talked for a couple more minutes before hanging up. I contemplated what I had to do and how much I hated this particular type of incident.

"You all right, Kristin?" Trent asked quietly.

I peered at him and noticed his eyes looked very dark. Was he worried about something? Alex's eyes always turned darker when he was worried. "I hate these calls. They are the absolute worst calls to deal with, but yeah, I'm fine."

We drove the rest of the way in silence. When I pulled up in front of the house, I sat examining the dark windows of the two-story house. Slowly, I took a long, deep breath and reached for the door handle. "Trent, do me a favor and stay in the car on this. It's hard enough for a family to deal with me. Having another stranger see their pain will just make it harder on them." He took my hand, giving it a gentle squeeze. I felt a burst of sympathy from his touch. What was up with the skin contact?

"Thanks," I said as I climbed out.

At the front door, I took another deep breath and knocked. My hands shook, but they always did on these calls. I had to bang loudly and ring the doorbell three times before a light came on upstairs.

I stepped away from the door and made sure that I was visible to the little window next to it. My flashlight pointed at my chest so they would clearly see it was the police and not a stranger. I saw the light-weight curtains pull away from the window and then fall closed. The door locks immediately started turning, and the door was pulled open.

"Can I help you, officer?" the man said to me, trying to clear the rest of the sleep out of his eyes as he blinked at me. I saw his wife start down the stairs.

"Mr. Reynolds?" I asked him quietly.

"Yes, that's me." He was watching me, and his wife was still coming down the steps, her hand holding her robe closed at the top.

"Mr. Reynolds, I'm Officer Greene of the Fawn Hollow Police Department. I apologize for waking you." I spoke calmly and quietly.

"That's not a problem. What can I help you with, officer?" he asked. By now, his wife had gotten to the bottom of the steps. She grabbed his arm, her eyes open wide. The fear that came from her told me she knew exactly what I was about to say. Women's intuition.

"Mr. Reynolds, do you have a son by the name of Robert?" Both of them gasped, and Mr. Reynolds nodded.

"Mr. and Mrs. Reynolds, I am sorry to tell you this, but your son Robert was killed in a car crash tonight." I stepped forward just as Mrs. Reynolds start to fold. I grabbed her arm before she could fall to the floor. As my hands made contact with her arm, stark grief struck me and I wanted to let go of her. But I clenched my jaws and kept hold of her arm as I stepped into the house, quietly pushing the door closed behind me.

It was twenty-five minutes later before I left the residence and made my way back to my truck. My shoulders were tall, my stride was steady, but inside, I was a total mess. I knew Trent was watching me, but I didn't make eye contact with him. I flipped open the top of my MDC and just before I started to type to clear myself, Trent grasped my shaking hand. I snapped my eyes closed because the tears began to spring up at his simple touch. The pain I felt coming from the mother had been so intense. It reminded me of the night I was told Trevor was dead.

Trent's hand on mine was calming. He didn't say anything, and neither did I. He knew what I was thinking. Could feel what was going through my body. I realized that must be his gift. The same way that Gabe could calm you with a touch, and Alex could feel all emotions, Trent must be able to feel things through touch, and now

175

that we were mated, so could I. I squeezed his hand back and nodded. Back in control again, I slipped my hand out of his and cleared myself from the call.

We drove in silence for a little while. I knew I needed to get back to the station to start my paperwork, but after the last call, I wasn't ready to think. I just wanted to drive. I turned the music up loud, trying to use the beat of the dance tune to clear out the pain and sadness from my last call.

I was slowly calming down when Trent looked at me and spoke. "You like to dance?" he asked as I scanned the dark houses we were passing.

I was a little taken aback by that question. I laughed. "Yeah, I love to dance. Why?"

He shrugged. "No reason really. Just listening to this music made me wonder." He was looking out the passenger window as I glanced at him.

"You don't like this music?" I asked lightly. I felt better now, the sound of music having washed away some of the pain of what I had done earlier.

He chuckled. "No, I like this music fine. I like pretty much any music, actually. I can totally understand why you put this music on when you got in the truck." He winked at me. It was kind of neat that he understood my moods and knew why I was doing the things that I was doing. I appreciated that.

I drove a little longer, and then pulled up to the station. I needed to start on my paperwork. As we walked inside the locker room, Trent stopped me by taking my arm and turning me around. He was getting into a habit of doing this.

I watched him as he stepped closer to me. His hand slid along the side of my face, his thumb caressing my cheekbone before moving to my lips. His other hand went around my back and pulled me tightly to him. A small sigh escaped my lips as they met with his. I felt caring and passion and lust running from his hands into mine.

The kiss was gentle, soft lips touching, exploring one another. His tongue came out and swiped my lower lip and my mouth opened to invite him in, our tongues swirling around one another swiftly but gently. I rested my hands on his arms, gently holding him as his hand moved from my face to slide to the nape of my neck where he kept me in place.

It was a sweet kiss, nothing demanding or possessive about it. When he pulled back, his eyes remained closed. When he finally opened them the brightness of the green made my knees weaker than his kiss did.

"Kris..." He seemed to struggle saying something and closed his eyes again. I would have stood there all night waiting for him to speak again, to say my name or to reel me in and bring our lips and our bodies back together, but my dispatcher had other ideas for me.

"Thirty-One-Paul-One," the male voice called out into the silence that was between us.

Really? Come on, can't a girl get a little quiet time here? I hissed and answered my dispatcher as I turned away from Trent. "Thirty-One-Paul-One."

"Thirty-One-Paul-One, ten nineteen Maple Grove Road, you have a missing juvenile. Mother states the seventeen-year-old took off after a fight and hasn't been seen in about four hours."

"Damn, Jacob," I said, and then told my dispatcher that I was on my way.

Trent followed me out of the station. "You know the kid?"

"Yeah, I know him. He's a good kid going through a rough time. His dad died a couple of years ago, and his mom can barely afford to keep the home they live in. His older brother got involved in drugs and has been in and out of jail for a while. Now Jacob has been using heavily, and I've been trying to help his mom get him into a drug rehab facility."

I sat thinking about where he might be at this time of night. A thought came to mind and I pulled out of the station driveway and went in the opposite direction from the residence. I pulled my cell phone off my belt and dialed his mom's phone number.

"Hello, Theresa? It's Kristin Greene." I spoke as soon as I heard the woman say hello.

"Oh, thank God it's you, Kristin. You're the only one who seems to be able to reach him these days."

"He's a good kid, Theresa. I'm glad I can help him. Look, I'm going to go check a few places before I stop over your way." I was heading toward Valley Spring Creek. Jacob liked the water, and I had the feeling he might be there.

"Thank you, Kristin. You are so good to us both. Thank you." I knew she was close to tears. She wanted to help her son, but he had been pushing back against her and getting more involved in the things he shouldn't.

I said good-bye and hung up the phone. As I got closer to the creek, I slowed down and pulled off the roadway into a small dirt area used for people who wanted to view the small waterfall in the area. Trent and I exited the truck and headed in the direction of the water.

I managed to get down over the rocks without too much effort and went toward the underside of the bridge. I knew Jacob was there, I heard his heartbeat. I also knew he wouldn't hear us with the sound of the rushing water moving over the jutting rocks; it would no doubt hide the sound of our steps to someone with human ears.

I glanced back at Trent, and he appeared to be very alert. He didn't know what we were walking into, but I smiled at him and he seemed to relax a tad.

As we got to the edge of the bridge, I held up my hand behind me to stop him. I stepped out around the edge of the bridge, and I saw Jacob. He was huddled against the underside, arms tight around himself, tears running down his face.

"Jake," I said softly, and he jumped. He swiped at his tears. I waited until he had done that before I snapped on my flashlight. I'd try to let the kid keep as much dignity as I could.

"Hey, Officer Greene," he said in a deep, husky, emotional voice.

"Hey," I answered back as I shuffled forward. "What's going on, Jake?" I kept the flashlight pointed in his direction, but off of him. It was very dark here, and I didn't want to take away his night vision totally. I didn't need the light to see his tired face and the small pupils.

The pupils were smaller then they should have been with the poor lighting conditions, and I knew he was probably high.

He didn't say anything for a while, but then he shook his head and squatted down to pick up a rock. He skimmed it out over the water, and I waited for him to gather his thoughts.

"Had a fight with my mom. No big deal." I could tell from his voice that it was a big deal. He hated fighting with his mother.

"Over what?" I asked, as he picked up another rock and threw it.

He looked over my shoulder, and I felt his fear spike. I looked over my shoulder, my own heart skipping a beat until I realized it was only Trent.

"It's okay, Jacob. He's here with me. He's a friend of mine. You have nothing to fear from him, I promise," I said soothingly, trying to get him to rein in his fear.

"Hi, Jacob. My name is Trent. I'm riding with Kristin tonight." Trent stood next to me, and it wasn't until then that I realized just how large and threatening he might be to a young human boy.

Jacob examined him from head to toe.

"It's okay, I promise. He's not going to hurt you, just like I have never hurt you."

Jacob took a few seconds to consider. "You're freaking huge, man," he said, but he was no longer afraid. He trusted me and knew I wouldn't lie to him.

"Come on, Jacob, let's go get in the truck and get you warm. It's cold out here. We can talk on the way home." I waited while he looked at both of us again, and then hung his head. He knew he couldn't not obey.

As we all made our way up the rocks, we stayed quiet. I opened the back door for Jake to climb in, but before he did, he turned sad eyes on me. He was taller than me by about four inches. His features were still soft from his youth, but his eyes looked so old. I put my hand on his arm to let him know I was there for him. Pain and failure coursed through my body as my hand touched him.

Tears sprung to his eyes, and I immediately put my arm around him. He came to me easily, and I held him as he cried. I didn't know why he was crying, but I knew that at that moment, he needed contact. Needed to know someone cared and was there for him. I felt Trent tense behind me, but I knew he was doing it more because he was worried about my safety.

I let Jake cry for a few moments, and then he pulled back, embarrassed by his display; I rubbed his arm gently and waited while he climbed into the backseat. Then I closed the door and turned back to Trent.

He was relaxed once again, and his eyes seemed intense as they bore down on me. I didn't know what he was thinking, but I could feel a possessiveness coming from him. A shiver ran down my back as I remembered his words, *"you belong to me,"* and I went around to the other side of the truck.

What was that look about? Was it just the bond that we had now that caused that possessiveness to come out? Had he really meant those words last night, or was he jealous that I was trying to help this kid, that I put my arms around another male? I didn't have time to think about that, and I pushed it away from my mind.

After I turned up the heater in the car, I flipped the spring lock on the prisoner screen behind me to slid open the little window that made it easier to talk to the people in the backseat.

"So, tell me now…Why were you fighting with your Mom?" I put the truck in gear.

I could feel fear coming off of him again, and I figured it was because he didn't want to tell me something.

"Why, Jake?" I asked again when he didn't answer me.

I heard him take a deep, shaky breath before he answered me. "Cuz she found out I was dealing."

I had just pulled out onto the road, and I immediately slammed on the brakes, causing everyone in the car to slam up against the seat belts that secured them in. "You what?" I turned to glare at Jake through the prisoner screen.

CHAPTER TWENTY-FOUR

TRENT

*A*s we drove to her disabled vehicle incident, Kristin asked me what my last name was. It was out of the clear blue, and I hadn't expected her to ask such a simple question after what had just happened. I was mulling over what I was thinking about doing when Alex came back.

I looked over and answered her. "Myers, why?"

"No reason. Just trying to get to know you. I figured it couldn't hurt seeing as we have no idea how long we are going to be in this position." She stopped talking, and then chuckled quietly.

"What's so funny?" I had no idea where her mind had gone after that comment, but I couldn't find anything in it to laugh about. Especially when I thought about what it would be like if she actually took my name—Kristin Myers...I liked that. Damn. That was never going to happen.

"Nothing, was trying on the name for size. Kristin Myers. Funny, huh?" She laughed again, then looked at me. She mistook my startled expression as one of "Are you crazy?" instead of the "I was just thinking about that," and then started talking about the guy in front of us with the flat tire. I let the conversation go.

Helping the old man with his tire felt good, and with Kristin in such a light-hearted mood, it was even better, until the man mentioned children. Then her mood flipped and tension filled both of us. We fed off each other's emotions, that was obvious.

I watched her talk and laugh with Ian and Stefan, trying not to feel jealous of the camaraderie that she had with them. I ended up talking to Ian in-depth about the difference between Glocks and Smith & Wessons and found we had a lot in common.

Her adrenaline was racing, fierce and strong, as she drove to the cardiac arrest. I felt every drop of it. While I have felt my share of adrenaline surges of my own, I'd never felt one coming from someone else. It was amazing. I was spellbound as she worked, in awe of how she handled every incident to perfection. No matter what the circumstances, she adapted and did what she had to.

"That was one of the most beautiful things I have ever seen," I told her before I leaned down and kissed her at the back of her truck. I didn't care who saw us, or what was going on around us. At that moment, I needed to tell her how amazed I was at all of this. How amazed I was at the feelings the bond between us created. I would have said more, but her radio came to life and called her once again.

Her next call was brutal. She had just helped save a man's life and now she was going to go tell parents that their child's life had been cut short. I had known plenty of cops in my time, and I had heard stories, one after another, but I never sat a night in their shoes. How the hell did they do this day after day? How could you live with life and death constantly and not have it affect you?

Kristin's compassion for mortals was astounding. I had never known a vampire who cared about people as much as her. I stayed in the car while she spoke with the parents, but I watched every second of her approach to the house, how she'd spoken at the door, and when she cringed as she disappeared behind the door. I wasn't worried about her safety; I was worried about her state of mind. I couldn't imagine having to tell a parent their child had died. Especially in something as avoidable as a drunk driving accident. I wondered how it must feel to lose someone you loved. I had never had to deal with that, other than my mother and little sister, but that was a long time ago. Since then, I have never really gotten close to anyone else except for Alex. Well, Alex and Kristin now.

The whole time she was inside, I kept a close vigil on her emotions, so I was not surprised when she climbed into the truck and cried. She had been on the verge of that for a few minutes, and I felt something else that was deeper causing her even more pain. Something that I didn't understand and didn't want to ask about, not yet. After driving around, she relaxed. The moment we were behind a closed door, alone, I had no hesitation in bearing down on her and kissing her. The longer the night went on, the more I craved the touch, the taste of her.

I felt the desire in her as I knew she could feel in me. Our tongues gently rolled over each other's as we stood in the locker room. I wanted to tell her so much, wanted to ask her things, find out more about her, tell her that I wanted to be with her. I pulled away slowly and took a second to get myself under control. When I opened my eyes, I found her watching me.

"Kris..." I started to say, but once again, her radio mic came to life, and I saw the flash of disappointment in her eyes as she stepped away from me and answered the call. She explained a little about the young man as we drove, and I listened as she made the phone call to his mother.

I was still amazed at how much she cared about people. Every place we had been tonight, she had shown over and over again that she cared about these people. The little old lady with the dog, the elderly man with the flat tire, the guys she worked with, the strangers hurt in the car accident, and the man who had collapsed at his house in front of his family. She cared about each and every single one of them.

I had always been a social person, and I liked being around humans. I don't think that I ever really cared that much about them, but I liked them. Seeing how she interacted with all of them made me see them as more than just mortals. They were people with very fragile lives.

I was nervous for a few moments when she disappeared under the bridge. The kid was on drugs, what if he tried to hurt her. I stayed out of sight as long as I could, then joined her and surprised the hell out of the kid.

Jealously spiked through me when she held him, but I stomped down on it. This was a child, a mortal child, and she was trying to help him. As much as I wanted the jealously to stop, I was compelled to feel as if this boy was invading my territory. She belonged to me, and he was holding her, crying on her, needing her. I didn't want another male to need her.

She looked over and gave me a tight look. I backed away and got in the truck.

"So, tell me now…Why were you fighting with your mom?" She started to drive, but I knew she could feel the fear coming off of the kid, just as I could. "Why, Jake?" she asked again.

"Cuz she found out I was dealing," the kid said very quietly from the backseat. If we didn't have the exceptional hearing that we did, we might not have heard him.

It was obvious that Kristin heard it just as I had because she slammed on the brakes, and I was glad that I had put the seat belt on. Not that I would've been hurt, but I would have been thrown into the glass of her windshield.

"You what?" Kristin screamed at him as she spun around in her seat. Okay, this was a similar rage to what I'd seen in the bedroom after she woke up and found that we'd mated. She was furious. I could feel the spikes of her anger digging into me, and I squirmed in my seat.

No one said anything. Kristin glared at him. I'm not sure if he looked at her or not. She was trying to rein in her anger. I could feel it.

"Please tell me that you didn't just say that you were dealing," she said toward the backseat.

He was quiet for a moment. "It's not what you think, Officer Greene," he said quietly.

"Not what I think? Jacob…let's take a look at this, shall we? You're a user, you say you want to get clean, but you keep using. Now you're selling the crap to keep up with your habit. What's there to think about?" She was angry, but she had calmed down and was talking in a lower tone.

"Really, it's not what you think. It's hard to explain," he said.

I was watching Kristin's face. Her eyes were light gray.

"Well, you have about five minutes to figure out how to explain it, because when we get back to your place, you better be able to put it all in words for me." She turned back around, and I heard the kid exhale a loud breath behind me.

A few minutes later, he spoke again. "Officer Greene, can I ask you a question?"

"Yeah, Jake." She didn't take her eyes off the road. I knew she was trying to stay calm.

"Why don't you have kids?"

I couldn't help but peek at Kristin. Her lips were tight, and she was gripping the steering wheel even tighter.

"Wow, Jake, what does that have to do with what's going on?" she asked after a few more seconds.

"Nothing really, but I was just wondering. You just care about kids, that's all. You'd make a great mom."

I watched as she inhaled deeply, letting it out again slowly. "Thanks, Jake. Maybe someday I will." After she had spoken the words, she glanced over at me, her eyes now blue. The emotions in her eyes were stark, and it caught the breath in my lungs. What the hell was that in her eyes?

She looked away before I could figure it out, and we pulled up in front of a small house. She didn't look at me again. The conversation with Mr. Albertson earlier tonight rang in my head about how beautiful our children would be. For the first time in my life, I could almost picture myself as a dad.

CHAPTER TWENTY-FIVE

ALEX

I woke up before the woman. I heard her breathing softly, and I tried to stretch out to get the stiffness out of my body from lying on the hard concrete floor. As I moved, the air around me shifted and her scent came to me.

I could still smell her blood. Her sweet minty scent collided with mine, and I felt the hunger in my body for her blood. The stress of being locked in here, injured and unfed, was playing havoc with my body, and it wanted relief in all ways.

I tried to block her scent from my mind. It brought up thoughts of Kristin, but I instantly realized that was the wrong thing to think about, as my arousal grew even harder with the picture of her in my mind.

Then I remembered the adrenaline I felt from Kristin earlier and the desire that had raced through her body. I had felt that desire coursing through someone else, too. Was it a coincidence, or were they together? I told Julian to break the bond with Kristin or to have Trent do it. I never would have thought that Trent would not only break the bond, but mate with her. Pain lanced my heart at the thought of Kristin being with someone else.

Anger from that thought raced through me which only seemed to enhance the throbbing in my pants. I shifted to ease the tightness over my arousal. I heard the woman move in the bed.

She was so close, her scent drifting off of her in waves as I realized she was awake and afraid. I swallowed hard and tried to keep my teeth from pulling down. Closing my eyes, I concentrated hard. I heard her sit up in the bed.

"You could have slept up here on the bed. There is enough room for the two of us," she spoke softly. It was the first time I heard her voice. The delicate sound with a sweet Southern accent did nothing but make my arousal throb harder.

"I'm fine here," I said roughly.

She was quiet for a minute, and I saw her moving around on the bed. She put her legs over the side and stretched her back. Her body was lean and tone, her arms tight and strong.

"I know the concrete can't be comfortable. At least come sit up here now." She moved over on the bed to make room for me.

I wasn't sure if I would be able to be that close to her right now. My need for blood and for a sexual release was dangerously close to not being controllable.

"I said I was fine." I spoke roughly again. I didn't mean to sound that way.

"Okay," she replied quietly. She seemed to think for a few moments, and then she turned toward me, but kept her face down. "Thank you."

I knew what she was thanking me for. I was still torn about whether or not I had made the right decision. "How are you feeling?" I tried to change my voice, make it not so husky.

"Amazing, actually." I saw her touch her chest where she had been stabbed. She pushed down on it, and I assumed it was healed because her face didn't change any as she put pressure on it.

"Please…Please don't sit on the hard floor. Please come sit up on the bed." She sounded almost as if she was begging, and the soft Southern lilt of her voice pulled me.

I sighed and slowly stood, my arms heavy with the weight of the cuffs on them, my wrists raw from the constant friction. I walked over to the bed and sat down, feeling extremely weak. I pushed myself all the way to the wall so that my back was resting against it. Being this close to her was not making it easier. My mouth watered, and her scent was stronger now that she was moving around.

She was twisting her fingers in her hands; agitation and fear were heavy in the air around us.

"What's your name?" I asked to lighten the silence.

"Courtenay. My name is Courtenay. You're Alexander," she said looking down at the bed. Her voice was so soft, and it reminded me of Kristin's after we made love. I closed my eyes to push that thought away.

"Yes, I'm Alexander. How did you know that?" I asked carefully.

"The guys who brought me here said I was going to be your dinner." She seemed embarrassed by that.

She moved back onto the bed and sat beside me. My body stiffened at her closeness. I tried to breathe lightly through my mouth so that I wouldn't get any more of her scent into my nose than I had to. I didn't speak.

"I'm glad I wasn't your dinner. Thank you again for saving me." She peered at me then. It was the first time that she looked up into my face. My eyes widened as they took her in. Her face was beautiful. The bruises were healed, although there was still some dried blood there. I was tempted to reach out and wipe it off. Her hair hung down gently on both sides of her face, and her eyes were a bright clear blue.

She studied me carefully. "You're hungry," she said quietly. "I can feel your hunger." I could only stare at her. Her soft features were pulling me in. Her scent drowning me, dragging me under. The need in me was alive and begging to be fed.

She kept her eyes on mine as she slowly pulled her hair back over her shoulder, exposing her long thin throat to my eyes, the vein in it pulsing, and I felt my body responding. I didn't move though. I sat still and took her in. I examined her face, her scent, her vein, and her eyes, especially her eyes.

She sat still as my eyes traveled over her. Slowly she sat up on her knees and came closer to me. I was afraid to move. I was afraid that if

I did, then the dream in front of me would disappear. She came closer and climbed over my legs, straddling them, but still her eyes watched mine.

Her scent struck me like a viper, and I almost grabbed her and pulled her to me, my fangs now long and throbbing as I kept my mouth closed tightly. She slowly slid up my legs to where she almost rested against my chest. My heart was beating hard and fast, my arousal straining against my pants. My teeth were threatening to rip through my lips, but I sat still and focused on her eyes. The closer she got to me, the darker they got. As she pushed herself up against me and began to lean forward, they turned an even darker shade of blue.

I struck so fast that I heard her yelp. My teeth dug into the soft tissue of her neck and my hands gripped her hips to push her down on my arousal, she gasped lightly and pushed herself tightly against me. When the first pull of her blood washed over my tongue, I thought that the gates of heaven had opened up and welcomed me home. It was pure, simple, and fresh.

The sweetness and hint of mint in her blood washed down my throat, and I could not hold back the groan. She pushed harder against me, then let up. She tried to push away from me, but I held her tightly.

"Alex, I need to feel you," she rasped out. I groaned against her throat as I took another pull of her blood. She pushed back from me again and I felt her hands go to my pants. She pulled at the button on my slacks and quickly unzipped them. I didn't want to take my teeth out of her neck, but at that moment, I needed to feel her too, so I pulled my teeth out and quickly pulled her shirt over her head. She started to unbutton my shirt, and I moved to her pants.

The clothing came off fast, and then she moved back to my lap, pressing her body against me as soon as there was nothing to keep us apart. When I had pulled my teeth out of her neck I had not taken the time to close the holes. Small lines of blood ran down her neck and I bent to lick them off. She moaned softly as my tongue ran up her neck and my teeth slid back in through her skin.

I felt her rise up over me, and she took my rod in her hand, positioning it under her. As I pulled deeply from her, I was not thinking of what the consequences would be for my actions. I was only thinking of what I needed at this moment, what I wanted. I felt her slide down over me. My body shook from the feel of her body around me.

I pulled deeply from her neck and started to move within her. She pushed hard against me, taking me in deeply and as we moved, I felt my body coming close. She was kissing my neck, licking over a vein that was throbbing. I wanted to tell her no, but I was lost in the feel of her. She licked my neck one more time, and then I felt her teeth bite hard against my neck, breaking the skin. My body climaxed at that moment, and my mind blew to pieces.

Drawing from her neck as I throbbed deeply inside of her, she pulled from my vein. Her sweet scent mixing with the smell of our sex made me dizzy. She pulled once more from my vein and then reluctantly pulled herself back, licking my neck and putting kisses down my throat to my shoulder.

I pulled my teeth out of her skin and licked the twin holes to close them. I looked up into her eyes. They were a deep dark blue, and as I watched them, they turned a bright blue again. My heart was still racing and my mind was going frantic as I looked at the woman in front of me. She smiled shyly at me and put her arms around me to hold me close.

My hands still rested on her hips. The metal bracelets making them heavy, but not as heavy as they had been before I fed. I could feel my strength building and knew that although what I had just done had changed so many lives, it might have just saved mine.

I inhaled her scent again and wondered exactly who this woman was with me, and how I was going to deal with the consequences.

CHAPTER TWENTY-SIX

KRISTIN

I screamed at Jake from the front seat. I was lucky that it was very early in the morning. If it hadn't been, then I would have just caused a traffic accident with the way I stopped dead in the street.

"Not what I think? Jacob…let's take a look at this, shall we? You're a user, you say you want to get clean, but you keep using. Now you're selling the crap to keep up with your habit. What's there to think about?" I was trying hard not to yell and to calm myself down. It was a very hard thing to do at that moment.

I watched him over my shoulder as he looked down at the floor to avoid my eyes. I wanted to reach back and shake him.

I told him he had five minutes to come up with an explanation, and it had better be a good one. Then I turned around and drove toward his house. I was focusing on breathing, focusing on driving; doing everything I could not to focus on what he just said.

I had just about calmed down when Jake spoke again. "Officer Greene, can I ask you a question?"

I had to keep the lines of communication open, no matter how upset I was with him. So I let him ask his question. What he asked was not what I was expecting. At all! What the hell was it with people bringing up comments about children today?

His compliment about me caring for kids was nice, but I was still reeling from the whole conversation. I glanced over at Trent and saw that he was observing me. The memory of what he said to Mr. Albertson earlier tonight ran through my mind. *"I'm sure they will."* Again, hearing those words made me think about what a child with Trent would be like.

I had to get a freaking grip on myself! I pulled up in front of Jacob's house and got out, slamming the truck door just a bit harder than I meant to. I was angry at Jake, angry at Alex, and angry at myself.

I walked around to the back door and opened it. Jacob looked at me as if he was afraid. Probably because he could feel the anger coming off of me and thought I was going to take it out on him.

"Let's go, Jacob. I'm not going to kill you out here. I want witnesses to this, so let's go inside and do this in front of your mom." I stepped back and waved him out of the truck. Trent chuckled behind me. I turned to give him a stern look, and he laughed again.

We followed Jake up to the house, and as we got to the porch, the door swung open and his mother ran out to Jacob. Jake put his arms around his mom as she held him tight. I could smell her tears.

"Jacob, honey, you gotta stop running. We need to find a way to deal with this. Please!" she begged him.

"Theresa, let's go inside. The neighbors don't need to see any more than they have." I put my hand on her arm and felt the gratitude she had for me and the love she had for her son.

She looked over my shoulder and her eyes opened wide as she saw Trent beside me. "Theresa, this is my friend Trent. Trent, this is Theresa Nolan."

"You're a friend of Officer Greene's? Or are you a social worker or something?"

I knew she would be concerned that he might be someone trying to harm her family. *"Trent, say something to make sure she understands you aren't here to hurt Jacob."* I sent the message to him quickly, hoping he didn't have walls up and would hear me.

I saw him blink, and then he said, "Mrs. Nolan, I'm not a social worker. I'm actually Kristin's fiancé. I thought I would come out tonight and watch her in action." His smile was deep and friendly, and I felt Theresa relax, although my pulse tripled in speed.

"Hey, you didn't tell me he was your fiancé!" Jacob looked at me accusingly.

"I said he was a friend. Can't a fiancé be a friend?" I replied dryly.

He thought about that for a second. "Yeah, I guess. So now that you're getting married, you can have kids." He gave me a lopsided smile.

I heard Trent snort beside me, and I wanted to hit them both. I'd had enough kid comments today.

I pointed at the door. "Let's go, Jake. You have some explaining to do." He huffed once but went into the house. I followed him, and Trent held the door open for Theresa. She still seemed a bit concerned about Trent.

We went into the small, clean kitchen and sat down around the square table. I rested my arms on it and looked over at Jake. "Well?" I asked.

"Well, what?" He looked at me all innocent and wide-eyed.

"Oh, Jake, we aren't going to play that game. It's been a long night, and I just don't have the patience for that. Why are you dealing?" I looked him straight in the eye and waited. He wiggled in his seat, but finally, after several heavy breaths, he looked at me.

"I know this is gonna sound bad, but I'm doing it for a good reason." I raised my eyebrows at him. I didn't speak, and his mother looked back and forth at both of us. She had seen me in action enough to know not to interrupt me. She would get a chance to ask her own questions later.

He looked down at his shoes under the table. "I'm selling so I can pay for my rehab." His voice was so quiet, I wasn't sure if his mother had heard him, but when I peeked over I saw the tears and I knew she had.

"Seriously? Jake, that's seriously why you're selling the dope?" I looked at him. I wasn't sure if I believed him or not.

"Yeah, Officer Greene, I swear. I figured you can make so much money selling this stuff that I could make enough to put myself in rehab, maybe help my mom out some." He glanced at his mom, and I watched as the tears spilled down her face.

I heaved a heavy sigh. I wasn't lying when I said I was tired. It had been a long couple of days, and I was mentally worn out from tonight's shift.

"That has got to be one of the craziest excuses I have ever heard." I wiped my hands over my face and held up my hand when he tried to speak. "I'm not saying I don't believe you, I'm just saying it's crazy and stupid."

Everyone was quiet for a minute, and I stared at a scratch on the table. "Where's your stash, Jake?" I eyed him carefully.

"What? I can't give you my stash!" He was alarmed now, and his mother reached out to grab his wrist.

"Jake, I'm not going to ask you again. Where is it?" My voice raised up a notch from friendly to business. I could be friendly, but when it came to doing my job, professionalism ran through and through.

His eyes were wide, and he looked at me and then Trent. I'm not sure why he was looking at Trent, but then I realized the fight-or-flight mode was kicking in and he was trying to see who he could get around quicker.

I felt Trent tense next to me just after I did. He had picked up on it too, or he had picked up on me. Jake continued to study both of us, and I stood ready to grab him if he moved. Trent stayed seated, but I knew he would move in a flash if Jake looked ready to bolt.

"You're not going anywhere, Jake, so just tell Officer Greene where the stuff is," Trent said softly next to me. Jake looked at him long and hard, then sighed an incredibly long and hard sigh. The fight-or-flight emotion ebbed away.

"It's in my room," he said as he hung his head.

"Trent, can you stay here for a minute. I need to go out to my truck." I went to the back of my truck where I kept evidence bags and pulled one out before I returned to the house.

"Let's go, Jake. Show me where it is." Jake stood and I sent Trent a silent message. *"Stay here with his mom. I'll be okay."* He nodded at me ever so slightly.

When we got to the second floor, Jake pushed open a door at the top of the stairs and I stepped into his room. It was neater than most teens' rooms. His mom made sure that he kept it clean. He went over to where his stereo sat and pulled down one of the large speakers from the shelf. He popped the back off and pulled out a bag. I was not surprised he had it hidden there. It was a favorite place for many people.

As he pulled the bag out, I pulled out a pair of Nitrile gloves that I kept in my back pocket, slipped my fingers into them, and took the bag he handed me. His eyes were so sad.

"Jake, we'll come up with something. Don't do it this way." I pulled open the top of the bag and looked inside and my mouth fell open when I saw the small baggies with the red powder inside. There must have been about fifty of them.

"Jake, where did you get this stuff?" I could barely speak as I gaped at the powder, the same powder I had been finding in many of my drug busts recently. The same one the drug labs couldn't figure out the ingredients to. The very same one that was turning people into raving lunatics, worse than PCP, and killing them after they ingested it several times.

"Guy in the city," was his only response.

I swallowed and looked up at him. "Jake, is this what you've been taking?"

I almost sagged in relief when he shook his head. "No, I haven't touched it. That stuff is scary. I got enough of a problem with weed. I don't need that."

"Good. Stay the hell away from it. This is bad stuff, dude. *Real* bad." I put the bag he gave me into my evidence bag and folded the top closed.

"Anything else?" I asked him. He shook his head again.

"Jake, we will find another way. I know your mom can't afford the rehab, but we'll find a way."

Trent was standing in the kitchen when we got downstairs.

"You have to promise me you won't try to sell any more of this. Promise me." I gave him a pointed look.

"Yeah, I promise." He sounded so dismal when he said it, but I knew that he would not break a promise to me.

"And I promise we will find a way." I reached out and touched his arm, and felt a flair of helplessness in him. Just before I let go, I felt a sense of hope, too.

"Hold on, kiddo, we'll get you help." After saying good-bye to his mother, we left.

"His mom says the rehab costs fifteen thousand and she doesn't have any insurance to pay for it."

I nodded. "Yeah, I know. I've been calling around to find someplace that might take him. If I could do it, I'd pay for it in a heartbeat." I rolled my head around. "Thank God this night is almost over. I've got just enough time to get this stuff back to the station and log it in before we can go home." As I said that the words, I inwardly flinched. It was my home, but it wasn't his. Would he catch what I just said? I was afraid to look at him.

He stayed quiet for the ride to the station, and we walked inside after I grabbed my camera bag out of the truck. I sat down at the computer and told Trent there were plenty of magazines for him to look through while I tried to get a little bit of paperwork done.

Intermittently, I thought I felt his eyes on my back, but then I would hear a page flip and I figured it was just wishful thinking. I tried to concentrate on what I was doing. I glanced up at the clock. Another twenty minutes and my relief would be here. I was exhausted and fought back a yawn.

I grabbed the evidence bag that I had taken from Jacob's house and stepped into the locker room. I had a work table there that I used for processing evidence. I put on another pair of Nitrile gloves, pulling them tightly over my hands, and then pulled the bag that Jacob gave me out of the evidence bag. I snapped a couple pictures of it.

I glanced up through the window of the room into the patrol area. Trent was leaning back in a chair reading an article in one of our police magazines. I watched him for a second, and I guess he knew I was looking at him because he looked up and winked. I chuckled. There was that silly feeling again. He put the magazine down and came over to stand in the doorway, his arms crossed over his broad chest.

God, he was amazing looking. He was so tall, and his blond hair was spiked short across the top of his head; the sides were just long enough that it would tickle your palms as you ran them over it. My fingers were dying to reach out and touch his strong cheekbones.

"You need to stop looking at me like that," I heard inside my mind. My eyes popped open wide. "Sorry," I muttered out loud, but I really wasn't. I closed my eyes for a second, trying to bring myself back to the here and now and not the fantasyland I had slipped into. Man, I was so tired.

I turned my attention back to the evidence I'd gotten from Jacob. I couldn't believe that he had been selling this deadly stuff. I was going to go back tomorrow night and talk to him some more. Try to find out where he had gotten it. It would be awesome if we could catch the supplier.

"I'm not sure where Jake got this stuff, but I intend to find out. I've been busting guys left and right with this stuff recently. I just had a really large bust about a week ago on a traffic stop. We haven't figured out where it's coming from or who it's going to yet, but I intend to figure that out. Our labs don't even know exactly what it is."

I reached into the bag and pulled out a handful of the small clear bags that held the red powder. As I put them down on the processing table, I heard Trent's sharp intake of breath. My eyes darted up to his face. His eyes were huge and he stood rigid as he stared at the packets.

"What?" I asked as I looked at him. I didn't know what was so wrong.

"Kristin..." He looked up at me. I could hear his heart beating rapidly. I was waiting for him to finish. He swallowed and looked back down at the bags. "I think we just figured out the connection." It took a second before I figured out what he was saying.

"Burke?" I whispered.

CHAPTER TWENTY-SEVEN

TRENT

*W*hen we got out of the truck at Jake's house, I stayed quiet. Kristin was still tense from the conversation in the truck about the drugs and the kids; I didn't want to get in her way. She opened the back door of the truck for Jake, but the look on her face kept the kid from climbing out. I couldn't help but laugh at what she told him.

I watched as his mother rushed out of the house and hugged him. It was obvious that she was very worried about him, and she was even more worried about who I was. I felt her tension mount immediately. I was not surprised by what Kristin mentally asked me to do. Going back to what we had said earlier seemed like the easiest thing to do. The look that she gave me after he mentioned kids again had me wanting to double over with laugher, but I contained most of it.

I watched as Kristin questioned Jake, and felt her more than him when he started moving into fight-or-flight mode. I would have jumped into a fight quickly to protect her, but I thought he would more likely try to run.

"You're not going anywhere, Jake, so just tell Officer Greene where the stuff is." I wanted him to know he wasn't going to get by me.

As Kristin left the room with Jake to get the drugs he had stashed, I stayed at the table and spoke with Mrs. Nolan.

"Kristin mentioned that you are trying to get help for Jacob," I said lightly.

She studied me intently for a few moments. "Yes, I don't have any insurance and no one will take him. It will cost me at least fifteen thousand dollars to get him the treatment that he needs, and I can barely make ends meet now."

I wanted to reach out to calm her as I had seen Kristin do, but I held back. Kristin made it look so easy, and it seemed to be that easy—until you tried to do it, then it felt strange. I gave Kristin a lot of credit for putting herself out there to others.

"You don't have any family who can help you?" I queried. It wasn't really any of my business, but I felt as though she wanted to talk.

"No family that's worth anything." She clenched her hands on the table. "His father died a couple of years ago, and our older son is in jail now for this very problem. Jake is an incredible kid. He's smart, and he's talented. I want to see him go somewhere in life." She picked at her fingernails and grew quiet.

I heard Kristin coming down the stairs and stood to wait for her. She made Jake promise not to buy any more of the stuff, and then she reached out to him and told him to hold on. It was so easy for her to reach out to others. I wished that I could have done that to his mom. I wished that I could reach out to her.

We left and I told her about the conversation I had with Jake's mother. She seemed to know the problem. I wasn't surprised when she said that she would have paid the money for him if she could have. I knew she had the money. Alex was very wealthy. Why didn't she just ask him for it?

When we returned to the station, she got busy with her pile of reports. I dug through a stack of magazines and paged through one. I wasn't much into reading at that moment; I was more interested in watching her. She tried to concentrate on what she was doing. Every once in a while, she would pause and look over her shoulder. I would go back to looking at the page I was on, as though I was interested. I couldn't have cared less about what was on the page. It was her I wanted to know about.

She stood up and yawned, stretching her back and raising her arms over her head to relieve her tired muscles. I let my eyes trail down her body, and felt a swift kick in my groin. It had been a long night and I had a feeling that once we got back to the house, it was only going to get longer. I wasn't sure I would be able to sleep thinking of her in another room, alone.

I followed her into the other room at the station, and she turned, her eyes soft, but full of lust. I didn't trust my voice out loud so I told her mentally, *"You need to stop looking at me like that."* She laughed, and I was so tempted to take her in my arms so that I could feel her body vibrate against mine. The sexual tension crackled in the air between us. Yeah, it was going to be hard to sleep today.

"I'm not sure where Jake got this stuff, but I intend to find out. I've been busting guys left and right with this stuff recently. I just had a really large bust about a week ago on a traffic stop. We haven't figured out where it's coming from or who it's going to yet, but I intend to figure it out. Our labs don't even know exactly what it is."

I watched as she reached into the bag and pulled out a handful of small clear packets that had red powder in them. My body froze solid as I pushed off of the doorjamb and stood upright. "What?" I heard Kristin say.

I swallowed. "Kristin..." I looked at up at her, and my heart jack-hammered in my chest. I swallowed, trying to force the bile down. "I think we just figured out the connection."

Her wheels started turning in her mind. Her eyes changed color from light blue to steel gray.

"Burke?" she whispered.

I was nodding at her when the side door opened and her relief walked in. She flicked a glance my way as she shoved the little drug bags into the bigger bag. I snatched one before she could put them all away and slid it into my pocket with a small shake of my head to her.

John had his back to us at his locker, and I listened tensely as she told him about the night shift. She told John she was exhausted and would finish her paperwork when she came back in tonight. She tossed the evidence bag into her locker and clamped the lock closed.

Her smile was forced, almost brittle, as she tried to control the shaking in her hands. I led her out of the station and into the driveway after she said good-bye to John. She threw me the keys to her Challenger, and I pulled it out of the garage so that she could back her work truck into the bay. She climbed into the passenger side of her Challenger without a word, and we remained silent, lost in our thoughts on the way back to the VMF house.

I glanced at her when we pulled into the driveway; she was still in full uniform. "You forgot to change," I said softly.

She looked down at herself. "Damn...I was a little distracted." I pulled into the garage, and when she came around the side of the car, I laced my fingers with hers and we entered the house.

Now that I knew what the connection was, I could understand why Burke was gunning for Kristin, and I was going to do everything to protect her and keep her by my side. At least, that's what I told myself as I peered down at our entwined hands.

I called out to Julian the moment we entered the foyer, and heard him reply from the kitchen. I was still holding Kristin's hand as we walked in and found the room full of people. Julian sat on one of the stools and next to him was another agent by the name of Cameron. Gabe and Olivia were also seated up at the counter. My eyes took them in, and then noticed that there was another man whom I didn't know standing by the window. I eyed him carefully.

My instincts were high and tight right now. Kristin was checking out the occupants too, and started to pull her hand from mine. I squeezed it and pulled her closer to my side. I wasn't going to let her go, at least, not right now.

"What's going on, Trent?" Julian eyed us carefully He noticed our hands, and I saw his eyes tighten.

"Kristin, are you okay? You look really pale," Olivia said as she peered around Gabe.

"Who is that?" I pointed my chin toward the window.

"That's Fitz. I think you remember Cameron, right?" I knew the name Fitz, but I had never met him. I nodded at him, and then looked at Cameron. "Hey, man, been a while."

"Trent, what's going on?" Julian asked again, and I knew he could feel the tension running off of Kristin and me.

"I figured out the connection," I said as I walked further into the room and tossed the small baggie of red powder onto the counter, pulling Kristin along with me.

All eyes went to the baggie, and then looked back at us. "The VBC? How is that the connection?" Cameron asked. I assumed that Julian had filled everyone in on what was going on.

Kristin started talking before I could open my mouth.

"I've been doing some major drug busts lately. Most of it has been that stuff. What did you call it? VBC? What is that?" She looked between Cameron and Julian.

Julian's eyes were huge, and his jaw dropped. He put his hand up over his face and wiped it down.

"Why didn't we know about this?" He glared at Kristin.

Kristin's anger flared. "Why? Why would you know? Who would think to ask me what I was doing with my life? You all are so hell-bent on making my decisions for me that no one cares what I'm doing or what I want!"

Okay...So that was a lot of mixed information, not all having to do with the drug busts, but I could see her point. Julian flinched, and I almost did too. She tried to free her hand, but I held fast.

"That's not what I meant," Julian said quietly. "What I meant was, why didn't someone think to look into what was going on in the drug market in this area." He picked up the little packet of the powder.

"To answer your question, Kristin," Cameron stated, "VBC stands for Vampire Blood Cocaine. They mix a pure form of cocaine with vampire blood, and then dry it out and cut it."

"That's why the labs don't know what it is, the vampire blood," Kristin stated. She looked so tired.

"Kristin, why don't you go up to bed? You've had a really long night." I said it quietly to her, and she darted a look at the fridge.

"I need to eat first. I haven't eaten all night." Everyone watched her, and I wanted to pull her behind me and shield her from them.

As she looked inside, she sighed, stepped back, and closed the door. "Actually, I don't feel very hungry. I think I'll just go upstairs and take a shower." She didn't look at anyone as she left the room. Olivia was watching her and touched Gabe on the arm before she followed Kristin.

Cameron spoke after they left. "So now we know why he threatened Kristin. Burke must have made the connection between Kristin and Alex after she started busting the deliveries."

"Yeah, but that still doesn't tell us where Alex is," Fitz said. It was the first time he had spoken since I entered the room. There was something about him I didn't trust.

Olivia returned sooner than I expected. "Is Kristin all right?" I asked as she moved back to Gabe's side. Gabe's eyes traveled over her body as she approached him. Huh…interesting.

"Yeah, she said she just wanted a long hot shower and some sleep." She didn't seem concerned, and she knew her a lot better than I did, so maybe I shouldn't be either.

Yeah, right…

We talked a little bit longer about what we had found out and tried to figure out how we could locate where Burke was keeping Alex. Finally, my own exhaustion hit me and I excused myself. I wasn't sure how Kristin had made it through the entire night doing all that she'd done. I was worn out just from watching her.

Everyone talked about turning in for the night, and as I walked up the stairs, I wondered if I should check on her. I almost walked to her door and knocked, but I decided that she probably wanted time alone. We had been together for the last thirteen hours nonstop. She was most likely tired of me.

As I stepped under the hot water of the shower, I tried not to think about her doing the same thing just across the hall. No matter how tired I was, I couldn't stop the thoughts, and I wondered how I was going to fall asleep knowing she was there, and that she was my mate, and I wanted her, but that I couldn't have her.

CHAPTER TWENTY-EIGHT

KRISTIN

The shower helped relieve some of the tension from my body, but my mind was still going a mile a minute. I needed to find a way to relax before I even attempted to sleep.

I felt trapped in my room and decided to head to my office on the second floor, maybe surf the Internet or play a game to relax my mind. As I walked out of my door, I heard the shower running in Trent's room. I imagined what the water would look like as it traveled over his perfect chest and down his ribbed abdomen. I groaned. I didn't need to be thinking this way. It was not going to ease my tension.

As I continued down the hall, I noticed that all the bedroom doors were closed, and it was quiet in the house. Everyone must have turned in for the day. I was glad because I was only wearing a pair of cotton sleep pants and a thin camisole. Too many men in this house to be wearing such clothing.

In my office, I went to the window and peered out. The sun was beginning to rise. I pulled back the lightweight lace curtains to look out over the eastern sky.

The sky's kaleidoscope of colors—oranges, pinks, blues, and purples—were glowing on the horizon as the sun climbed over the edge of the earth. I stood, watching, my arms wrapped around myself, lost in the moment of beauty before me.

"Kristin, are you all right?" I jumped when I heard Trent's voice behind me. I'd been so focused on the colors before me that I tuned out everything else around me.

Trent put his hands on my shoulders gently. "I'm sorry. I didn't mean to scare you. I guess you were deep in thought. "

"It's okay."

His hands were so soft on my shoulders, warm from his shower. His scent heady in the room.

"Are you okay?" he asked me again. I felt the heat from his chest radiating over my back. Thoughts of hearing the water running in his bathroom flashed back to my mind. I needed to put some distance between us. I rolled my shoulders to dislodge his hands and moved to the other window in the room.

"No. No, I'm not all right," I said quietly as I looked out over the new morning sky. Morning used to be my favorite time. I had always loved to watch the sun come up and think about how a new day had started. Now I guess I needed to think that way about sunset.

"What can I do to help?" he asked quietly, and came up behind me again. His warm skin gave off his delicious scent, making my mouth water. I wish that he had stayed across the room, but part of me wanted him to touch me again. He stood a foot behind me, and I fought with myself as the urge to move back into his arms became so strong.

I shook my head. "Nothing...There's nothing you can do."

"Talk to me, Kristin. Please tell me what going on inside your mind." He stepped close enough that his chest was now against my back.

Why would he care what was going on inside my mind? Was he that loyal to Alex that he would go above and beyond what he had already done to make sure I was okay?

"What's going on? What's going on is that this is all my fault." I watched as the top edge of the sun broke over the horizon, shimmering gently.

"This isn't your fault. How could you even think that?" I felt his breath on my neck. It was like a caress.

"It's not?" I blurted and spun around, angry at the situation and how attracted I was to Trent. "How can it not be? Look at what's happening to Alex. That is all my fault. I led Burke right to him."

"You had nothing to do with that. Alex has been working on this case for months. Yeah, you're right that he found out you two were together, but he has probably been following Alex around for months."

I looked over my shoulder at the window. The sun was coming up fast. I moved toward the door.

"Where are you going?" Trent asked.

"To my room. The sun's coming up. It's going to be uncomfortable for you in here in a minute," I said over my shoulder as I headed for the stairs, Trent's footsteps following.

We didn't speak as we went upstairs, and I entered my room, leaving the door open behind me. He closed the door quietly and came to stand by the edge of the bed. "You can sit down. I promise I won't attack you." I saw a flicker of something run through his eyes. Was that anger, disappointment, or humor? Trent went around to the other side of the bed and lay down so that he was on his side propping his head up with his hand.

It wasn't until then that I noticed he only had on a pair of cotton lounge pants. They had the Tasmanian devil on them and I chuckled.

"What?" he said with a scowl.

"I like your pants. Taz is one of my favorites." I watched the scowl change into a lopsided grin.

I rested my head back against the wall, looking at him through half-closed eyes. "I know that not all of this is my fault, but a big part of it is. I know that Burke has been trying to get my attention, and now he's using Alex to get it."

Trent watched me for a minute. "Why do you think that?"

"The other night, the night Alex was supposed to come down, I went out to the bar and met my friends. While I was there, that woman, Angie, she was there. Right after I felt the stabbing pain through my bond with Alex, I saw her leaving quickly."

"So, why does that make you think Burke was trying to get your attention?" Trent asked suspiciously.

"Just as my head was clearing from the pain, I saw her heading out the door to leave. She was on the phone, and I saw her say, 'Yeah, she got the message.' I was too freaked out by what had just happened or I would have followed her."

Trent was quiet for a moment. I watched as he ran a finger over a design on my quilt. "Okay, so maybe he is trying to get your attention." He glanced up at me, and then went back to watching his finger trace the design.

I watched him do it too, but got distracted when I noticed the muscles in his arm flexing as his hand moved. My eyes went up over his arm to his shoulders and down his chest. His chest was so perfect; tight, strong-built muscles that were just crying out to be caressed. His stomach would have been flat if it wasn't for all the ribbed muscles that traveled across it. I ached to reach out and draw my fingers over it as he was drawing his fingers over the design.

As that thought entered my mind, I realized that he was no longer drawing the design and I studied his face. His eyes were bright, bold, and dark green. His mouth was slightly open, and he was watching me. I felt my body warm as he looked deep into my eyes.

"Kristin...I told you before to stop looking at me like that." It was spoken silently.

"Maybe I can't," I answered him back the same way.

Trent slowly reached out with the hand that had been drawing the designs and put it on my leg. His hand was hot over my lounge pants. He slid it up my leg to my knee, stopping there for a moment, watching me. I didn't move. I just watched him, my heart beating a little faster. He moved from his position on his side to being on his hands and knees, and he crawled slowly toward me, looking like a predator moving in for the kill. My heart skipped a beat, and I knew my eyes were changing color to a deep dark green that matched his.

When he got closer, he spoke again. *"Then if you can't, I can't be held responsible for what's going to happen."*

I had a moment of panic and thought, *What am I doing? What about Alex?* But just as quickly as those thoughts came, I pushed them away. I knew what I was doing. I knew that my time with Trent was limited, and I wanted to take advantage of it. He wanted the same thing. We were already mated. It wasn't as if anything else could get screwed up.

"I take responsibility for my own actions," I said as he climbed over me, his hands on either side of my hips. Not touching me, but close enough that I could feel the heat of his body radiating toward mine.

"You aren't going to regret this, are you?" Trent asked me quietly, out loud.

He was inches from my face, his spicy chocolate scent flooding my senses. "Never..." I lifted my hands to touch him, one hand on his face and the other behind his neck, leading him in. Our lips were a fraction of an inch apart. His eyes darkened and grew smoky. A low growl vibrated in his chest, and I tingled from head to toe. This man couldn't get any sexier.

With his growl still reverberating through his body, he closed the distance between us, one hand cradling the nape of my neck. Our bodies fused on contact, and within seconds, we were rolling onto the bed, pushing ourselves as close to each other as we could.

My hands roamed every inch of his body; his head, neck, shoulders, back, hips, even his legs begged for my touch and I gave it to him. He moaned into my mouth as I scored his back once again with my nails. I guess I really did have nails after all.

It did not take long to remove what little clothing we wore and we lay side by side, chest to chest, legs wrapped around each other, touching, tasting, needing.

His hands traveled over my body, teasing me, making me want to beg for more. He used his thigh to push open my legs and eased himself in between, sliding kisses down my neck and over my chest.

My hands never stopped, and if I could have pulled him closer, I would have. His mouth went lower as I arched up underneath him, his fingers sliding between my wet folds below. I wanted to cry out instantly, but he kept me from going over the edge. He continued to tease and tempt me. The craving to sink my teeth into his neck was starting to burn in my throat.

He kissed around my belly button, licking the skin and making it burn for him. His fingers entered me over and over, driving me wild. He moved lower, licking the inside of my thigh. I watched him with hooded eyes. A sly smile crept over his lips just before his fangs came out. Without warning, he bit into the major artery on the inside of my thigh.

Holy God! I'd never had anyone do that, never felt something so intense as he took his first pull. I flew over the edge into the heavenly abyss. Prisms of light exploded behind my eye lids, and he took me higher than I had ever been. I heard him moaning as my climax flowed through him, his fingers never stilling from their movement.

When I could finally breath and open my eyes again, I pushed him away. I wanted more, I wanted him. I flipped him over so that he was now flat on the bed. I was over him in a second, and it was my turn to give the pleasure.

I reciprocated the smile and nipped at his lips. His eyes were filled with desire, and I licked at a drop of my blood the trailed down from his lips. He closed his eyes briefly and I moved down to his neck, kissing the soft skin, nipping at the pulsing vein. I licked my way down his chest, letting my hands roam lower over his tight stomach, following the ridges of his hard abs, my tongue teasing his nipple, then moving on to the other one.

I took him in my hand, the smooth, hard, silky flesh made every nerve in my body tingle. He pumped his hips as I moved my hand up and down on him. I kept up my assault with my tongue as I moved down between his legs. His mouth was open, his lips wet as he watched me. I saw the wish in his eyes, and I knew what he wanted.

My fangs were long and tight, longer than they had been before, throbbing with the need to feed from him. When I bit down into the inside of his thigh, he hissed and his entire body tensed as I brought him over the edge with my hand in just a few slight strokes. I fed till his heartbeat calmed. He was still breathing heavy as I pushed up and gazed at him.

He grabbed me by the arms and pulled me up, flipping me over so that I was once again under him. His cum, hot and wet on his stomach, allowed our bodies to slide over one another. His eyes were so intense, but he said nothing as he bent down to kiss me. It was a gentle kiss, a passionate one. The kind you had before you had sex. Our tongues slid over each other, tenderly, as his hand caressed the side of my body. I loved the way he touched me, the way he made me feel.

As our kisses grew from gentle to more intense, our bodies responded to each other again as if we had known each other a lifetime. "Trent, I need to feel you inside me, please..." I begged him.

He didn't need any further words as he slid inside of me and we moved in harmony, like this was all there was, like we were made to be together. We fit so perfect, loved so magically, and we exploded into the abyss of ecstasy.

I wanted to feel this forever. I never wanted to let his go, so I held on to him until he was sound asleep. How could I go back to what I had with Alex, after what I felt with Trent? Even the passion with Julian was nothing compared to the incredible desires I felt in Trent's arms. But it wasn't just the desire, it was the way he looked at me as a woman. How he saw me at work, accepted me for who I was, what I did.

How could I ever let him go?

A single tear rolled from my eyes as I lay snuggled up against his warm, solid body. I wanted to hear him say I belonged to him again, but there would never be a forever with this man. I belonged with Alex, and Trent was only with me because of his need to protect me and because of his needs as a man. They had nothing to do with me. This was all I would ever have with him.

A second tear fell.

CHAPTER TWENTY-NINE

TRENT

I walked downstairs after my shower, in search of blood. I intended to head to the kitchen for a warm mug, but then I felt Kristin's presence on the second floor; her sweet scent filled the air and my mind as I entered her home office. She stood, silent and still in front of the window, the colors of the morning sky glowing around her. She was breathtaking. I memorized the way she stood, how her shoulders were so wide, her back so straight, and swore I would remember this moment forever.

"Kristin, are you all right?" She started and I saw her hands fist. I went to comfort her, the sadness and stress radiating from her begged for help.

I placed my hands on the bare skin of her shoulders and inhaled slowly, drawing her sweet scent deeply into my lungs, another memory I did not want to forget. She shrugged out of my hold, but I refused to allow her to push me away. The bond we shared would not allow me to leave her alone. She was trying to be so damn strong, so independent. She didn't want help, especially if she had to ask for it, but I would do everything I could for her; until I had to leave her, I would do anything, anything she asked.

How could she think that Alex's kidnapping was her fault? She had no clue that we had been watching Burke for months, knew that things were changing and that it would come to a head soon. It wasn't her fault, none of this was her fault. I followed her out of the office and upstairs, my thought of food long forgotten. I hesitated at the door, but not for long. She climbed onto the bed and leaned against the wall, her legs stretched out in front of her. God, I shouldn't be here. This was too tempting.

"You can sit down. I promise I won't attack you."

I wasn't worried about her attacking me, I wasn't sure how long I could keep my distance. With each tick of the clock hand tonight, my desire for her had grown. I can do this...I can be here for her and not ask for more. I lay down on the other side of the bed and my stomach muscles tightened when she laughed. The sound was magical to me, made me feel happy, content, wanted, when it came over her lips.

I was catching on to the way her eyes and emotions were linked. The soft light blue shade of her irises now displayed the sadness she felt. I already knew her anger came through in gray, and passion in green. I wanted to see the green now, I wanted it as much as I wanted my next breath. I ran my finger along the stitching pattern of the quilt, pretending it was her skin I was drawing on while she talked about her thoughts. "Okay so maybe he is trying to get your attention." I peeked up at her and then back to the design.

She was quiet, and I felt liquid warmth reaching out to me. Jesus, her eyes were roving inch by inch over my arms and chest. Did someone turn the temperature up in the room, or was that my internal body furnace on scorch?

"Kristin...I told you before to stop looking at me like that." I would not have trusted my voice to speak that out loud.

"Maybe I can't." In my mind, her words were whispered, seductively, erotically, a temptation of epic proportions. I touched her leg, feeling the warmth and desire as my hand went up to her hip. I didn't break eye contact, and watched as the color I wanted to see so much filled her eyes. She was mine.

"Then if you can't, I can't be held responsible for what's going to happen."

I crawled over her body, wanting to cover it with mine. The green glowed back at me, sucking me in.

"I take responsibility for my own actions."

I was completely over her now, my hands on the sides of her hips, not touching her, but close enough to feel the heat of her skin.

"You aren't going to regret this, are you?" I asked out loud. If she had said yes, I would have stopped. I would have found the strength to pull away. I would not do something to hurt her, not on purpose, ever.

Her hands moved in slow motion toward me as she whispered. "Never..." Jesus, I wanted this woman so badly, and I took her in ways I had never taken another.

After we made love, I could not deny how much I felt for Kristin. She completed me in a way I never thought could happen. Walking away from her was going to kill me. Hadn't Julian warned me about just this? What if I refused to give her up? Would Alex fight me? Would Kristin want me? I wanted to be with her, wanted her to belong to me forever. I never wanted her to go, but I also knew that I never got what I wanted, and the day would come soon when I would walk away from her and our time together would have to last me a lifetime. I fell asleep holding her tightly to me, wishing I never had to let go.

When I woke up hours later, I carefully slipped out of her bed. Kristin was so peaceful and serene in her sleep. My heart already felt as if it was breaking as I turned and walked out the door.

Julian was in the hallway when I turned from closing the door softly. His eyes narrowed and we stared at each other for a long time, neither of us speaking. I could see in his eyes understanding and pain. His love for Kristin was so plain to see, and he could not have her. In that moment, I knew he could see how I felt, and compassion filled his eyes. I could not have her either.

He cleared his throat. "I'll put on the coffee."

I went back to my room, showered, and dressed again in the same kinds of clothes as last night. Kristin was working again, and there was no way I would leave her side, not now, not until I had to.

Cameron and Fitz were already seated at the kitchen table, both working on laptops. Fitz nodded; he was a man of few words.

"I think we have the location narrowed down to three places," Cameron said to everyone in the room. I was pouring my coffee when Gabe walked in.

"What are they?" Julian asked as he sat down at the counter.

"We've been able to locate three properties that come back to Burke. One in New York near Binghamton, one in the Poconos, and one in New Jersey," Cameron stated. "Okay, I'll send some guys out to each of those locations to scout. Trent, I assume by the way you're dressed that you're going with Kristin to work again tonight."

I nodded since my mouth was full of coffee.

"Okay, keep a close eye on her. Burke is going to know that we are getting close, so he might try to get to her. I'll be up in Kristin's office making those calls." Julian turned and almost walked right into Kristin as she entered the kitchen.

"Whoa," Kristin said as she moved to avoid the hot coffee that was spilling over the edge of the mug. "Sorry, Jules, you turned around faster than I thought you would."

Julian stood stock still, his eyes wide as Kristin passed by him. His nose flared ever so slightly. His eyes flew to mine, shock evident in them. His Adam's apple bounced in his throat as he swallowed and he looked as if he was going to say something, but instead he shook his head and left.

What the hell was that about?

Kristin went straight to the fridge, snagged a blood bag, and tore it open with her teeth. She drank it straight from the bag. "You know it does taste better when it's warm," I said to her as she finished it off in record time.

She shrugged. "I was starving. Guess I should have had some last night."

You did, I silently said, and her face turned scarlet red. She peeked over her shoulder at the two men sitting at the table, but neither of them was paying any attention to us. She checked Gabe and found him smirking. She glared at me, but couldn't stop the smile that crept over her lips.

I laughed out loud, and Gabe chuckled. She smacked him on the arm. His arm snaked out and wrapped around her waist and pulled her in to his chest to hug her. The affection between them was priceless, and it made me jealous as hell.

Gabe froze very similarly to how Julian just had and Kristin found her escape and wiggled out of his arms. "Let's go, Trent. I need to get going. I have a few errands to run before work starts." She left the room without looking back. Gabe continued to stare at me, his jaw slack.

"What?"

He shook his head. "Dude, you are in so much trouble."

"Let's go, Trent!" Kristin yelled from the other room. I gave Gabe a confused look and went to catch up to Kristin who was already climbing into her Challenger.

I inconspicuously sniffed the air when I sat down next to her. All I could smell was Kristin's sweet rich scent, maybe it was a little stronger, but I couldn't catch anything else. I'd have to ask them later.

The sun was still above the horizon, so I stayed in the car while Kristin ran a few errands. The dark tint of her windows kept me comfortable while she popped in and out for a few minutes at a time.

When we got to the station, I sat at the little round table in her patrol area and went back to paging through the stack of magazines. She dove right into her reports from the night before. The desk phone rang and she leaned over and picked it up without even looking at the caller ID.

"Fawn Hollow Police Department, Officer Greene speaking." She was so damn professional; I beamed from across the room.

She held the phone between her shoulder and her ear, making a tight seal, so I wasn't able to hear the other side of the conversation.

"Sure, Trooper Reynolds, what can I help you with?" She rolled her chair to a clear spot on the desk and picked up a pen and paper. "Go ahead." She listened for a moment. "Yeah, I know that address. It's mine." I felt a trace of her discomfort slither through our bond. I dropped the magazine, preparing for what might be coming our way. *Coming our way?* As if I was a part of all of this and not just some innocent by-stander along for the ride. Wow…I needed to take a step back. This wasn't my job; protecting her was.

"What?" she said quietly into the phone.

I moved closer to her, pulling up another office chair and straddling it. Did this have something to do with Alex?

"Yes, I know her. She is the sister of a friend of mine. He's staying with me right now." Her hand shook. She listened for a few more moments and then paled.

"No, Courtenay wasn't involved with any drugs that I know of. Did you find something in her car?" she asked. She glanced at me quickly and pulled the phone away from her ear so that I could hear.

"There were a couple of little baggies in the car. Looks like some fancy new variation of cocaine."

Oh shit!

"Is it a red powder?" Kristin was staring out the window in front of her, but I knew she wasn't seeing anything. Her eyes looked glassed over. I put my hand on her arm. It wasn't just her hands that were shaking, her whole body was.

"Okay, thank you. Yes, I'll let her brother know. Here, take down my cell phone number. If you need anything or find anything out, please call me right away."

"What's going on, Kristin?" I said as soon as she started to put the phone down.

"Gabe's sister was kidnapped." She swallowed. "It looks as if she was on her way down here. The police found MapQuest directions in her car with my address on it."

Crap. "What else did they say?"

She stared at the floor for a moment, lost in thought. "There were two little baggies in her car with VBC in them." She swallowed and I felt the quake of her body vibrate through our bond. "They have Courtenay."

I didn't know her, but if they had Gabe's sister, this was bad.

Before I could reply, Kristin's phone rang on her belt. It took her a second to break out of her haze and unclip it. She glanced at the screen and answered it, putting it on speaker. "What's up, Olivia?"

"Hey, Kristin, you know those cars you like to stop? Well, I have one. I'm getting ready to stop it. You want to come over?" she said in a sing-song voice over the speaker.

Before Olivia finished the sentence, Kristin was racing to the back door. I was right behind her, not exactly sure what the hell was going on, but I had a hunch.

Another officer pulled up as we were dashing to the car. "Where you guys running to?" he asked.

"We're going to back Olivia up on a traffic stop," Kristin called out, never pausing.

Kristin was tense, and she threw the car into drive before I had the door closed. She didn't even bother to put on her seat belt, something I noticed she did every time she got in the car. It wasn't until we were moving that she replied to her friend. "I'm on my way. Where are you?" She threw on her lights and siren and took off from the driveway.

"I'm going to stop it at Route 50 and Airdale Road," she said.

"Olivia, you listen to me. You stay in your car until I'm there. Do you understand that?" Her adrenaline was exploding through our bond; my heart beat as fast as hers and I had no clue why.

"I will."

I heard the sound of a siren over the speaker. Kristin raced around cars as she rushed to get to Olivia, driving at speeds that were not safe in the Expedition on curvy roads, but she didn't care. She was intent on getting to Olivia, and as fast as possible. I snapped the seatbelt around me and held onto the door handle. She knew how to antici-pate the vehicle's movement since she was controlling it. I, on the other hand, was getting slung all over the passenger seat. Thank God I didn't get motion sickness.

We heard Olivia call the stop out over the radio, and before the dispatcher acknowledged Olivia's stop, Kristin was telling them she was en-route to back her up. We arrived within two minutes and found Olivia sitting patiently in her car watching the vehicle in front of her. Her car angled with the front engine compartment slightly into the road for protection.

It was a black Volvo sedan with extremely dark window tint, and I saw that the car had Florida plates. An uneasy feeling wormed its way up my spine.

"Olivia, listen to me, and listen carefully. I want you to get on the speaker in a minute and tell the driver to step out. Whatever you do, do *not* get out of your car, you got it?"

"Yep. Got it…Tell me when," came the cellphone speaker.

Jesus! What was she about to do? Kristin turned her attention to me for the first time since the phone call. "Trent, I need you to trust me on this and stay in the car until I say so." I didn't want to listen to her, but I would. She seemed to know better than me on this. I nodded once.

She opened her door just enough to slide out and dropped to the ground in a crouch. What the hell was she doing? I saw her move up behind Olivia's car, and saw her put the phone to her lips. All hell broke loose in the next three seconds. Olivia called out over the loud speaker from inside her car, telling the driver to climb out with his hands up. The driver's door opened and a man stepped out of the vehicle. He sniffed the air and morphed into attack mode. My instincts had me releasing the seat belt and the door at the same time.

My door began to open and I was twisting to get out when the passenger door of the Volvo opened and another man exited at top speed. Kristin stood, her shoulders squared, her feet planted firmly, and she fired off two shots at the driver. They struck him directly in the face, and he flew back against the open car door, bouncing before he landed on the ground.

I was in the process of getting out of the truck, but couldn't pull my attention away from the scene in front of me. Kristin swung to the right and delivered two more rounds to the passenger. One to his chest, center mass, the second to his thigh. He held his chest and dropped to his knees. The smell of the gun smoke hit me as I rounded the door, running toward the man on his knees.

I smelled traces of platinum and titanium. She had used our special bullets. Kristin darted to the driver, and I saw her disappear from view. After what I had just seen, I was not in the least bit worried about her safety. She said very calmly into my mind, *"Don't kill the passenger. We need him."* Her calmness was almost eerie.

Not a second later, I heard the specific whooshing sound of the vampire on the driver's side go up into ash. She had staked him.

I reached the passenger and pinned him to the ground. Kristin rounded on us. "Get him off the ground!" she said through gritted teeth.

As I pulled him up, I looked into her face. Holy shit! She wore a mask of rage, her eyes burning a shade of gray I had never seen before. They were shining so brightly that I had to look away, but not before I saw her fangs hanging low in her mouth. I felt mine throb.

"Where is he?" she yelled into the man's face. I heard footsteps behind us, but I was so enthralled with Kristin that I didn't give it a second thought.

The man didn't answer, and Kristin pulled her arm back and punched him in the face. His head spun to the side, and blood flew out of his mouth. "Where is he?" she asked quieter, hissing at him.

The man spit onto the ground. Blood splattered up onto her shoes. "Don't know what you're talking about."

I was holding him around his throat in a choke hold. He was almost as large as I was, but with the two bullet holes in his body, I knew his strength was nothing compared to mine. I applied some pressure to his throat. "Tell the officer what she wants to know," I growled through my teeth, the combination of my anger and hers causing my canines to extend with a vengeance.

Kristin lifted the compact Glock that she held in her hand. Where had that gun come from? She carried a full-sized Glock on her belt. I had no idea she carried a backup weapon. She placed the muzzle to the guy's temple. At that point, I shifted away in case she fired and it went through his skull. I didn't need to get injured in this.

"I'm going to ask you again, and you can either tell me where he is, or you can die like your buddy. You tell me where he is, and I will let you leave so that you can take a message to your boss." Her eyes were glowing silver.

The man thought about it for a few seconds. "Harvey's Lake. They have him at Harvey's Lake." Kristin shot me a look and I gave her one nod—the guy was telling the truth.

"Move," I heard her say, but I knew she wasn't talking to the guy, she was warning me. I released him and twisted away as her eyes flashed a metallic silver. As I twisted away, I saw the male cop from the station watching in horror beside the Expedition. Fuck! I turned back when the body thudded to the ground. For two seconds, she stood over the body and then faster than I could have, she slammed a stake through his heart. He burst into dust.

I heard a strangled noise from behind me and found the officer wide-eyed and pale. He was staring at Kristin, fear etched over his features.

"What the hell are you?" He swallowed as he stared at us.

I put my hands up in front of me and willed my fangs to retract. "Officer...this is not a good time to explain all of this."

Kristin stopped beside me. "Mick, we're vampires. You've been asking me for a long time to tell you what was wrong with me. Well, now you know." She passed him and he practically jumped out of her way as Olivia joined me.

"Liv, you all right?" Kristin asked as she bent down and stowed her gun on her right ankle. I glanced at Mick, and he was gawking at her with his mouth wide open.

"Yep, I'm good. Kris, your eyes are freaky...They're glowing!" Kristin lifted her other pant leg and I saw another holster around that one with a stake inside it. She slipped the second stake into another pocket and stood up, dusting off her pants.

"Liv, " Kristin said, glancing over at Mick, "Do you mind explaining this to him? We need to get out of here."

As Kristin walked away, I spoke to Livy. "Thanks, Olivia. We owe you one." I hesitated beside Mick. "She might be a vampire, but she's one of the best damn cops I have ever seen. You remember that." His nod was jerky, his mouth still at the position to catch flies as I walked away. While Kristin was pulling away, Olivia was putting her arm around his shoulders and leading him to her car. I stared at the Volvo as she picked up speed. That was one of the best kills I had ever seen. I wondered if she could feel the pride I had for her seeping through our blood bond.

CHAPTER THIRTY

ALEX

*M*y eyes were open, and my senses stronger than they had been for days. My body felt physically and mentally sated. I listened to Courtenay breathe quietly next to me as she slept.

What had I just done? I put my arm behind my head, trying to get comfortable, even though the metal bracelets made it hard. I closed my eyes and berated myself. *What have I done?*

I needed the strength, needed the blood. What happened beyond that I could not ponder. I didn't want to think about it. I ground my teeth together, fighting the urge to roar at the injustice of everything that had happened.

I didn't know the woman beside me. What if she was a plant? What if Burke had thrown her in with me just to get this outcome? He knew I would try to get my strength back, while still attempting to save the woman. He knew that bloodlust would've come easily. I might be an elder, but it hit me the same as the younger vampires, especially in these types of circumstances. Burke had planned to break my mating with Kristin, and it had worked. Was this woman connected to Burke in some way? Was she part of this whole plan? The questions bombarded me, making my head spin.

I could easily break the mating. When I got out of this, I would go back to Kristin and take her back. There was no way that Trent would want the responsibility of having Kristin in his life. But what if he did?

The woman stirred next to me. "Alex?" she said huskily.

"Yes…" I answered her in the same way.

"Are you all right?" She lifted her head off my shoulder where she'd been resting. Her eyes were questioning, but soft.

It took me a few seconds before I answered with a simple, "Yes." She was feeling curious, and I could see it in her eyes as she looked over my face. "Wait…You're Alex Armstrong? You're the head of the VMF?"

Warning bells clanged in my head. How would see know that? "Why would you ask me that?"

"Because I've met you before. I didn't realize it until just now." She cleared her throat. "I'm Gabe's sister. He brought me to the VMF to show me around one time when I was visiting, and you called him into the office." She smiled as she spoke. "I knew you looked familiar, but I didn't place you right away."

I did remember meeting her briefly. That was right before Gabe and Julian were sent to Florida to watch Burke's warehouse.

"Wait…You were mated to that girl, Kristin, that's her name, right? Gabe told me about her. Oh God!! What did we just do?" Her heart rate spiked and she moved away from me. "Oh, Alex, I'm so sorry! I never meant for that to happen. You know that, don't you?"

Tears sparkled in her eyes. Her emotions wafted through the air and over our bond consistently with the way she should be feeling with surprise and remorse. If she was acting, she was damn good.

"Don't worry about it, Courtenay. Kristin will understand the circumstances." At least, I hoped she would. "I'm sorry you got thrown into this. How exactly did they get you?"

"I was heading down from New York to see Gabe in Fawn Hollow. He said he was working a job and told me I could come see him. I stopped to get gas, and two men asked directions. Before I knew it, they had thrown me into their car."

"Where were you when they found you?" Maybe I could finally figure out where I was.

"I was at the exit at Route 81 and 309."

"How long were you in the car before you got here?" I quickly asked.

"Not long; thirty, maybe forty minutes. They blindfolded me, but I could smell a lake when I got out of the car."

I wasn't too far away from Fawn Hollow, but how was I going to get that information to Julian and Trent? I wasn't. I had to hope like hell they figured it out.

"You didn't say anything to them about where you were going, did you?" I was worried they would go down to Fawn Hollow and find the VMF house.

"No, I wouldn't tell them anything. That's why they beat me up." She sat up straighter and moved against the wall.

"I'm sorry you had to go through that. All of it." I watched her as she looked aimlessly around. We were quiet for a few minutes.

"Why did you save me? You could have just finished me off and gotten all of your strength back." She studied me while she asked the question.

"Trust me, the thought crossed my mind, but I couldn't do that." I looked away, not wanting her to know how close I had been to doing just that. "My job is to protect. I couldn't put myself before you if I knew I could help you."

"Well, thank you for not making me your dinner." She laughed softly, and I listened to the way it rang out through the air. It was sweet and mellow and touched a piece of me down deep.

"You're welcome."

She burst out laughing at my response. "Gabe is not going to believe this! What a mess I've gotten myself into now; well, the mess I've gotten us both into." She shook her head and pulled her knees into her chest.

Wait a second, Gabe... "Did Gabe know you were coming down to see him?" I looked at her eagerly.

"Yes, but I wasn't sure when I could get away. He knew it was going to be soon, but not exactly what day. I was actually trying to surprise him."

Damn. If Gabe had known she was coming, then he would've known what route she was taking and that something had happened to her. It might've given them an idea of where I was. Although, how would they know she had been taken by the same people? There was no way. I was grasping at straws.

"Alex, I'm really sorry for all of this trouble," she said quietly.

"Courtenay, you need to stop apologizing. This is not your fault. Burke used you. He was hoping you would break my bond with Kristin. It was just another way for him to get to me." I stared up at the ceiling.

"Why did he want to do that?" she asked.

"I'm not sure why he has it out for Kristin, but for some reason, he thinks she's involved with his drug trade. Breaking the bond between us was just a way to punish me." I blew air out through my mouth in a huff.

She stopped apologizing, and we started to talk. It was casual conversation about who she was and what she did. She told me stories about Gabe, and I found myself relaxing and laughing as much as I could in our situation. She was funny, and the conversation was light-hearted. It was nice to think about something that wasn't doom and gloom.

It was good to not think about what would happen once I was out of this cell. I had an uneasy feeling that things were not going to turn out the way I originally thought.

CHAPTER THIRTY-ONE

KRISTIN

I woke up, but pretended to be asleep. I felt Trent standing over me. I wanted to open my eyes and pull him back into my arms, but I didn't. I listened to his soft footsteps as they moved toward the door and went through it. I slowly peeled open my eyes, rolled over, and stared at the ceiling. Wow, I felt amazing today. It had to be because of the blood I shared with Trent, or maybe it was because I had chosen to be with him last night and didn't have any regrets about that. None.

I felt strong and alive in a way I never have before. I rolled over and put my face into the pillow he slept on. His scent filled my nose and my body responded to it immediately. I allowed his rich chocolate and spice scent to fill my senses. I wanted to lie there all day, but I had other things I needed to do. After one last quick draw of his incredible scent, I climbed out of bed.

I had to work tonight, and I needed to drop off some dry cleaning and pick up some things from the drugstore before I went in for my shift. I turned on my stereo, jumped in the shower, and got dressed quickly.

On a whim, I grabbed my compact Glock and strapped it to my ankle, but not before I pulled out the magazine and made sure I had my special rounds in it. Then I clicked it back into place inside the gun. I grabbed another rig and put it on my other ankle. This one was for the two metal stakes I would carry. With everything that was happening, I couldn't be too careful.

The upbeat sounds of Rihanna played loudly from the speakers and helped to keep me in a good mood. I was still beaming as I skipped down the stairs.

I almost ran straight into Julian. "Whoa...Sorry, Jules, you turned around faster than I thought you would." I bypassed him, feeling light on my feet and singing the chorus of one of Rihanna's songs in my head.

Man...I was starving! I passed Julian and headed straight for the fridge, grabbing a bag of blood out of the compartment inside. I didn't even take the time to warm it up.

I passed a few flirtatious glances over to Trent, and embarrassed myself when I realized all these guys were asleep on the top floor—right near my room—while Trent and I made love last night. What must they think of us? Whatever, I'm an adult, I can do what I want.

Gabe grabbed me around the waist, being playful and laughing at me as he pulled me close to give me a hug. I felt Gabe stiffen and figured it was the usual male jealousy with Trent in the room. I didn't even acknowledge it and walked out the door, grabbing my shoulder bag from the foyer and yelling over my shoulder, "Let's go, Trent!"

Trent was quiet as I ran my errands and did my paperwork. Unlike with some people, the silence with him did not feel strained or strange. It was actually comforting. It is a rare person whom you can be around who doesn't feel the need to talk all the time. I liked people who didn't feel the need to prattle just because the air between them was silent.

I was digging into my reports from the night before, documenting everything we did from the time we arrived, to the people we dealt with, and how the incident ended. As I looked over my shoulder, Trent was reading behind me and seemed really engrossed in his article.

I just started the last report when the phone rang.

"Evening, Officer Greene. This is Trooper Reynolds from the State Police Hazelton barracks. I need some assistance from your department, if you don't mind."

"Sure, Trooper Reynolds, what can I help you with?" I grabbed some paper and my pen.

"I believe that four twenty-five Valley Springs Road is in your jurisdiction. Do you know that address?" His voice was solid, professional.

I blinked and put my hand up to the receiver to hold it as I straightened my neck. "Yeah, I know that address. It's mine," I responded, but my hackles were rising. I gripped the phone receiver harder.

"We found a vehicle yesterday in the area of Route 81 and 309. It had MapQuest directions in it to that address."

"Okay?" I said quietly.

"Do you know a Courtenay Montgomery? The vehicle is registered to her." I acknowledged the fact that I knew her, or more importantly, knew her brother Gabe, and my nerve endings began to tingle.

He took a deep breath. "We think she was possibly kidnapped."

"What?" The word barely came out of my mouth when Trent came over and sat down beside me. Courtenay was kidnapped! Did this have to do with Alex's kidnapping? What did Courtenay have to do with Alex or Burke?

"Videotape from the gas station shows she had just finished refueling her car, then two men walked up to her and pulled her away. We can't find any witnesses and the video is pretty bad. We have no idea where they took her or what kind of car they got into." He seemed frustrated. I knew the feeling.

"Amazing that no one said anything or came forward at the time. How did you guys get the call?" I asked, letting my frustration be heard in my voice now.

"Gas station attendant called to complain about someone leaving their car in front of the gas pump." He kind of laughed when he said it, but got serious very quickly as he asked the next question. "Do you know if she was involved with drugs?"

"No, Courtenay wasn't involved with any drugs that I know of. " I glanced at Trent and pulled the phone away from my ear so that her could hear. "Did you find something in her car?" I tried to keep from crushing the phone receiver in my hand. *Oh, please...Please don't say it.*

"There were a couple of little baggies in the car. Looks like some fancy new variation of cocaine."

My heart dropped.

"Is it a red powder?" I asked, as I stared absently out the front window. I knew what the answer would be. I knew what it meant. I couldn't help but shake, and I was thankful for Trent's touch right then.

"Yes, it is...I guess you know about it then. Well, we were going to ask you to make a notification to the person whom she was visiting, but I guess that has already been done. Will you tell her brother about what is going on? We'll be in touch when we know anything further." His voice was still radiating professionalism.

"Okay, thank you. Yes, I'll let her brother know. Here, take down my cellphone number. If you need anything or find anything out, please call me right away."

"What's going on, Kristin?" Trent watched me intently as I put the phone back into its cradle.

"Gabe's sister was kidnapped." I could barely get the words out, and I swallowed, hard. "It looks as if she was on her way down here. The police found MapQuest directions in her car with my address on it."

"What else did they say?" he asked pointedly.

I looked up at him. "There were two little baggies in her car with VBC in them." I swallowed again before I could get the next words out. "They have Courtenay." *Oh, God...Gabe's going to freak.*

I heard my phone ringing, but my hands felt frozen; it took me a second to get them to work. I removed my phone off of the belt clip. The screen said it was Livy. "What's up, Olivia?"

"Hey, Kristin, you know those cars you like to stop? Well, I have one. I'm getting ready to stop it. You want to come over?" Her voice was clear, and she sounded excited. My heart sped to a gallop as her words registered in my head. I was running out the station before I responded.

"I'm on my way. Where are you?" I responded. I was putting the car into drive as Trent closed the passenger door. Somewhere in my mind it registered that Mick had seen us. Would he follow us? I hoped not! I flipped on my overhead lights and turned the dial on my center console to start my siren.

"I'm going to stop it at Route 50 and Airdale Road," she said.

"Olivia, you listen to me. You stay in your car until I'm there. Do you understand that?" My heart was racing, pumping faster than my car was driving.

"I will," Liv replied, and I heard her siren over the speaker as she started to make the stop.

I drove more recklessly than I would have liked, but this was my chance, and I wasn't going to lose it.

I listened as Olivia called the stop out over the radio. Before she was done talking, I had the radio mic in my hand and told the dispatcher I was on my way to back her up. It took less than two minutes before I had her in my sights. I pulled up behind her and saw her sitting up straight in her seat watching the vehicle in front of her carefully as she was trained to do. Her eyes flickered to her rearview mirror as I stopped behind her.

I turned off my overhead lights. I didn't want to draw any more attention to our stop than was necessary. She had found a good place to pull them off, a side street with no homes near the roads.

The black Volvo sedan had the standard limo-tinted windows and Florida plate that I was used to seeing. My adrenaline was sky high.

"Olivia, listen to me, and listen carefully. I want you to get on the speaker in a minute and tell the driver to step out. Whatever you do, do *not* get out of your car, you got it?"

"Yep. Got it…Tell me when," she replied calmly.

I looked at Trent quickly. Would he do as I asked, or would he fight me? I knew what I was doing, and I needed him to trust me. "Trent, I need you to trust me on this and stay in the car until I say so."

He nodded once. I wondered for only a moment if my adrenaline was affecting him.

I opened my door, dropping to the ground in a crouch. Carefully, I reached for the backup weapon that I strapped on earlier. Was it only instinct that I wore it today? My Glock 27 felt heavy in my hands as I pulled it out. It was only a .40-caliber handgun, but with the special ammunition in it, it would serve my purpose.

I pulled it out of the holster and gripped it tightly. I moved between the police cars at a crouch. I needed to stay out of sight for as long as I could and keep my scent low. I whispered into my phone, "Go."

Olivia's voice came over the car's loudspeaker. "Driver, step out of the vehicle and put your hands in the air where I can see them." The door opened and the driver stepped out. I knew I would have only one chance at this, so it had to be perfect. He sniffed the air as I knew he would and immediately began to crouch, reaching for a weapon, probably very similar to what I was using. But he was too late; I was prepared and ready. I stood and took my shot as the passenger began to open his door.

I pulled the trigger twice and struck the driver in the head both times. He bounced back against the door from the thrust of the bullets striking his skull. I barely saw him fall to the ground as I spun on the passenger who was now standing upright beside the car.

At the same moment, I heard the door to my truck open and knew Trent was moving in to assist. I fired off two more shots at the passenger, placing one in his chest and the other in his leg to keep him from running; I needed him to be able to speak. As Trent reached me, I told him quietly, but loudly enough that I knew he would hear me, *"Don't kill the passenger. We need him."*

I dropped down on one knee beside the driver, and yanked a stake off my boot. I hissed as I slammed it right into the driver's heart and his body disintegrated before my eyes.

Before the dust even settled, I was rounding the other side of the car. "Get him off the ground!" I could barely say the words as the anger took hold of me.

Trent pulled him up off the ground.

"Where is he?" I yelled into the man's face. Trent had his arm wrapped tightly around the man's neck, keeping him upright.

The man didn't respond, and I threw a punch that any boxer would have been proud to call his own. I heard the crack and saw the blood spatter away from his mouth as his head spun sideways. "Where is he?" I asked again, more in control now.

He spat at the ground. "Don't know what you're talking about," he said.

Trent squeezed the man's throat tighter. "Tell the officer what she wants to know."

With my right hand, I slowly put the muzzle of my gun to his temple. I distantly noticed Trent shift his position behind the guy. I had to make sure I warned him before I fired into this man's head. I did not want to accidentally hurt Trent.

"I'm going to ask you again, and you can either tell me where he is, or you can die like your buddy. You tell me where he is, and I'll let you leave so that you can take a message to your boss." I felt his fear then.

He looked at me, pleading for his life. "Harvey's Lake. They have him at Harvey's Lake."

I looked at Trent. Trent nodded once to me, letting me know he spoke the truth. Oh, how I loved that he could do that.

"Move," I said quietly, and I knew he would know what I meant. Trent released the man and spun out of the way. As I fired the shot into his head, the man collapsed. As his face fell out of view, a new face came into my sight. Mick.

Mick stood there with disbelief written over his face, shock making his eyes wide and his skin pale. Oh man, this was not how I wanted my partner to find out about me. A gurgle from the ground brought my attention back to what I'd just done.

I stood over the man, looking at the wound I just put in his head. He wasn't dead yet, but I had seriously injured him. With a vengeance, I bent down and slammed my stake through his chest to make contact with his heart. I relished the whoosh of sound that came as his body disappeared before me.

I was still down on one knee, staring at the dust as it got caught in the air movement around us. Mick spoke from behind Trent. "What the hell are you?"

I looked up to see Trent raise his hands in a calming gesture. "Officer...this is not a good time to explain all of this."

I moved next to Trent. What was the use in hiding it anymore? Might as well tell it how it is. "Mick, we're vampires. You've been asking me for a long time to tell you what was wrong with me. Well, now you know."

As I got closer to him, his eyes just got wider. I turned to look at Olivia as she walked around her car. "Liv, you all right?"

"Yep, I'm good. Kris, your eyes are freaky...They're glowing!"

I shrugged. I didn't care what my eyes looked like right now. I knew something now, something that would help us to find Alex. I holstered my gun and stake. "Liv," I said, and glanced over at Mick, "do you mind explaining this to him? We need to get out of here."

Olivia laughed. "Sure, I'll try to explain it to him. You guys get out of here. You know where Alex is now, so go. I'll deal with Mick."

As I walked away, I saw Olivia glance over at Mick, his eyes practically popping out of his skull. I heard her say, "Oh, Mick, relax. I'm human! I'm not going to hurt you. I'm just going to fill you in on what you need to know."

Trent stayed and said something to Olivia before climbing into the truck beside me, and I drove away from the scene. I took my phone back off my belt and pulled up my chief's contact information.

"Yeah, Kristin, what's going on?" came his reply shortly after I hit him up.

"Chief, I have a family emergency. I need to get out of here. Mick's out on the street. Just wanted to give you a heads-up."

"Everything all right?" he asked, sounding sincere.

"Yeah, nothing I can't handle." I knew I was being rude, but I didn't have the time to be anything else.

"Let me know if I can help with anything." He sounded concerned, and it was probably because I was being so short. I never acted this way.

"Okay, thanks. I might need to take tomorrow night off. Can you find someone to cover for me?"

"Yeah, I will," he responded.

"Thanks, Chief." I put my phone back on my belt and made my way to the station. I had not looked at Trent or said anything to him since we left the traffic stop. I didn't know what was going through his mind. I had acted like a crazy woman, and I wasn't sure what he thought about all of that. It really didn't matter what he thought; I tried to tell myself that, anyway.

As we pulled up to the station, I walked inside to do a quick report for the assist I had just done. Of course, I lied through my teeth on it. Then I started to break down out of my uniform. Trent stayed outside, saying he needed to call Julian and let him know what was going on. I slammed my locker shut and ran out of the station without looking back.

Trent was waiting for me to throw him my keys to start the Challenger, and I put the truck into the bay. When I jumped into the passenger seat, Trent took off.

We knew approximately where Alex was. Now we just needed to get him. Fear and anger raced through my blue-blooded veins with every pump of my heart. I looked out the window into the darkness around us and wondered what was going to happen once we got him back.

CHAPTER THIRTY-TWO

TRENT

*K*ristin was almost in a trance as she drove back to the station. The intensity of how she had just dealt with the situation stunned me. Her anger possessed her in a way I had never seen on anyone. The way she moved, the way she shot, the way she took down the two men was astounding! Before tonight, I thought she was an excellent officer, but seeing her deal out justice for our way of life, well, it just made her a true warrior in my eyes.

I loved this woman. Jesus, I loved every single thing about her. From her magical eyes that changed with each and every emotion to her zeal for life and the way she fought. The fact that I just concluded that I did love this woman scared the hell out of me. It would only lead to heartache for me. How could I fall so hard, so quick?

As hard as I tried, I couldn't take my eyes off her as she drove. Her eyes were slowly going back to a normal color, but they still remained a deep shade of gray. She never looked at me, and I realized that now that she had an idea of where Alex was, she was totally focused on that. She might not even remember that I was sitting in the car with her.

She climbed out of the truck and went right into the station, not even turning around when I told her I was going to stay outside to call Julian.

The entire ride back to the house, she looked out the window, somber, intent, and lost in her own mind. I wanted to reach out to her, speak with her as I knew our time was limited to only a few more hours together, but I kept quiet. I kept my thoughts to myself.

We entered the house, and Kristin went straight to the kitchen. Everyone was gathered inside, and they stopped talking and watched as she went straight to the fridge and grabbed another bag of blood. She tore it open and downed the bag before she turned to them. "When are we leaving?" she asked as she looked at Julian.

Julian exchanged a glance with Gabe, and then looked at me. I saw something that I didn't like. Julian turned his attention to Kristin. "We're leaving in a few minutes, but you're not going, Kristin."

Oh, man…That was *not* going to go over well at all. The strange glow came back to her eyes for a second as she stared him down from across the room. Julian visibly flinched under her look, but he held his position.

"Yeah, wrong answer. I'm going, Julian." She stood ram-rod straight—her shoulders squared, her chin tipped up—and glared him down. I felt the tension running through the bond she had with me, and I almost walked up behind her to try to calm her down. Almost…

"No, you need to stay here, Kristin. I'm not going to put you in any more danger," he said evenly.

"It's not your choice. We are going after Alex. Alex is mine. I'm going." She stalked closer to him as she spoke. When the words "Alex is mine" came out of her mouth, every eye in the room flicked to me, every eye except for hers, and it took everything in me not to react.

Kristin was almost the same height as Julian, and while she was nowhere near as wide as he was, she looked formidable standing there staring him down. Julian glanced over at me. *"Trent, you have to talk some sense into her. She can't go. We can't afford for her to get hurt."*

"I see no reason why she shouldn't go, Julian. If you don't want her to be there, then you need to talk her into staying." I turned and left the room.

"Trent, there is a perfectly good reason she shouldn't go! You just can't see

it yet! You need to talk her out of it. She'll listen to you," Julian said more forcefully, though still silently.

"Nope. She's not my problem anymore. And after what I saw tonight, she can handle herself just fine." I was shaking as I got to the stairs. No, now that we were going to get Alex, she wasn't my problem anymore.

"Trent!" Julian shouted in my mind. I ignored him and took the stairs two at a time.

When I got to the third floor, I refused to look toward Kristin's room. I walked into the room I had been using and packed my things into my duffle bag. A few minutes later, I heard Kristin's door close across the hall and I went downstairs to put my bag into the back of one of the trucks that we would be taking.

My heart was heavy, but I squared my shoulders and headed back into the kitchen. I listened as Julian gave out the orders and spoke on the phone to a couple of the guys who were already up in the area keeping an eye on the place. They had seen a lot of movement, and it looked as if we had the right place.

As we were getting our final orders, Kristin came in dressed in black BDUs, a tight-fitting thermal shirt, and a different pair of work boots. She wore two firearms strapped tightly to her sides in a pretty fancy shoulder holster. Her face was more determined than I had ever seen it. She glanced at me briefly, and I thought I saw something flash across her face before she looked away. She looked beautiful standing there, a warrior angel among us.

She went to Gabe and put her arm around his waist, squeezing gently. Gabe looked murderous; there really was no other word for it. Now that he knew his sister was a victim in this, the nice guy image was replaced by a violent warrior who was ready to fight to the death. He held Kristin close, shooting me a menacing look before he surrendered to her comforting arms.

"You stay by my side, Kristin, you got that?" Gabe said as he held her. She nodded and pulled back from him. She stayed by his side in the kitchen until it was time to leave.

As Julian once again confirmed where we were going and who would be doing what, we exited the house and climbed into the two

Tahoes that were parked in the driveway. Julian was driving one of them while Cameron drove the other. I was riding with Cameron.

I followed Fitz over to the truck and tried hard not to look over my shoulder as I heard Kristin speaking softly to Julian behind me. As I got to the rear door, I couldn't hold back anymore.

Kristin stood at the rear passenger door talking to Julian, quietly but fiercely. Julian huffed and turned to climb into the truck. Kristin glanced my way, and in that moment, I wanted to tell her to stay here. I wanted to tell her to wait here, for me. I wanted to tell her I loved her and I didn't want to lose her, but once again, I didn't.

She stared at me, and pain crossed her face. I saw something else too, but I didn't want to believe it. *"Be safe, Trent,"* she whispered as she turned and climbed into the Tahoe without looking back.

"You too," I answered as I climbed into the truck next to me.

"Always..." she responded.

"For life..." I said to her as the trucks started to move. Sadness washed over me, and I was not sure if it was mine or hers.

I put my head back against the seat and put up my mental wall. I needed to focus. My heart was breaking, but I would do everything in my power to make sure that hers did not. I would make sure that she got Alex back, and that she was happy. It was all I had left to give her.

The rest of the ride to the Poconos was quiet. Last-minute details came from the headsets we all wore, but for the most part, everyone kept to themselves. It did not take long to get to our meeting place where we picked up two other men who climbed into the truck with Kristin. I didn't see her, and I didn't try to communicate with her.

I already said my good-bye.

I watched as her truck took off and we waited a few moments for them to get ahead of us. Two black Tahoes traveling so closely together would alert someone who might be watching. A few minutes later we pulled out and made our way to the address we had obtained, a chalet out in the woods near Harvey's Lake.

We parked a couple of miles away and got out on foot. We were as silent as the forest around us, moving lighter and quicker than humans could even think possible. It was colder up here in the mountains, but not cold enough for the ground to have totally frozen yet.

We slowed as we got closer to our destination. We knew that the other group, the one with Kristin, was close to making contact with the target from the other side. They just reported seeing multiple threats in the front and side yard, vampires and humans alike. A moment of fear passed through me, not for myself, but for Kristin. What if she got hurt? What if she was killed? I should have sided with Julian and tried to get her to stay.

Cameron put his hand on my arm and very quietly said, "Don't think about it." He turned and walked silently toward the house. How did he know what I was thinking?

"I can read your mind. I can read everyone's mind, walls or not," he said as he walked away.

*Damn...*Should I be embarrassed at the thoughts I'd had in his presence?

I heard him snicker. Yeah, he heard that, too.

I followed him. We barely had visual when I heard gunshots coming from near the house. We moved in from our side, and within seconds, we took out a few of the vampires that had come our way.

Fitz was carrying an AR-15 rifle, and he took down two from a safe distance. The guys who were outside the house were neutralized, and I heard glass breaking as the other team made entry into the back of the house.

I had not seen Kristin in the action and wondered if Julian had talked her into staying in the truck. I doubted it, but maybe.

We got closer to the house and took time to stake the vampires that had fallen from our hits. They quickly disappeared into dust as we approached the house. Two human bodies remained. We would take care of them once business was finished.

I heard shots coming from inside, and then someone yelled. I heard two pairs of feet running toward the woods, and I ran to see a man and woman moving fast in the opposite direction. The woman was the same one we had seen in the bar, Angie, Burke's daughter. I didn't know who the man was with her, but I knew it wasn't Burke.

They took off into the woods, running at a speed only vampires could achieve.

I took off after them. "Cam, I got two taking off toward the north," I called out over the headset.

"Copy...coming your way." I heard him behind me, and we set off into the woods on the other side. They had a good head start, and we heard car doors slamming and an engine starting as we raced through the woods. An instant later, we got a visual on them as they sped off down a dirt lane.

Cam fired off a couple of shots with the rifle, but it wasn't enough to stop the vehicle, and it got away. We would hunt her down and find her later.

We turned to go back toward the house. Gabe came over the headset. "We've got Alex and Courtenay. They're alive." I stopped dead in my tracks, almost tipping over at the abrupt halt of my forward movement. Of course I wanted them to be alive, but I realized that part of me had been wondering if, just maybe, I might still have a chance.

We jogged back and Cam headed toward the house, while I made my way to the other side. There was no way I could face either one of them right now, so I headed back to the truck.

As I stepped into the woods on the other side of the property, I heard Cameron behind me ask someone, "Did we get Burke?"

Gabe laughed as he answered through the headset, "Yeah, Kristin wiped him out!" So Kristin had been in there. I turned around to look back at the house. It was quiet now, peaceful here in the woods, but I felt no peace.

I caught Cameron's eye. *"I'm going back to the truck,"* I thought, and he nodded. Then I yanked the earpiece out of my ear from the headset. I didn't want or need to hear anything else.

I was numb as I arrived at the truck. I should have been satisfied that we accomplished our mission and rescued Alex and Courtenay. Sadly, I leaned back against the side of the SUV and looked up at the stars. A memory of the night we stood under them near the lake came back to me, and I remembered the taste of her as I ran my tongue down her neck. I shivered and felt pain lance through my heart. I would never know that taste again.

I was still staring up at the stars when Cameron, Fitz, and the other four men we picked up came back to the truck. Cameron studied me but said nothing. Neither did I. We all piled back into the truck and drove down to the highway.

"You need to go back to the house, Trent?" Fitz asked me quietly from the front seat.

"No, I have nothing left there. I'll just go with you all and find my way to an airport." I put my head back against the seat.

Kristin did not belong to me any longer...She was back with Alex. I really had nothing left there.

Fitz looked over the seat at me. "You sure about that?"

I fisted my hands and stared out the passenger window. "Yeah, I'm sure."

CHAPTER THIRTY-THREE

KRISTIN

hen we arrived back at the house, I still had not said anything to Trent. He was stone-cold quiet next to me. Ever since I had taken those two vampires out on Olivia's traffic stop, he hadn't said a word. He probably thought I was possessed. Maybe at that particular moment, I was.

I didn't know what to say to him. My thoughts kept running back to Alex and the fact that we now had a pretty good idea of where he was. What was going to happen when we found him? How was Alex going to react when he found out I had mated with Trent? How was I going to handle it when Alex took me back? I didn't have answers for these questions. Did I even want to go back to Alex now that I'd shared something so incredible with Trent?

I was starved and went straight for the fridge, grabbing a bag of blood and tearing it open. I couldn't believe that I could be hungry right now, but maybe it was the extra use of adrenaline that had caused me to burn through the blood I consumed earlier today. Although, even after feeding off of Trent last night, I still felt hungry this morning. Maybe my body was starting to transition more. Who knew? I would figure it out later.

"When are we leaving?" I felt the shift in the room as Julian glanced at Gabe and Trent. I realized that we were about to have a problem. I steeled myself for what I knew he was about to say.

"We are leaving in a few minutes, but you are not going, Kristin." I felt the earlier anger whip through my blood. Julian actually flinched as I looked at him.

"Yeah, wrong answer. I'm going, Julian." There was no way I was staying here. I had every right to go. I could take care of myself.

"No, you need to stay here, Kristin. I'm not going to put you in any more danger." Julian stared me down, his jeweled eyes bright.

"It's not your choice. We are going after Alex. Alex is mine. I'm going." I stepped closer to him as I spoke. *Oh crap...Did I really just say, "Alex is mine"?* It took every ounce of my strength not to look at Trent when everyone else did. I felt the tension spin almost out of control.

Julian looked at Trent, and I knew they were talking. I waited as anger washed over Julian's features, getting worse as Trent stalked out of the room.

I almost hung my head. No matter what he felt for me, my words had hurt him. I felt the betrayal he'd experienced zip straight to my heart. My intention was not to hurt Trent, but to make Julian realize I had every right to be there. Alex being in this trouble was my fault. I owed it to him to be there.

I almost called out to Trent, but I needed to finish this with Julian. Julian turned back to me. "Kristin, do you have any idea how mad Alex will be at me if you are there?"

"Do you know how much I really don't give a fucka?" I said quietly. "I'm either going with you, or I will go on my own. I am just as trained as some of the people who are going. I think I proved that today."

I was not joking, I knew where we were heading, and if I had to go on my own, I would. I kept glaring at Julian, waiting for him to say something. Julian glanced over at Cameron. I saw him nod out of the corner of my eye.

"Julian, let her come. I'll take responsibility for her," Gabe said from behind me. I didn't need someone to be responsible for me, but if it got me there, then fine.

Julian looked at Gabe. "Okay, she's with you, but if you let anything happen to her, I swear I will kill you before Alex even gets the chance."

I almost smiled at my victory, but I spun on my heel and rubbed Gabe's arm as I passed by and went to change clothes. My shoulders sagged the moment I left the room. When I got to the third floor, I stopped. Should I try to talk to Trent now, or should I just wait till this was all over?

I was about to step toward his door when I chickened out. I hung my head and went to my room, closing the door. I would apologize to him after it was over. Try to get him to understand.

I pulled out a pair of my training BDUs, grabbed a long-sleeved thermal Under Armour shirt, and laced up my thermal boots. We would be traveling through the woods, and I knew the Poconos were colder than where we were, especially at night.

After that, I grabbed one of my shoulder rigs, a special black leather rig that held two full-sized Glock 22's snuggly against my sides. I strapped it on and pulled two firearms from the safe where I kept them. I released the magazines that were inside and replaced them with ones that contained the ammunition I would need tonight. Then I tucked the extra four magazines into the holders I had clipped to my belt.

I stopped and looked in the mirror before I left my room. I looked tough, mean, and yes, possessed, my eyes a shade of gray I had not seen before. When I went back down to the kitchen everyone was there, including Trent. I glanced at him. I wanted to tell him we would talk later, tell him that I was sorry, tell him that this was painful for me, but I didn't. I looked away.

I knew that Gabe was hurting; I could see it in his eyes. Gabe needed me more than Trent's bruised ego did. He pulled me into his arms, and I felt him shaking, the anger almost uncontrollable. I knew what he was feeling too well, way too well.

"You stay by my side, Kristin, you got that?" he said to me as he pulled back. I listened as Julian told all of us who was riding with whom and how the raid would play out. It was exactly like any police briefing would be as the SWAT team was getting ready to move.

We left the house, and I followed Gabe and Julian out to our truck. Julian asked me again to stay behind, but I told him there was no way in hell that was going to happen. He shook his head knowing he was beat.

Trent was watching me. The thought of not seeing him again when this was over, of never being with him, never making love to him again, was like a knife cutting through my chest. I realized at this moment that I felt more than I ever wanted to about him.

"Be safe, Trent," I said the words softly from my mind to his. It was what all cops said as they went into a raid. I climbed into the truck and pulled the door closed without looking back. If I had looked at him, he might have seen the tears in my eyes.

"You too," he whispered back to me.

"Always..." was all I could say in response.

"For life..." came very softly to my mind, and a painful sob left my throat. I closed my eyes and threw up the wall around my mind. I couldn't hear one more thing from him. I was not strong enough for that. I opened my eyes to find Gabe observing me, and he reached back and put his hand on my knee. I felt a calmness seep into me.

I reached into one of the pockets of my BDUs and pulled out a set of headphones that I plugged into my cell phone and turned on my music. I needed to prepare myself for what was to come. Would Alex be alive? Would Burke be there? Would we get to Courtenay in time?

I put my elbow on the door handle and rested my chin on my fist. A song by Placebo, "Running Up That Hill," started playing in my ears. The beat of the tune so close to that of a heartbeat caused my thoughts and memories to race through my mind like the blood running through my veins.

Pictures of my life seemed to flash to the beat; pictures of my mother, the beautiful woman I never got to meet in person. Only through the few photographs and stories from her friend Rose had I known her. The father I also never knew, the man who left before I was born. Images of Rose, the woman who raised me, birthdays, holidays, shopping, laughing, and the day I sat by her bed when she lost the fight with cancer.

My time in the police academy, the feeling as if I had found something I was good at, knew that I had chosen the correct career. Meeting Trevor, my human husband; the memories of our wedding, the pain of his funeral.

The night my life changed: Dawn's death, Julian's eyes, Alex's explanation of whom I was and why I was different. My memories of Calista and the life-and-death fight with Damon. The choice I made between Julian and Alex, and finally feeling as if I belonged someplace; as if I know whom I might really be.

The thoughts just kept coming, faster and faster, flipping through my mind's eye at epic speeds. As the thoughts raced, my emotions from the past roared through me and tore at my soul.

The loss, the loneliness, the love all pulled at me now. The frustration of feeling as though Alex didn't really know me; that Julian still looked at me as if I was Calista. The constant pressure from Alex to finish our bond, even though I always said I wasn't ready. The pain I felt from him through our bond, and now knowing that I had something to do with why Burke had taken him.

Trent's eyes flashed into my mind, so similar to Alex's, but different too. The color the same, but the depth in his eyes was deeper, like you were reaching down into his soul and not being held at arm's length. The words he had spoken while we joked at work. The sound of his voice was so clear in my head along with the feel of his lips against mine. His scent forever imprinted in my memory.

I watched the bare trees blur past us as we drove; headlights from other cars racing by. My music played on and on in my ear; the memories and moments of my life flashing like the car lights across my face.

We stopped after I don't know how long and picked up two other men who were going in with us. I nodded at both of them, but I honestly didn't care who they were. I had no words to say to anyone at this moment. I went back to looking out the window, forcing myself to focus on the job before us.

We would be coming in from the north through the woods. Our team would make the first contact, and head directly to the chalet after we took out as many people on the outside as we could. It was our job to get to Alex.

As we got closer, I felt my heart pumping steadily, the adrenaline slowly leaching into my body, but not running swiftly yet. I knew that it would soon. We pulled up to the spot where we would get out on foot, and Gabe walked around to me as I made sure my firearms were loaded and ready to go one last time. He put his hand on my shoulder, but I knew it was not to calm me down. I was calmer than I expected to be.

Quiet instructions were given over the headsets that we all wore, and we spanned out and started heading toward the chalet where Alex was being kept. With Julian to my left, and Gabe to my right, slightly closer, we moved silently through the dark, cold woods. After about twenty minutes, we could all pick up on the scents from around the house. One of the other guys whom we picked up earlier put his hand up to stop us. We all stood still at his signal and waited for him to move forward to get eyes on the target.

He flashed fingers to show us how many were outside. We would not use our headsets this close; they would hear us. When the signal was given, we moved forward, silently traveling through the brush and trees until we all had eyes on the people around the house.

I had one of my firearms out, low by my side. I trained my eye on one subject that was directly in my line of sight. Then I slowly raised my gun, looking down my front sights and lining them up with his head. I was not the first to shoot, but I was right behind the first trigger pulled.

The cracking of guns being fired was quick and proficient. All the men in front of us quickly went down. The smell of gunpowder hung heavily in the air. I inhaled it, a slight smile on my lips as we quickly moved forward. Someone spoke over the headset; we moved faster, taking out all of the men in the front, human and vampire alike.

I followed Julian's lead as we moved toward the back side of the house. Gabe was right behind me. We were cautious, looking in all directions as we moved, listening to every detail that we could. Julian fired two shots into the back sliding door and the glass shattered and fell to the ground. We moved in.

I stepped into the room, moving to the opposite side from where Julian entered, and cleared the space. I saw movement coming around a corner and immediately fired two shots taking down the male vampire that had been entering the room. I moved to his side, glanced around the corner to make sure there were no more threats, then grabbed a stake off my belt with my left hand and plunged it into his heart. The whoosh of his body left me feeling high.

We continued to move, clearing rooms. We heard Trent speaking over the headset. Someone was running through the woods to the north. It was the job of the second group to clean up and take out anyone who got outside once we were inside. Hearing Trent's voice made me stumble a second, but I quickly caught my balance and moved silently down the hallway.

I felt a pull going through my body. It made me focus on a door at the end of the hallway. I moved toward it, and felt someone behind me. It was probably Gabe. I didn't turn around to look. Instead, I focused on the door in front of me.

I reached the door and listened. No sounds were coming from the other side, but the pull was strong, and I grabbed the doorknob. As the door swung open, I saw steps to the basement. Was this where they were keeping Alex? I glanced behind me and saw not only Gabe, but Julian too. Gabe nodded and the three of us moved down the stairs slowly, listening intently with all our senses for any other presence.

We saw no one as we got to the bottom, but the pull was strong for me here. The room had large lights set up around a circle. Inside the circle was a wooden chair with dried blood caked to the ground around it. Anger welled up inside of me, and I forced myself to breathe.

On the other side of the room was a large metal structure, a cell. We knew this was where Alex was. Julian and Gabe moved around me and started toward the cell. My feet felt frozen to the ground. We had found him, and yet I could not move forward. I watched as they closed the distance to the door and started to open it up.

I realized as I stood there watching them that the pull was not coming from the cell; it was coming from *behind* me. I was about to turn to see what was calling to me and heard the whoosh of movement before I felt it. Before I could react, an arm wrapped tightly around my throat and I was being held against someone. My handgun was ripped from my hand and thrown across the room.

The magnetic pull I felt was coming from the man who was clutching me. I looked up to find both Julian and Gabe staring at me with wide eyes. Alex stepped quickly through the now open door.

His dark green eyes flashed to my face, and then to the man who held me. His body was rigid with anger, matching the stances of Julian and Gabe. I had only enough time to realize that Alex was alive and well before he spoke to the man holding me.

The arm around my neck tightened, and I couldn't have spoken if I wanted to.

"Burke, let her go." Alex's voice was as hard as steel. Burke...

The pull I felt had led me to him. Had led me down the stairs to where he was. How had my body known to feel for him? How had I not known he was behind me? I tried to keep myself calm, but the pulse in my body was deafening as it drummed heavily in my ears, causing my tension to ratchet up a notch.

Burke laughed from behind me, the movement causing his arm to tighten even more around my throat. "I don't think that's going to happen, Alex. You might be free, but there is no way Kristin is walking out of here alive."

Julian was staring at me. Maybe he was trying to talk to me, but I had my wall up. I would not drop it down. I did not want to hear what anyone had to say, did not want to think about what they were thinking, and the last thing I wanted to do was to alert Trent. I had put myself in this position, and I would get myself out of it.

I saw a woman walk out of the cell behind Alex and move toward Gabe. Courtenay. Thank God, she was safe. Gabe had his eyes locked on Burke, as did Alex.

"I'm not leaving without her, Burke," Alex said tightly.

"Why do you even care, Alex? You are already mated to someone else now. She's of no use to you." Burke sneered at Alex.

I froze at his words. I know my eyes were wide from surprise. Alex had mated with Courtenay? Holy crap! I saw Gabe glance at Alex, and then back to me. Julian's head turned quickly to look at Alex, and then he looked back at Courtenay, too. She actually looked embarrassed as she peered around Gabe at me.

I focused on Alex. He never made eye contact with me. He stared at Burke with hatred burning in his eyes. I could feel his tension from across the room. I was not expecting the twisted smile that came over his face, the slight upturning of his lips, nor was I prepared for the next words that left his mouth.

"You will not hurt your daughter, Burke."

What the hell did he just say? His daughter? What drugs had they given Alex while he was locked up?

I felt the tightness around my neck loosen just a tiny bit. Was it possible? The pull...knowing I needed to come down here. Was I drawn to Burke's blood? If Burke had let go of me then, I would have fallen to the ground in shock.

"What? Burke, you haven't figured it out yet? Kristin is Angelina's twin sister, your *other* daughter. You can't see it? Can you feel it? I can from all the way over here. I feel your bond with her, can smell your blood in her body," Alex spoke angrily. He glanced at me once, but looked back at Burke just as fast.

Even though his hold on me had loosened, I felt as if I was choking, felt as if I was running out of air. My mind started to spin, started to blacken around the edges as if I was going to pass out. *Burke's daughter...*I thought I was going to be sick, but he was right. I could feel the pull my body had to his. The natural pull to be close to its own blood.

Angelina was my twin sister? There was no way. I would deny that pull till the day I died. I would die today before I allowed this man to be a father to me or to accept that Angelina was my sister. My mind instantly began to clear, started to form a plan.

"It doesn't matter if she is my daughter. It's obvious that she's on the wrong side of the line. She means nothing to me." Burke spit out the words with venom.

It only further steeled my resolve. Everyone was focused on Burke. I shifted ever so slightly to the side, turning my head so that my chin faced into his elbow, sliding my right shoulder back just a tiny bit so it was flat against his chest. I braced my feet the best I could against the hard concrete ground.

"You would kill your own daughter, Burke?" Alex asked coldly.

I waited for his answer, although it would not matter what he said. My plan was solid. It was only a matter of a simple movement and I would put it into action.

"Of course I would kill her," he spat at Alex.

Yeah, wrong answer, asshole, I thought right before I moved. My eyes locked on Alex. *This is for you. Or, maybe, this is for me.*

In a move that I learned back in the police academy, I reached up and grabbed the arm that held my neck tightly. Then I bent my knees, while simultaneously rounding my back, causing Burke to go slightly off balance.

Immediately, my chin dug into the space near his elbow so that I could pull the arm off my neck as he fell. I continued in a swift fluid movement and held his arm tightly as I continued to round my spine and flip Burke straight over my back.

Burke, unprepared for my action, flew over my head and onto the floor in a quick flip. It all happened so fast, but I saw it in slow motion as it happened: the look on his face as he went to the ground, his other arm reaching out to grab something to stop his downward descent.

I held his right arm tightly as my left hand reached to my belt. I pulled the stake out without thought, and as Burke's body made contact with the ground, my eyes found his. We were upside down looking at each other. My eyes watched as his changed color from blue to gray. His mouth opened in surprise as I dropped to one knee.

Without words, thoughts, or emotions, I stabbed Burke through the heart with the stake I held in my left hand. The pressure of the strike went deep into his chest, right into his heart, and I fell to both knees as the whoosh of his demise swallowed me for a brief second. Pain raced through my blood and into my mind, and I roared. My hands fell to the ground into the ash of his existence.

My father, the man I wondered about my entire life, had been my enemy. The scum of this earth and I had taken his life. I should have felt proud, but at that moment, I was numb.

No one spoke, no one moved. I knew all eyes were on me as I sat on the ground on all fours, staring down into the dust of the man who created me.

Julian came to my side and pulled me up. I was not sure if I would be able to stand. My legs felt like jelly under me. He kept his arm around me as I looked up into the eyes of Alex.

CHAPTER THIRTY-FOUR

ALEX

*C*ourtenay and I lay on the bed, speaking for hours, talking about everything and nothing in particular. She was a smart woman who had a passion for life. Family was important to her, and it was obvious how much her brother meant to her. I could only imagine the relationship they had together.

Does Gabe know she's missing? Does he have any idea that Burke has her? What will Gabe think when he finds out that I mated with his sister? Man, what was Kristin going to say?

We just started talking about places she wanted to visit around the world when a tension started to run through my body. Somewhere in me, I felt a stirring. I sat up straighter on the bed. Something was going on, and my instincts were telling me things were about to change very quickly.

"You okay, Alex?" Courtenay asked.

"Shh…" I said quietly. I listened intently, trying to reach out as hard as I could, to fight against the walls that held me. A sound came from the other side of the wall, a small popping sound. Gunshot?

I stood up. "Courtenay, stay there. I want you to stay as far back as you can."

She didn't question me and I heard her move back into the corner of the bed. I almost laughed. If that had been Kristin, she would have not only asked, but demanded to know what was going on.

I did not hear anything else for a long time. Then suddenly, someone was at the door and it was opening. As soon as it opened, I felt Gabe, Julian, and Kristin on the other side, but there was someone else there also.

As Gabe pulled open the door I stepped out, just as Burke grabbed Kristin around the throat. The sight of Kristin in his arms burned deep into me, and I felt fire ignite in my veins.

"Burke, let her go," I said through clenched teeth.

I did not respond to what he said about my mating; instead, I used the little piece of knowledge that I had been able to figure out. The eyes so similar, the way they moved, the smell of their blood. I didn't think he had any idea, and this would be to my advantage.

"You will not hurt your daughter, Burke." I didn't look at anyone else. I continued to talk to him. "What? Burke, you haven't figured it out yet? Kristin is Angelina's twin sister, your *other* daughter. You can't see it? Can you feel it? I can from all the way over here. I feel your bond with her, can smell your blood in her body," I almost yelled at him. I couldn't help but glance at Kristin as I finished my sentence.

Her eyes were wide, a shade of gray I had never seen before, almost silver. I looked back at Burke.

His eyes flashed a darker gray, and his lips lifted in an evil sneer. "Of course, I would kill her."

Kristin began to move, her eyes staring deeply into mine, glowing in the strange silver color they had become. I watched as she flipped Burke to the ground over her back. The look of surprise on his face was priceless.

She was down on her knee as soon as his body touched the ground. A stake raised high in her left hand. She slammed the stake down through his chest, and his body instantly disintegrated around her. She fell to her knees, and I knew the pain she must feel from the blood bond she just destroyed. He was her father, and she would feel an incredible pain as his body went to ash.

She fell to the ground with a roar I had not thought her capable of.

Hands and knees on the ground in Burke's ashes, she stared down, not moving. Julian went to her side as Gabe reached behind him and grabbed his sister fiercely in a hug.

I watched as Julian pulled Kristin up off the ground. She was unsteady and leaned into him. He wrapped an arm around her as she caught her bearings and looked up at me. I was unprepared for the amount of pain and anguish that was in her eyes. I felt my feet responding before I consciously made the decision to move.

I pulled her into my arms. Closing my eyes, I leaned down to bury my face into her neck and froze. The scent that hit me was not what I was expecting. I knew she was mated to Trent—I could feel the bond in my blood—but *this* I had totally not expected.

I heard Julian in my mind. *"She doesn't know, Alex...Be careful what you say."*

"How could she not know?" I shot back to him.

"She's been kind of busy lately; she hasn't figured it out yet."

I stood and kept Kristin tight to me, letting her rest her head against my chest. I looked at Julian over Kristin's head.

"Does he know?" Julian's response to my question was a small shake of his head. I clenched my eyes shut as I heard Gabe talking behind me.

"Yeah, Kristin wiped him out!" He must have been talking over the headset, because Kristin reached up and yanked the earpiece out of her ear.

"Did you find Angelina?" I asked Julian as I stood there still holding Kristin. She stiffened in my arms.

"No, she got away with another male," Gabe said from behind us. "Trent and Cameron chased them in to the woods, but they got away."

Kristin pulled away, not meeting my eyes. She turned and tried to walk away, and I pulled her back. "Kristin, are you okay?" I tilted her face up to look at mine.

Her eyes were no longer glowing, but they were still a strange color, almost liquid silver. She swallowed and I thought she was going to speak, but she pulled out of my grasp and walked to the stairs.

"Give her some time, Alex. A lot of shit just happened here," Julian said as he watched her walk away.

We all followed her up the stairs and out the back door. She stayed several feet in front of us. Gabe and Courtenay were talking quietly behind us. I turned to check on her, and she smiled at me. Gabe gave me a look that was loaded with questions. Questions that I didn't have answers for.

Someone had brought one of the Tahoes to the house, and we all climbed in. I sat up front with Julian, while Gabe sat in the back between Kristin and Courtenay. Kristin was seated behind Julian, so I could easily turn and look at her. She avoided my eyes, putting in earphones and resting her head against the window. She had not said a word to me yet.

As she closed her eyes, I could tell she was trying to shut out the pictures of what happened tonight. I saw her try to hide the emotions as they traveled over her face. She was in pain, immense pain, and I could do nothing to help her. Gabe reached over to Kristin and put his hand on her knee.

She pushed his hand off. Gabe and I both sighed, and I turned back around to talk to Julian about how they had figured out where I was.

During the ride home, Julian and Gabe filled me in on everything they had found out. I was shocked to realize that Kristin had been so deeply involved in this, just as Burke had stated. I had had no idea that she was involved. Actually, there was very little I knew about what she did in her job.

Everyone in the car was careful not to mention Trent. None of us were aware of how much or how little Kristin was paying attention to our conversation. I looked over my shoulder again to see that she had not moved since she got into the truck. Was she sleeping or just lost in her thoughts?

When we arrived back at the VMF house, Kristin got out without a word and walked into the house. She walked straight up the stairs, and I bent down to pet a very excited Garda who rubbed up against my legs to welcome me home. I watched Kristin as she disappeared on the second-story landing turn that led to the third-story flight of stairs.

Everyone stood in the foyer until we all heard a door close. Gabe spoke first. "Court, let's go get you cleaned up, then we'll get you some food." He took her arm and started to head up the stairs. Courtenay glanced at me, a shy smile on her lips. I managed to return the gesture.

I followed Julian into the living room where he walked over to the bar and poured two large glasses of Crown Royal. I sank down in one of the chairs and reached for the glass as he handed it to me.

"How bad was it, Julian?" I asked him as he settled down onto the couch.

He raised his eyebrows while he took a drink from his glass. "It could have been worse," he said after he swallowed. "Of course, she freaked out when she found out you told us to break the bond."

I thought about the bond and remembered it had been more than the bond breaking; it had been a mating. "Did he intentionally mate with Kristin?"

He shook his head as soon as I started to speak. "No. Trust me, he was pretty upset about the whole thing, at first." He looked down at his drink.

"At first?" Why just at first? Why not now? I took a sip of my drink, enjoying the burn the whiskey had on my throat.

"Don't get me wrong here, Alex. He never intended to mate with her. He was just doing as you asked." He looked up at me. "The thing is, the two of them just kind of hit it off after that. It seemed different with them. Different than it was with Calista and me, and even different than the way things were with you and her."

They had hit it off. Of course they would hit it off, Trent and Kristin were so much alike. "Why didn't you do it, Julian?" I asked as I looked at the empty fireplace.

"Alex, if I had done it, I would not have been able to give her back to you. You know how I feel about her. I thought it would be easier if Trent did it." He laughed. "I guess it just got messed up all the way around."

Wasn't that the truth? I nodded, finding the irony in it all. "So why isn't Trent here?"

He shrugged. "Probably because he assumed that as soon as you returned, you'd take Kristin back. Little did he know how many things might be in the way of that idea."

I chuckled once quietly. "Yeah, just a couple." We both grew quiet for a few minutes.

"So what are you going to do, Alex?"

I knew what he was talking about. I thought for a long moment.

"I'm not exactly sure yet. I need to talk to Kristin, but I need to take a shower first." I finished my drink in two long swallows, closing my eyes as the burn ran down into my chest, and stood up.

CHAPTER THIRTY-FIVE

KRISTIN

I could not move as I looked up into Alex's eyes. The deep rich green reminded me of Trent, and I wondered if he was all right. Alex pulled me into his arms, and I held on to him. I felt him tense as he leaned down. I was sure it was because he smelled the mating. He didn't let go though, and we stood like that for a few moments.

I listened to Alex's heartbeat, allowing the sound of it to calm me. I wasn't ready to think about anything at this moment. I just needed time to calm down.

Through the earpiece I heard someone ask if we got Burke. The thought that his ash was still on my palms, rubbed into the material of my pants, made me angry, and I ripped the earpiece out just after Gabe responded. I didn't want to hear any more.

"Did you find Angelina?" Alex asked Julian, and I could not help but tense up from head to toe. My sister...the sister who would be my enemy until the day that I hunted her down. I would send her on to the same place that Burke now was.

I pulled away from Alex, but he grabbed my arm and pulled me back to face him. I could not force words to come to my mouth. I turned slowly and walked away from him, back to the stairs. I needed to get out of this place.

I was numb, and I barely remembered climbing into the truck. I put my headphones on and cranked my music up loud. Gabe reached over to calm me, but I needed to feel this anger, this pain. I had to deal with this alone, and I pushed his hand away without a word.

I shut the world out and got lost in the haunting melody of Evanescence. The memories that I was reliving now were much different from the ones I thought of on my way here.

Burke had been my father, the man who left my mother before I was born, or so I'd been told. Maybe that wasn't true. Angelina was my twin. Obviously, she was not my identical twin, but I had felt a strange feeling coming from her the first night I saw her. Could it have been our blood bond?

I thought about the fact that for my entire life I had lived within the law, and now, it was my job to make sure others followed those same laws. Burke and Angelina were exactly what I never wanted to be. I could only be thankful that I had not been raised in that environment or I might have turned out differently.

Burke was dead. Would he really have killed me? Had I not meant anything to him as a daughter? How could I have meant anything to him? He hadn't known anything about me. He didn't even know I existed. How had Alex figured it out?

Alex…The sight of Alex had been overwhelming. To know that he was now safe meant the world to me. I never wanted him harmed, especially when I knew that it was partially my fault for him being there.

Now what were we going to do? Alex appeared to have mated with Courtenay. That was an unexpected twist to this whole saga. Would Alex choose to stay with her? How upset was he that I had mated with Trent?

Trent…I tried hard not to physically sigh. I didn't want anyone in the car to pay me any attention. As I thought of Trent, I remembered the look in Alex's eyes, the shade of green as they looked at me while he crossed the distance in the basement. Trent's eyes were the same shade of green as his, but the feel of his arms as they went around me was all wrong.

Trent hadn't returned with us, and I kind of figured that he was not coming back. He probably didn't know what happened in the basement. Or maybe he did know, but it didn't matter to him. He had bonded with me on an order from Alex; he'd done as he was told. Yet why had it felt as if maybe it had been more?

The Tahoe pulled up outside the VMF house and my entire body trembled. I staggered out and went directly into the house and up to my room. I needed to be alone, needed to take a shower to hide the tears. No one spoke and no one followed me.

I knew I wasn't being fair to Alex, but I needed time for me right now. After everything that had happened, I had the right to be selfish. I closed my door a bit louder than I intended, the tears blurring my eyes as I walked to my bathroom and dropped my shoulder rig to the floor with one of my handguns still inside the holster. I kicked off my boots as the tears leaked silently down my face.

It wasn't until I was standing under the hot stream of water that I could no longer hold back the sobs, and I sank to the tile floor, wrapping my arms around my knees as my heart broke to pieces.

I had killed my father tonight. I had a sister I never knew existed. She was my enemy, and the man whom I was in love with, was not coming back.

I cried until I had no tears left, and then I sat there on the floor a while longer. The emotions of the day having finally taken a toll on me, I stood and finished my shower feeling numb, as if the water was ice cold, even though it was still running warm.

I dried off and shook my hair out. I didn't care what it looked like. I just wanted to go to bed. Exhausted, I pulled myself to my mattress and climbed under the sheets. Trent's face was smiling at me in my mind as I rested my head on the pillow he had used just last night, his scent still clinging to it, drifting up to me as my mind shut down and finally went to darkness.

I wasn't sure how long I slept, but as my mind was waking up, I heard the sound of my door click quietly. I listened to see if someone had just come in or just left. I heard footsteps outside my door and realized someone must have checked on me.

I opened my eyes and looked over at the clock. It was nine. I knew that it had to be nighttime. I climbed out of bed and went to brush my teeth, and pulled on a sweatshirt over my camisole. Slipping on a pair of Crocs, I took a deep breath, then opened my door.

I was strong enough to deal with it now. I had released the emotions, dealt with my anger, and it was time to talk to Alex about what would happen now. As I walked downstairs, I could hear voices coming from the kitchen. The sound of a woman laughing stopped me for a second, but I steeled myself and continued down the stairs.

I entered the kitchen and tried as hard as I could to put a genuine smile on my lips as I looked over at Gabe, Courtenay, and Julian at the table.

"About time you woke up, Kristin," Gabe spoke, and grinned at me. Leave it to Gabe to always find a way to relax me. Julian joined me, taking me by the shoulders.

"How are you feeling?" Jules. I could always count on Julian.

I lifted my hand to his face. "I'm fine, Julian, thank you." I turned to the fridge, glancing over at the table as I pulled the door open. Courtenay was staring at the table, her body rigid with tension. I pulled out some blood and, like yesterday, was absolutely famished. As I was finishing up my bag, I heard footsteps come into the kitchen. I swallowed the last mouthful and looked at Alex. He looked as tense as Courtenay. I'm sure he was waiting to see what my attitude was like today. I gave him a tight-lipped smile as I tossed the bag away.

I approached him and stared up into his beautiful green eyes. "Alex, I am so glad that you are all right." I put my arms around him and pulled him close. The tension in his shoulders relaxed, and he held me tightly to his chest.

"Kristin, I'm so sorry for everything you had to go through," he whispered in my ear.

"Not as much as I am for what you went through because of me." I chuckled.

"Yeah, how you got into all that mess is beyond me. Maybe if you had spent more time up in Poughkeepsie, you might not have gotten yourself in so much trouble." Even though that was normally a sore subject, I laughed. Things between us had changed.

"Would you all excuse us? I think we need to talk for a little while," I said, as I turned and addressed the rest of the room. I winked at Courtenay as I make eye contact.

Alex and I went into the living room. Someone had turned on the fireplace and the flames were bright and wild. I watched them for a minute while Alex got comfortable on the couch next to me.

"Are you all right, Alex? You've been through so much." I didn't want to talk about the pain I'd felt. Was it only days before when it had all started?

Alex put his hand on the side of my face. I leaned into it, cherishing this tender moment with him. "I'm fine, Kristin, I really am." His thumb slid gently over my cheekbone. "I'm sorry that you had to go through all that you did."

I put my hand up to his and pulled it off, gently holding it in my lap. "It's okay. I have to admit, it was kind of crazy when it all started happening. Not knowing what was going on, and then finding out you had been kidnapped..." I looked down at our hands and pondered everything. "I owe you an apology, well, maybe more than one." I smiled sheepishly at him.

He shook his head gently. "No, you don't owe me anything. It's me who has to—" I put my finger up to his lips before he could go on.

"No. If I had come up to see you when you asked, maybe this all could have been avoided. I thought you wanted to get on my case about our mating." I watched as something passed across his face. It was so quick that I had no idea what it could have been.

"Kristin, if you had come up, then we both would have been taken. I'm glad that you weren't there. Things could have turned out a lot worse." He squeezed my hand.

I thought about that for a minute. "Yeah, you might be right, but that doesn't take away the fact that I should have come to you when you asked."

He laughed. "Since when have you ever done anything I asked?" I knew he was teasing, but what he said was also the truth.

I was quiet for a while, dwelling on all the other things we had to talk about. I watched the fire and wondered when we would get to the discussion of Trent and Courtenay.

"You finished your transition," he said so softly that I wasn't sure I had heard him. I looked at him quickly.

"What? No, maybe I'm just getting closer. All this different blood traveling through me probably just got me moving faster." I shook my head, thinking about how it was Trent's blood that was flowing through my body.

"No. Kristin, you haven't figured it out yet, have you? Julian said that he and Gabe figured it out right away. I did too as soon as I was close enough to smell you." He watched me carefully.

I stared at him. What was he talking about?

"Kristin, you're pregnant," he said softly.

I heard his words, and I almost laughed. *Pregnant...What?* I knew my eyes went wide as I stared at Alex. The feeling I had the other morning when I woke up, the intense feeling of strength, the feeling as if I was starving, the emotional breakdown I had last night. "Oh! Oh! Oh..."

I continued to stare at Alex, waiting for him to freak out. Waiting to see the anger across his face, but it didn't come. He continued to study me, and I saw that his eyes were not angry; sad, maybe, but not angry.

I didn't know what to say. I was pregnant, and it was Trent's child. I thought that when I was to be faced with this, I would have been upset, but as the realization settled in, I found myself almost excited. What would Trent say? Would this change the way he felt? Suddenly, the thought of what Trent would think scared the death out of me.

"Kristin, I think Trent will be very happy to hear about this."

How could he even think that?

"Alex, you don't know that. You have no idea how Trent would feel about this or if he would even want to have anything to do with a child."

"What, you don't think I would know how my own son feels about you?" He looked taken aback, but probably not as taken aback as I was at that moment.

"Your son? Trent's your son?" I choked out.

"You didn't know? They didn't tell you?" I shook my head wildly. "Julian! Julian, get your ass in here, *now!*" Alex yelled over my head toward the hallway. I didn't know why he was yelling. I knew they could already hear every word we were saying.

Why hadn't I figured it out? How many times did I think Trent's eyes were so much like Alex's? It was why I had been so drawn to him, his blood. I was so freaking blind!

I heard footsteps behind me and spun around on the couch, an accusing look on my face. "Yes, Alex?" Julian said very calmly.

"Why didn't you tell her Trent was my son?" I watched Julian as Alex spoke to him. He looked at the two of us.

"Um...It never came up." He shuffled his feet and Gabe stopped to stand beside Julian. He looked guilty as hell, too.

"Yeah, right!" I snorted at Julian, looking back at Alex.

Gabe laughed from the doorway and went to sit on the arm of the couch. He winked. I returned it.

"So...Mom...How you feeling?" He smirked at me.

"I can't believe you all knew about this and none of you told me anything." I shook my head. "I thought we were better friends." I laughed despite myself.

Somehow, knowing that Trent was Alex's son didn't upset me. It only deepened the feeling I had for him. It all made sense, and Alex didn't seem upset by any of this either.

"Aren't you upset, Alex?" I asked him, being serious again.

I wasn't the only one to get serious. The emotions in the room changed quickly as everyone waited for Alex to speak. He glanced around the room, his eyes stopping at the doorjamb. I looked over my shoulder to see Courtenay there. She looked pensive, probably waiting to hear what he was going to say, too.

Alex looked back at me. "Kristin..." He stopped, probably to figure out how best to say what he wanted to. "Tell me something. Do you want Trent?"

I looked deeply into his emerald eyes. They were waiting, and I knew that what I was about to say was the truth and while it might hurt him, I had to be honest. "I love him, Alex." I smiled slightly. "It's different from the way I feel about you. Different even from how Calista felt for Julian." I glanced at Julian and saw a brief sadness come over his face, but he smiled at me.

"Although I didn't have the opportunity to choose him, thanks to all of you, I would have chosen him. I still choose him; that is, if he'll have me."

Alex was still for a few seconds, and then he pulled me to him. "How could I be upset to know that my son has such an incredible woman in his life? Besides, I think I have some changes going on in my life, too."

CHAPTER THIRTY-SIX

TRENT

*M*y palms were damp as I pulled into the driveway. I hadn't been back to the house since we found Alex four weeks ago. I'd been surprised when Alex called and all but demanded I meet him here immediately. Of course, I assumed he was ready to take my head off, verbally of course, about mating with his woman. I guess if I thought about it, I wasn't surprised that he wanted me to meet him down here and not at his office. He was most likely spending more time with Kristin now.

Kristin...She had been on my mind every minute of every day. The bond we shared for that very short time had been incredible, and since the moment I climbed into the SUV to rescue Alex, I had not dropped my wall. At first, it was to protect myself from what I knew would be there, then it was to save me from knowing what wouldn't be. I didn't want to let the walls down and find that hollow emptiness on the other side where her mind had once connected so perfectly to mine.

I studied the three-story stone house that was owned by the VMF. Several lights were on in the downstairs, and electric candles burned in some of the second-floor windows.

Are you someplace in that house, Kristin? I was torn down the middle, of wanting to see her and the wish to avoid her so that I didn't have to feel. We had both been guilty of jumping straight into the fire on the second night we were together. Would she regret that now?

Not an hour went by that some part of those forty-eight hours didn't replay in my mind. When I closed my eyes, I relived the passionate moments of the one night we loved each other without abandon. Other times of the day, it was the moments I had watched her work. Her compassion, strength, intelligence, and willingness to help everyone still filled me with a sense of pride that she had been mine, if only for that short time. I put the car in park and climbed out. Garda came bounding around the corner of the house, barking excitedly when he caught my scent. I took a moment to greet him, before I knocked on the door.

A few moments later, I heard footsteps on the other side of the door, and felt my heart thud as Gabe pulled it open. "Trent...Hey, man, come in."

"Hey, Gabriel, how's it going?" I entered the foyer, the crystal chandelier above threw sparkles around the room, making it seem like part of a fairy tale. Not my fairy tale though. I didn't get happy endings.

"I'm pretty good. What about you?"

I looked in the hallway toward the back of the house to see if Kristin might be anywhere nearby. "I'm doing pretty good." I swallowed back the lie.

"What brings you back here? I heard you went out west again." Gabe clapped me on the back as we walked toward the living room.

"Yeah, I did. Alex called, said he needed to see me right away. Asked me to meet him here." I was casually trying to put my feelers out around the house, and I almost stumbled in mid-step when I caught her body signature here in the house. I snapped back into myself and turned to Gabe who had stopped a few steps back.

"He did, huh?" He snickered for a moment. "Well, have a seat...I'll be right back."

I watched him disappear up the stairs before I turned and stood in front of the gas fireplace. The flames were flicking up and dancing around behind the glass. She was here...Would she come down to see me?

"Trent." I spun so quickly that I almost made myself dizzy. She was twelve feet away, standing in the doorway, and it suddenly seemed like an ocean away.

"Kristin," I said on a sigh. She was even more beautiful than I remembered. She seemed radiant and glowing. Her eyes sparkled that incredible shade of blue that showed her love and happiness. There was something different about her, but it wasn't my business to ask about her life, not now.

"So, Alex told you to come meet him here?" She stepped into the room and motioned for me to sit on the couch. I did, and she sat facing me in one of the wingback chairs that she seemed to prefer.

"Yeah. He called me yesterday and told me it was important to meet him here. Is he not here?" I put my arm over the back of the couch, trying to appear relaxed. I was anything but, and I was sure she would know that by the feeling in the room. Alex felt everything about everyone. I'm sure she was just as strong.

She smirked before she shook her head no. "Alex...He just doesn't stop, does he?" She appeared to be talking to herself.

I had no clue what to say.

She lifted her beautiful eyes from her lap to me. "Alex isn't here, Trent, and he's not supposed to be here for a while." She tilted her head to study me. "I think he wanted you to come here so that we could talk."

"Oh." That wasn't a very intelligent response, and I was well aware of that, but I couldn't think of anything else to say. My heart sped, and yet she appeared so relaxed, so at ease. I got lost in her crystal clear blue eyes for a moment.

"Trent, can I ask you a question?" She could ask me questions all night long, as long as I got to hear her voice and look into her eyes.

"Yes," was the only word I let escape my lips.

"Why did you leave that night without talking to me?" She didn't look upset; she seemed pensive. Her eyes were still blue, but darker and deeper. Jesus, I wanted to close the space between us and get lost in them up close. This, this was why I didn't come back, I wanted to shout. Because being close to you tears me to pieces.

Do I tell her the truth or do I lie? "I didn't want to get in the way." It was a half-truth.

She contemplated my words, then her gorgeous lips tipped into a sweet smile. "You missed a lot that night."

"What did I miss?" I was still staring at her, taking in every inch of her body, every movement, every breath. Her scent filled the room now, and it seemed sweeter than I remembered.

"Well, you know that I killed Burke; you were there for that." She leaned her head back against the chair and pulled her legs up under her. She looked so damn precious sitting there, the firelight reflecting off her sparkling eyes.

"What I don't think you know, is that Burke was my father." She said the words directly, not seeming to be affected by them, but I was.

"Burke was your father?" I was shocked to hear that. How would she have felt after she killed him, and then found out he was her father?

"Yes, he was, and no, I'm not upset about killing him."

I checked my walls real quick, how did she know what I was thinking?

"I knew that would be your next question." She laughed. "Burke was a bad guy; I'm a cop. I put the bad guys away; doesn't matter if they are family or not." She shrugged.

I was amazed at how easily she said that, but everything about her amazed me.

"Oh, and before I forget, Jacob and his mother say hello and thank you. You have no idea how surprised they were to find Jacob accepted to the rehab program, especially when they heard it was paid in full." She laughed. "You didn't have to do that, you know."

I grinned. "I'm glad I could help. I knew that they mattered to you."

She considered me for a moment as if deciding on what she was going to say next. "You matter to me, too," she said softly.

My heart skipped a beat. I wanted to ask her just how much I mattered, but I couldn't seem to find the words.

She examined the fire, still relaxed and radiant looking. I longed to go to her, pull her into my arms.

"There's a lot more you don't know, Trent." She turned to me with a serious expression.

I shifted in my seat. "Like what?"

She took a deep breath. "Well, like the fact that I finished my transition." She watched to gauge my reaction. I'm not sure how well I covered the look that passed over my face.

"You did?" I nodded absently. "Well, that's good. I guess congratulations are in order." My heart fell, split in two, and I stared at the floor to get a grip on myself. I guess that's why she looked radiant and smelled differently.

The last thing I expected her to do was laugh; so when she did, my head snapped up. I knew there was no way she could not feel my emotions swirling in the room. How could she treat my feelings so blasé?

"Trent, it's not Alex's child," she said softly.

I focused hard on her. *Not Alex's child? Was it Julian's? Son of a bitch... Wait. Was it mine?* My eyes had to have expanded as the thoughts tumbled through my mind. "Who's the father?" I spoke, barely above a whisper.

She tilted her head to the side. "Funny you should ask..." She watched me for a moment. I wasn't breathing. "I hope they have your eyes."

In the moment that she said that, my heart soared for a few beats, but then slowed back down again. I swallowed.

"Don't worry. I don't expect anything from you," she said quietly, and looked away as if she was disappointed.

I was torn between wanting to shake her and pull her into my arms. "What do you mean you don't expect anything from me?"

"Trent, life is all about choices. I would never take your choice away from you." She spoke calmly.

"You didn't give me a choice here, did you? You weren't going to tell me." I was angry about that.

She shook her head. "No, I had every intention of telling you. I just needed time to figure things out first."

I thought about that for a second, and then another thought burst into my head. "Who's been feeding you?" I sounded harsher than I meant to.

"Your father. I mean, it only made sense to have the strongest blood next to yours." She knew he was my father. She didn't seem upset.

"I'm sorry I didn't tell you about him. Julian didn't want me to." I scanned the room, feeling as if I betrayed her and not sure how to make it up to her.

"I know. Julian explained it to me." She had a serious expression on her face when I looked back up.

"Why didn't you go back to Alex?" That part wasn't making sense. I was totally unprepared when she laughed.

"Well, this is the best part of the story." She bit her bottom lip and tried not to grin. "It seems that when Alex was being held captive, he had a roommate."

I knew she could tell I was confused again. She continued before I could ask anything. "You remember Courtenay? Gabe's sister?"

"Yes," I said slowly.

"Well, they were locked in the same cell together. Burke had stabbed her, and Alex healed her, but then she, in turn, saved his life and fed him. The rest is history." She shrugged her shoulders again, as if it was no big deal.

"Alex *mated* with Gabe's sister?"

"Yep, Alex and Courtenay are mated and not only that, but are expecting a child of their own."

I took a minute to think about what she said. Alex was mated to someone else. He was mated to Gabe's sister. Talk about ironic twists of fate. My head spun.

"So, why didn't you mate with Julian? I know he loves you." I looked up at her cautiously. What if she told me that was what she was going to do?

She smiled. "Jules..." She chuckled as she said his name. "Jules still thinks of me as Calista. The last four months have been so crazy and confusing." She looked down at her hands in her lap. "Four months ago, when I learned that I was a vampire, everything got so confusing between Julian, Alex, Damon, and who I really was. "

"But you chose Alex after all that happened," I said quietly.

"Well...I think I went to Alex after that incident because I couldn't be with Julian. I knew what we had shared forty years ago, and it wasn't what or who I was now. I guess I assumed that Alex would help me figure it out, but I constantly felt as if I was being told what to do. He was making my choices, and when I did get to make a choice, he always felt that it affected our relationship, badly. Maybe that's why I didn't want to finish the transition with him." She rubbed her hands down her jeans.

"Why didn't you try to contact me? You know I would have come to help you," I said quietly.

"I know." She smiled sadly. "Somehow, I felt that if I came to you and told you everything, told you that I was pregnant, then it would have taken away your choice. I wanted you to come to me." She blurted out a laugh. "Of course, your father had to get involved and make the choice for both of us, again."

She finally looked back at me, her eyes a soft blue, almost gray; she was worried. "Trent, I don't want you to feel you have to do anything for me. I wanted you to know, but you have already had so many choices taken from you. The first was being stuck with me, then finding out Alex tricked you to get you here, and now to find out you have a child you never asked for..." Her voice trailed off as she turned toward the fire.

I watched her talk, watched her laugh and smile, and I realized that there was no choice to be made. This was where I wanted to be. For the first time in four weeks, I allowed the walls in my mind to slowly crumble to the ground. Our connection seared into my mind, as if we had just completed it. I felt the life in her, the life that I helped create.

"Kristin, what if I have already made my decision?" I felt my hands shake. Would she accept me? Would she allow me in her life as her mate?

She slowly looked back at me, and for the first time, she seemed unsure of what to say. I stood and approached her. Every step closer made me even surer of my decision. I saw her swallow as I sank to my knees in front of her chair and reached up to take her face in my hands. Her body was shaking and her lips parted.

The wall that had been up since the moment I climbed into the SUV to find Alex was now gone, and I knew there was no doubt she could feel the rush of my love for her.

I had no doubts now. "I want you...I choose you," I whispered as I gazed into her eyes. As soon as the words left my lips, tears welled in her eyes.

"Then take me...choose me...love me, Trent," she whispered back as the tears rolled silently down her cheeks.

"I will love you. Forever, Kristin." I pulled her to me and sealed my promise with a kiss, a kiss that I had been dreaming about for weeks. A kiss that told me I made the right choice and found the destiny I wanted.

I gently wiped the moisture off her face after we pulled apart. I had to ask her another question. "Kristin, I always got the impression that you never wanted kids. Are you upset about this?" I was still on my knees in front of her.

She touched my face. "If it had been another's child, I would probably be upset. But when I found out I was pregnant, and I knew it was yours, it became the most important thing in my life."

My heart melted and I brought her to me again. I wanted to hold her, taste her, love her. "You know, I have been considering a career change."

She cocked her head to the side. "Yeah? To what?" she asked.

"Well, after watching you work, I was thinking about going to the police academy. I think I want to find out if my blood might really be blue, too."

My heart swelled as she threw back her head and laughed. "That would be so totally awesome! I could see us being partners."

"We already are partners, right?" I smiled at her.

She looked deeply into my eyes, and as she leaned forward to kiss me, she said softly, "Yes, we are partners...*for life.*"

Prepare yourself for the third book in the series: Mixing the Blue Blood coming soon.

ABOUT THE AUTHOR

Stacy Eaton is a USA Today Best Selling author and began her writing career in October of 2010. Stacy took an early retirement from law enforcement after over fifteen years of service in 2016, with her last three years in investigations and crime scene investigation to write full time.

Stacy resides in southeastern Pennsylvania with her husband, who works in law enforcement, and her teen daughter. She also has a son who is currently serving in the United States Navy and has two grandchildren.

Be sure to visit www.stacyeaton.com for updates and more information on her books.

Sign up for all the latest information on Stacy's Newsletter!

ALSO BY STACY EATON

Paranormal Romance:

My Blood Runs Blue, Book 1

The Pulse of Blue Blood, Book 2 (Short Story)

Blue Blood for Life, Book 3

Mixing the Blue Blood, Book 4

Blue Bloods Final Destiny, Book 5 (Spring 2020)

Garda ~ Welcome to the Realm

Domestic Violence – Crime - Suspense:

Whether I'll Live or Die**

Barbara's Plea

You're Not Alone**

Romantic Suspense:

Liven ~ No Evil

Second Shield

Distorted Loyalty**

Six Days of Memories

Second Shield II: The Return

Contemporary Romance:

Tempt Me Too**

Finding the Strength

Finding Love on Christmas Vacation

Heart of the Family Series

Mistletoe & Cocoa Kisses, Book 1

Roses & Champagne Kisses, Book 2

Orchids & Hurricane Kisses, Book 3

Carnations & Hot Toddy Kisses, Book 4

Heal Me Series

Cured, Book 1

Revived, Book 2

Mended, Book 3

Rescued, Book 4

The Celebration Series

Tangled in Tinsel, Book 1

Tears to Cheers, Book 2

Heathens to Hearts, Book 3

Rainbows Bring Riches, Book 4

Sweet as Sugar, Book 5

Making Mom Mad, Book 6

Sparklers or Spankings, Book 7

Raffles to Rattles, Book 8

Flirting with Fireworks, Book 9

Working under Wheels, Book 10

Masquerading at Midnight, Book 11

Blessings & Beans, Book 12

Velvet & Vows, Book 13

The Sometimes Series:

Sometimes You Win, Book 1**

Sometimes You Lose, Book 2**

Sometimes You Play The Game, Book 3**

Pleasure Your Fantasies Series

Mistletoe Fantasies, Book 1

Whispered Fantasies, Book 2

Secret Fantasies, Book 3

The Twisted Love Series

with Amy Manemann Co-Author

Love Lorn, Book 1 (Manemann)**

Love Torn, Book 2 (Eaton)**

Love Inked, Book 3

Love Drowned, Book 4

Love Carved, Book 5 (2020)

Love Trapped, Book 6 (2020)

Love Crossed, Book 7 (2020)

Love Twisted, Book 8 (2020)

Love Lies, Book 9 (2020)

Rise Again Warrior Series

Mission: Believe, Book 1

Loving a Young Series

Wesley, Book 1 (December)

Henley, Book 2 (January 2020)

The Unexpected Series

Unexpected Packages (2020)

Unexpected Catches (2020)

** These books are also available on Audio